MW01532819

# CASTE

Copyright © 2008 BiblioBazaar
All rights reserved

Original copyright: 1922

# William Alexander Fraser

AUTHOR OF
"RED MEEKINS," "BULLDOG CARNEY,"
"THE THREE SAPPHIRES," "THE LONE FURROW,"
"THOROUGHBREDS," ETC.

# CASTE

**BIBLIO**BAZAAR

# CASTE

# CHAPTER I

The three Mahrattas, Sindhia, Holkar, and Bhonsla, were plotting the overthrow of the British, and the Peshwa was looking out of brooding eyes upon Hodson, the Resident at Poona.

Up on the hill, in the temple of Parvati, the priests repeated prayers to the black goddess calling for the destruction of the hated whites.

Each one of the twenty-four priests as he came with a handful of marigolds laid them one by one at the feet of the four-armed hideous idol, repeating: *"Om, Parvati! Om, Parvati!"* the comprehensive, all-embracing *"Om"* that meant adoration and a clamour for favour. Even to Nandi, the brass bull that carried Shiva, he appealed, *"Om Shiva!"*

But down on the rock-plateau, where gleamed in the hot sun marble palaces, a more malign influence was at work. Dandhu Panth, the adopted son of the Peshwa, had come back from Oxford, and the English believed he had been changed into an Englishman, Nana Sahib.

Outwardly he was a sporting, well-dressed gentleman, such as Oxford turns out; but in his heart was lust of power, and hatred of the white race that he felt would make his inheritance, the Peshwaship, but a vassalage. His dreams of ruling India would fade, and he would sit a pensioner of the British. The Mahrattas had been stigmatised by a captious Mogul ruler, "mountain rats." As Hindus there was a sharp cleavage of character; the Brahmins, fanatical, high up in the caste scale, and all the rest of the breed inferior, vicious, blood-thirsty, a horde of pirates. Even the man who first made them a power, Sivaji, had been of questionable lineage, a plebeian; and so the body corporate was of inflammable material—little restraint of breeding.

And for all Nana Sahib's veneer of English class, mental development, beneath the English shirt he wore the *junwa*, the three-strand sacred thread, insignia of the twice-born,—the Brahmin.

From Governor General to the British officers who played polo with the Peshwa's son, they all accepted him as one of themselves; considered it good diplomacy that he had been sent to Oxford and made over.

There was just one man who had misgivings, the Resident at Poona. He was a small, tired, worn-out official—an executive, a perpetual wheel in the works, always close to the red-tape-tied papers, always. Strange that one not a dreamer, no sixth-sense, should have attained to an intuition—which it was, his distrust of the cheery, sporty Nana Sahib. That Hodson's superiors intimated that India was getting to his liver when he wrote, very cautiously, of this obsession, made no difference; and clinging to his distrust, he achieved something.

After all it was rather strange that the matter had not been taken out of his hands, but it wasn't. A sort of departmental formula running; "Commissioner So-and-So has the matter in hand—refer to him." And so, when a new danger appeared on the distressed horizon, Amir Khan and a hundred thousand massed horsemen, Captain Barlow was sent to consult with the Resident. That was the way; a secretive, trusty, brave man, for in India the written page is never inviolate.

Captain Barlow was sent—ostensibly as an assistant to the Resident, in reality to acquire full knowledge of the situation, and then go to the camp of Amir Khan with the delicate mission of persuading him not to join his riding spear-men to the Mahratta force, but to form an alliance with the British.

The Resident had asked for Barlow. He had explained that any show of interest, two men, or five, or twenty, an envoy, even men of pronounced position, would defeat their object; in fact, believing Nana Sahib to be what he was, he conceived the very simple idea of playing the Oriental's Orientalism against him.

Barlow would be the last man in India to whom one as suspicious as the Peshwa's son would attribute a subtlety deep enough for a serious mission. He was a great handsome boy; in his physical excellence he was beautiful; courage was manifest in the strong content of his deep brown eyes. Incidentally that was one of the reasons the Resident had asked for him, though he would have denied it, even to his daughter, Elizabeth, though it was for her sake—that part of it.

The affair with Elizabeth had been going on for two or three years; never quite settled—always hovering.

Indeed the Resident's daughter was not constituted to raise a cyclone of passion, a tempest of feeling that brings an impetuous declaration of love from any man. She was altogether proper; well-bred; admirable; perhaps somewhat of the type so opposite to Barlow's impressionable nature that ultimately, all in good time, they would realise that the scheme of creation had marked them for each other. And Colonel Hodson almost prayed for this. It was desirable in every way. Barlow was of a splendid family; some day he might become Lord Barradean.

Anyway Captain Barlow was there playing polo with Nana Sahib—one of the Prince's favourites; and waiting for a certain paper that would be sent to the Resident that would contain offers of an alliance with the Pindari Chief.

And this same hovering menace of the Pindari force was causing Nana Sahib unrest. Perhaps there had been a leak, as cautiously as the Resident had made every move. If the Pindari army were to join the British, ready at a moment's notice to fall on the flank of the Mahrattas, harass them with guerilla warfare, it would be serious; they were as elusive as a huge pack of wolves; unencumbered by camp followers, artillery, foraging as they went, swooping like birds of prey, they were a terrible enemy. Even as the tiger slinks in dread from a pack of the red wild-dogs, so a regular force might well dread these flying horsemen.

And it was Amir Khan that Nana Sahib, and the renegade French commander, Jean Baptiste, dreaded and distrusted. Overtures had been made to him without result. He was a wonderful leader. He had made the name of the Pindari feared throughout India. He was the magnet that held this huge body of fighting devils together.

Thus with the gigantic chess-board set; the possession of India trembling in the balance; intellects of the highest development pondering; Fate held the trump card, curiously, a girl; and not one of the players had ever heard her name, the Gulab Begum.

# CHAPTER II

The white sand plain surrounding Chunda was dotted with the tents of the Mahratta force Sirdar Baptiste commanded. And the Sirdar, his soul athirst for a go at the English, whom he hated with the same rabid ferocity that possessed the soul of Nana Sahib, was busy. From Pondicherry he had inveigled French gunners; and from Goa, Portuguese. Also these renegade whites were skilled in drill. If Holkar and Bhonsla did their part it would be Armageddon when the hell that was brewing burst.

But Baptiste feared the Pindari. As he swung here and there on his Arab the horse's hoofs seemed to pound from the resonant sands the words "Amir Khan—Amir Khan! Pin-dar-is, Pin-dar-is!"

It was as he discussed this very thing with his Minister, Dewan Sewlal, that Nana Sahib swirled up the gravelled drive to the bungalow on his golden-chestnut Arab, in his mind an inspiration gleaned from something that had been.

His greeting of the two was light, sporty; his thin well-chiselled face carried the bright indifferent vivacity of a fox terrier.

"Good day, Sirdar," he cried gaily; and, "How listen the gods to your prayers, my dear Dewani?"

Baptiste, out of the fulness of his heart soon broached the troublous thing: "Prince," he begged, "obtain from the worthy Peshwa a command and I'll march against this wolf, Amir Khan, and remove from our path the threatened danger."

Nana Sahib laughed; his white, even teeth were dazzling as the black-moustached lip lifted.

"Sirdar, when I send two Rampore hounds from my kennel to make the kill of a tiger you may tackle Amir Khan. Even if we could crumple up this blighter it's not cricket—we need those Pindari chaps—but not as dead men. Besides, I detest bloodshed."

The Dewan rolled his bulbous eyes despairingly: "If Sindhia would send ten camel loads of gold to this accursed Musselman, we could sleep in peace," he declared.

"If it were a woman Sindhia would," Nana Sahib sneered.

Baptiste laughed.

"It is a wisdom, Prince, for that is where the revenue goes: women are a curse in the affairs of men," the Dewan commented.

"With four wives your opinion carries weight, Dewani," and Nana Sahib tapped the fat knee of the Minister with his riding whip.

Baptiste turned to the Prince. "There will be trouble over these Pindaris; your friends, the English—eh, Nana Sahib—"

As though the handsome aquiline face of the Peshwa's son had been struck with a glove it changed to the face of a devil; the lips thinned, and shrinking, left the strong white teeth bare in a wolf's snarl. Under the black eyebrows the eyes gleamed like fire-lit amber; the thin-chiselled nostrils spread and through them the palpitating breath rasped a whistling note of suppressed passion.

"Sirdar," he said, "never call me Nana Sahib again. The English call me that, but I wait—must wait; I smile and suffer. I am Dandhu Panth, a Brahmin. The English so loved me that they tried to make an Englishman of me, but, by Brahm! they taught me hate, which is their lot till the sea swallows the last of the accursed breed and Mahrattaland is free!"

Nana Sahib was panting with the intensity of his passion. He paced the floor flicking at his brown boots with his whip, and presently whirled to say with a sneering smile on his thin lips:

"The English can teach a man just one thing—to die for his ideals."

"Yes, Prince, of a certainty the Englishman knows how to die for his country," Baptiste agreed in a soldier's tribute to courage.

"And for another nation's country," Nana Sahib rasped. "He is a born pirate, a bred pirate—we in India know that; and that, General, is why I am a Brahmin, because they alone will free Mahrattaland—faith, ideals. Forms! the gods to me are not more than show-pieces. That Kali spreads the cholera is one with the idea that the little red-daubed stone Linga gets the woman a male child, false; these things are in ourselves, and in Brahm. The priests sacrifice to Shiva, but I will sacrifice to Mahrattaland, which to me is the supreme God."

Jean Baptiste looked out of his wise grey eyes into the handsome face and felt a thrill, an awakening, the terrible sincerity of the speaker. At times the ferocity in the eyes when he had spoken of sacrifice caused the free-lance soldier to shiver. A blur of red floated before his eyes—something of a fateful forecasting that some day the awful storm that was brewing would break, and the fanatical Brahmin in front of him would call for English blood to glut his hate. It was the more appalling that Nana Sahib was so young. Closing his eyes Baptiste heard the voice of an English Oxonian that perhaps should be chortling of polo and cricket and racing; and yet the more danger—the youthfulness of the agent of destruction; like a Napoleon—a corporal as a boy. *"C'est la guerre!"* the French officer murmured.

Then, as a storm passing is often followed by smiling sunshine, so the mood of Nana Sahib changed. He had the volatile temperament of a Latin, and now he turned to the Minister, his face having undergone a complete metamorphosis: "Dewani," he said, "do you remember when a certain raja sent his Prime Minister and twenty thousand men to punish Pertab for not paying his taxes, and Pertab gave one Bhart, a Bagree, ten thousand rupees and a village to bring him the Minister's head—which he did, tied to the inside of his brass-studded shield?"

"Yes, Prince; that is a way of this land."

Nana Sahib drew forth a gold cigarette case, lighted a cigarette from a fireball that stood in a brass cup, and gazed quizzically at the Dewan. There was a little hush. This story had set Jean Baptiste's nerves tingling; there was something behind it.

The Dewan half guessed what was in the air, but he blinked his big eyes solemnly, and reaching for a small lacquer box took from it a Ran leaf, with a finger smeared some ground lime on it, and wrapping the leaf around a piece of betel-nut popped it into his capacious mouth.

"These Bagrees are in the protection of Rajas, Karowlee, are they not?" Nana Sahib asked.

"Yes, Prince; even some of Bhart's relatives are there—one Ajeet Singh; he's a celebrated leader of these decoits."

"And Sindhia took from Karowlee some territory, didn't he?"

"Yes; Karowlee refused to pay the taxes."

"I should think the Raja would like to have it back."

"No doubt, Prince."

Nana Sahib, holding the cigarette to his lips between two fingers gazed mockingly at the large-paunched Brahmin. Then he said; "I see the illuminating light of understanding in your eyes, Dewani—a subtle comprehension. Small wonder that you are Minister to the delightful Sindhia. If you are making any promises to Karowlee, I should make them in the name of Sindhia—through Sirdar Baptiste, of course. And, Dewani, this restless cuss, Amir Khan, might make a treaty with the English any time. The dear fish-eyed Resident has been particularly active—my spies can hardly keep up with him. I shouldn't lose any time—Ajeet Singh sounds promising."

Nana Sahib drew a slim flat gold watch from his pocket. "I now must leave you two interesting gentlemen," he said, "for I am to play a few chuckers of polo with—particularly, Captain Barlow. He is jackal to the bloodless Resident. I really thought a couple of days ago that he would have to be sent home on sick leave. One of my officers rode him off the ball in a fierce drive for goal, and by some devilish mistake the post hadn't been sawed half-through, so when Barlow crashed into it it stood up. As he lay perfectly still after his cropper it looked as though Resident Hodson had lost his jackal. But Barlow is one of those whip-cord Englishmen that die of old age; he was in the saddle again in two days. Well, *au revoir* and salaam."

When the clattering scurry of Nana Sahib's Arab had died out Baptiste turned to the Dewan, saying:

"Well?"

"I will write the letter to Raja Karowlee, but you must sign it, Sirdar; also furnish a fast riding camel and a trusty officer," the Dewan answered simply.

"But Nana Sahib was nebulous—we may be made the goat of sacrifice."

"It is a wisdom, Sirdar; but, also, it is from the Prince an order; and my office is always one of blame when there are excuses to make—it is always that way. When a head is required the Dewan's is always offered."

# CHAPTER III

In answer to the Dewan's request Raja Karowlee sent a force of two hundred Bagrees to Jean Baptiste's camp. Evidently the old Raja had run the official comb through his territories, for the decoit force was composed of a hundred men from Karowlee, under Ajeet Singh, and a hundred from Alwar, led by Sookdee.

The two leaders were commanded to obey Sirdar Baptiste implicitly; and Baptiste passed an order that they were to receive a thousand rupees a day for their maintenance.

In addition there was a fourth officer, Hunsa, who was a jamadar, a lieutenant, to Ajeet Singh. And if then and there the ugly head had been cut from his body, the things that happened would not have happened.

From the advent of the Bagrees, even on their way from Karowlee, Hunsa had been plotting evil. He was a man who would have shrivelled up, become atrophied, in an atmosphere of decency—he would have died.

Hunsa caused Sookdee to believe that he should have been the leader and not Ajeet Singh.

A document was written out by Dewan Sewlal promising that in the event of the decoits carrying out the mission they had come upon the estate would be restored to Raja Karowlee, and that he would be compelled to assign to the three decoit leaders villages within that territory in rent free tenure. The Dewan, with wide precaution, took care that the document was so worded that General Baptiste was the official promiser, putting in a clause that he, Sewlal, the Minister, would see that the General carried out these promises on behalf of Sindhia.

Baptiste set his lips in a sardonic smile when he read and signed the paper. However, he cared very little; no concern of his whether Karowlee attained to his lands or not—it would be a matter of the

King disposes. Even that the Dewan stood in Baptiste's shadow in the affair was another something that only caused the Frenchman to remark sardonically:

"Dewani, the English sahibs have a delectable game of cards named poker in which there is an observance called passing the buck; when a player wishes to avoid the responsibility of a bet he passes the buck to the next man. Dewani, you have the subtlety of a good poker player and have passed the buck to me."

The Brahmin looked hurt. "Sirdar," he said, "you are the commander of matters of war, which this is. You stand here in the city of tents as Sindhia; I am but the man of accounts; it is well as it is. And now that we have signed the promise the decoits will also sign, then I will make them take the oath according to their patron goddess, Bhowanee. They are just without—I will have them in."

When the three jamadars had been summoned to the Dewan's presence, he said: "Here is the paper of promise as to the reward from Sindhia for the service you are to render. You will also sign here, making your seal or thumb print; then it will be required that you take the oath of service according to your own method and your gods."

Ajeet consulted a little apart with Sookdee and then coming forward said: "We Bagrees are an ancient people descended from the Rajputs, and we keep our word to our friends; therefore we will take the oath after the manner of Bhowanee, beneath the pipal tree. If Your Honour will give us but an hour we will take the oath."

A mile down the red road from the bungalow, looking like a huge beehive with its heavy enveloping roof of thatch, that was Jean Baptiste's head-quarters, was a particularly sacred pipal of huge growth. It was an extraordinary octopus-like tree, and most sacred, for perched in the embrace of its giant arms was a shrine that had been lifted from its base in the centuries of the tree's growth.

And now, an hour later, the pipal was surrounded by thousands of Mahratta sepoys, for word had gone forth,—the mysterious rumour of India that is like a weird static whispering to the four corners of the land a message,—had flashed through the tented city that the men from Karowlee were to take the oath of allegiance to Sindhia.

The fat Dewan had come down in a *palki* swung from the shoulders of stout bearers, while Jean Baptiste had ridden a silver-grey Arab.

And then just as a bleating, mottled white-and-black goat was led by a thong to the pipal, Nana Sahib came swirling down the road in a brake drawn by a spanking pair of bay Arabs with black points. Beside him sat the Resident's daughter, Elizabeth Hodson, and in the seat behind was Captain Barlow.

At the pipal Nana Sahib reined in the bays sharply, saying, "Hello, General, wanted to see you for a minute—called at the bungalow, and your servant said you had gone down this way. What's up?" he questioned after greetings had passed between Baptiste, Barlow and Elizabeth Hodson.

"Just some new recruits, scouts, taking the oath of service," and Baptiste closed an eye in a caution-giving wink.

A slight sneer curled the thin lips of Nana Sahib; he understood perfectly what Baptiste meant by the wink—that the Englishman being there, it would be as well to say little about the Bagrees. But the Prince had no very high opinion of Captain Barlow's perceptions, of his finer acuteness of mind; the thing would have to be very plainly exposed for the Captain to discover it. He was a good soldier, Captain Barlow—that happy mixture of brain and brawn and courage that had coloured so much of the world's map red, British; he was the terrier class—all pluck, with perhaps the pluck in excelsis—the brain-power not preponderant.

"Who is the handsome native—he looks like a Rajput?" Elizabeth asked, indicating the man who was evidently the leader among the others.

"That is Ajeet Singh, chief of these men," Baptiste answered.

"He is a handsome animal," Nana Sahib declared.

"He is like an Arab Apollo," Elizabeth commented; and her tone suggested that it was a whip-cut at the Prince's half-sneer.

The girl's description of Ajeet was trite. The Chief's face was almost perfect; the golden-bronze tint of the skin set forth in the enveloping background of a turban of blue shot with gold-thread draped down to cover a silky black beard that, parted at the chin, swept upward to loop over the ears. The nose was straight and thin; there was a predatory cast to it, perhaps suggested by the bold, black, almost fierce eyes. He was clothed with the full, rich, swaggering adornment of a Rajput; the splendid deep torso enclosed in a shirt-of-mail, its steel mesh so fine that it rippled like silver cloth; a red velvet vestment, negligently open, showed in the folds of a silk sash a jewel-hilted knife; a *tulwar* hung from his left shoulder. As he moved here and there, there was a sinuous grace, panther-like, as if he strode on soft pads. At rest his tall figure had the set-up of a soldier.

As the three in the brake studied the handsome Ajeet, a girl stepped forward and stood contemplating them.

"By Jove!" the exclamation had been Captain Barlow's; and Elizabeth, with the devilish premonition of an acute woman knew that it was a masculine's involuntary tribute to feminine attractivity.

She had turned to look at the Captain.

Nana Sahib, little less vibrant than a woman in his sensitive organisation, showed his even, white teeth: "Don't blame you, old chap," he said; "she's all that. I fancy that's the girl they call Gulab Begum. Am I right, Sirdar?"

"Yes, Prince," Jean Baptiste answered. "The girl is a relative of the handsome Ajeet."

"She's simply stunning!" Captain Barlow said, as it were, meditatively.

But Nana Sahib, knowing perfectly well what this observation would do to the austere, exact, dominating daughter of a precise man, the Resident, muttered to himself: "Colossal ass! an impressionable cuss should have a *purdah* hung over his soul—or be gagged."

"One of their *nautch* girls, I suppose;" Elizabeth thus eased some of the irritation over Barlow's admiration in a well-bred sneer.

"Yes," Baptiste declared; "it is said she dances wonderfully."

"You name her the Gulab Begum, General,—that is a Moslem title and, from the turbans and caste-marks on the men, they seem to be Hindus; I suppose Gulab Begum is her stage name, is it?"

Elizabeth was exhibiting unusual interest in a native—that is for Elizabeth, and Nana Sahib chuckled softly as he answered: "Names mean little in India; I know high-caste Brahmins who have given their children low-caste names to make them less an object of temptation to the gods of destruction. Also, the Gulab may have been stolen from the harem of some Nawab by this bandit."

The Gulab suggested more a Rajput princess than a dancing girl. No ring pierced the thin nostrils of her Grecian nose; neither from her ears hung circles of gold or brass, or silver; and the slim ankles that peeped from a rich skirt were guiltless of anklets. On the wrist of one arm was a curious gold bangle that must have held a large ruby, for at times the sun flicked from the moving wrist splashes of red wine. Indeed the whole atmosphere of the girl was simplicity and beauty.

"No wonder they call her the Rose Queen," Barlow was communing with himself. For the oval face with its olive skin, as fair as a Kashmiri girl's, was certainly beautiful. The black hair was smoothed back from a wide low forehead, after the habit of the Mahratti women; the prim simplicity of this seeming to add to the girlish effect. A small white-and-gold turban, even with its jauntiness, seemed just the very thing to check the austere simplicity. The girl's eyes, like Ajeet's, were the eyes of some one unafraid, of one born to a caste that felt equality. When they turned to those who sat in the brake they were calmly meditative; they were the eyes of a child, modest; but with the unabashed confidence of youth.

Elizabeth, perhaps unreasonably, for the three of them sat so close together in the brake, fancied that the Gulab's gaze constantly picked out the handsome Captain Barlow.

An imp touched Nana Sahib, and he said: "I'd swear there was Rajput blood in that girl. If I knew of some princess having been stolen I'd say she stood yonder. The eyes are simply ripping; baby eyes, that, when roused, assist in driving a knife under a man's fifth rib. I've seen a sambhur doe with just such eyes cut into ribbons a Rampore hound with her sharp hoofs."

"Well, Prince," Elizabeth said, "I suppose you know the women of this land better than either Captain Barlow or myself, and you're probably right, for I see in a belt at her waist the jewelled hilt of a dagger."

Nana Sahib laughed: "My dear Miss Hodson, I never play with edged tools, and Captain—"

But Nana Sahib's raillery was cut short by a small turmoil as the bleating goat of sacrifice was dragged forward to a stone daubed with vermillion upon which rested a small black alabaster image of Kali; while a *guru*, with sharpened knife, hung near like a falcon over a quivering bird. Three times the goat's head was thrust downward in obeisance to the black goddess; there was a flash of steel in the sunlight, and hot blood gushed forth, to dye with its crimson flood the base of the idol.

A Bagree darted forward and with a stroke of his *tulwar* clipped the neck from a pitcher and held it beneath the gurgling flood till it was filled.

From where Elizabeth sat she looked across the shoulder of Nana Sahib as they watched the sacrifice; she saw him quiver and lean forward, his shoulders tip as though he would spring from the brake. His face had drawn into hard lines, his lips were set tight in intensity across the teeth so that they showed between in a thin line of white. The blood seemed to have fascinated him; he was oblivious of her presence. She heard him murmur, "Parvati, Parvati! There is blood, blood—wait, thou, Parvati."

The bay Arabs—perhaps their sensitive nostrils drank in the smell of fresh blood—sprang into their collars as if they would bolt in fright. The two syces, squatting on their heels at the horses' heads, had sprung to their feet, and now were caressing the necks of the Arabs as they held them each with a hand by the bit.

There was a curious look in the Prince's eyes as he turned them on Elizabeth; a mingling of questioning and defiance was in them.

Now the holder of the pitcher stood up and the *guru* drew upon it four red lines and dropped through its shattered mouth a woman's bracelet of gold lacquer beads. Then the pitcher was placed upon the Kali shrine; raw sugar was inclosed in a cloth and tied to a branch of the pipal.

The voice of the Bagree Chief, somewhat coarse in its fulness, its independence, now was heard saying: "Sirdar Sahib, and Dewan Sahib, we men of the nine castes of the Bagrees now make the sacred oath. Come close that ye may observe."

Jean Baptiste edged his horse to the side of the road, and the Dewan, heaving from the *palki*, stood upright.

Ajeet dipped a tapering finger in the pitcher of blood, touched the swaying bag of sugar, and laying the hand against his forehead said, in a loud voice:

"If I, Ajeet Singh, break faith with Maharaja Sindhia, may Bhowanee punish me!"

Sookdee and Hunsa each in turn took the same solemn oath of allegiance.

As Hunsa turned from the ordeal and passed the Gulab Begum to where the Bagrees stood in line, Nana Sahib said, "Do you know, General, what that baboon-faced jamadar made oath to?"

"The last one, my Prince?"

"Yes, he of the splendid ugliness. He testified, 'If I fail to thrust a knife between the shoulder-blades of Ajeet Singh may Bhowanee cast me as a sacrifice.'"

"He is jamadar to the other, Prince—but why?"

"He looked upon the Rose Lady as he passed, and as the blooded finger lay upon his forehead he looked upon Ajeet, and in his pig eyes was unholiness."

The cold grey eyes of the Frenchman rested for a second upon the burning black eyes of the speaker, and again he shivered. He knew that the careless words meant that Hunsa was an instrument, if needs be. But the Prince's teeth were gleaming in a smile. And he was saying: "If the play is over, Sirdar, turn your mount over to the *syce* and pop up here beside Captain Barlow—I'll tool you home. The Captain might like a peg."

The bay Arabs swirled the brake along the smooth roadway that lay like a wide band of coral between giant green walls of gold-mohr and tamarind; and sometimes a pipal, its white bole and branches gleaming like the bones of a skeleton through leaves of the deepest emerald, and its roots daubed with the red paint of devotion to the tree god. Here and there a neem, its delicate branches dusted with tiny white star blossoms, cast a sensuous elusive perfume to the vagrant breeze. Once a gigantic jamon stretched its gnarled arms across the roadway as if a devilfish held poised his tentacles to snatch from the brake its occupants.

When they had swung in to the Sirdar's bungalow and clambered down from the brake, Elizabeth said: "If you don't mind, General Baptiste, I'll just drift around amongst these beautiful roses while you men have your pegs. No, I don't care for tea," she said, in answer to his suggestion. There was a mirthless smile on her lips as she added: "I'm like Captain Barlow, I like the rose."

The three men sat on the verandah while a servant brought brandy-and-soda, and Nana Sahib, with a restless perversity akin to the torturing proclivity of a Hindu was quizzing the Frenchman about his recruits.

"You'll find them no good," he assured Baptiste—"rebellious cusses, worthless thieves. My Moslem friend, the King of Oudh, tried them out. He got up a regiment of them—Budhuks, Bagrees—all sorts; it was named the Wolf Regiment—that was the only clever thing about it, the name. They stripped the uniforms from the backs of the officers sent to drill them and kicked them out of camp; said the officers put on swank; wouldn't clean their own horses and weapons, same as the other men."

Then he switched the torture—made it more acute; wanted to know what Sirdar Baptiste had got them for.

The Frenchman fumed inwardly. Nana Sahib was at the bottom of the whole murderous scheme, and here, like holding a match over a keg of powder, he must talk about it in front of the Englishman.

When the brandy was brought Nana Sahib put hand over the top of his glass.

"Not drinking, Prince?" Barlow asked.

"No," Nana Sahib answered, "a Brahmin must diet; holiness is fostered by a shrivelled skin."

"But pardon me, Prince," Barlow said hesitatingly, "didn't going across the black-water to England break your caste anyway— so why cut out the peg?"

"Yes, Captain Sahib,"—the Prince's voice rasped with a peculiar harsh gravity as though it were drawn over the jagged edge of intense feeling,—"my caste *was* broken, and to get it back I drank the dregs; a cup of liquid from the cow, and not milk either!"

Baptiste coughed uneasily for he saw in the eyes of Nana Sahib smouldering passion.

And Barlow's face was suffused with a sudden flush of embarrassment.

Perhaps it had been the sight of the blood sacrifice that had started Nana Sahib on a line of bitter thought; had stirred the smothering hate that was in his soul until frothing bubbles of it mounted to his lips.

"I was born in the shadow of Parvati," Nana Sahib said, "and when I came back from England I found that still I was a Brahmin; that the songs of the Bhagavad Gita and the philosophy of the Puranas was more to me than what I had been taught at Oxford. So I took back the caste, and under my shirt is the *junwa* (sacred thread)."

A quick smile lighted his face, and he laid a hand on Barlow's arm, saying in a new voice, a voice that was as if some one spoke through his lips in ventriloquism: "And all this, Captain, is a good thing for my friends the English. The Brahmins, as you know, sway the Mahrattas, and if I am of them they will listen to me. The English boast—and they have reason to—that they have made a friend of Nana Sahib. Here, Baptiste, pour me a glass of plain soda, and we'll drink a toast to Nana Sahib and the English."

"By Jove! splendid!" and Captain Barlow held out a hand.

But Baptiste, saying that he would find Miss Hodson, went out into the sunshine cursing.

"Now we will go back," Nana Sahib was saying as the French General brought Elizabeth from among the oleanders and crotons.

# CHAPTER IV

The day after the Bagrees had taken the oath of allegiance to Sindhia the jamadars were summoned to the Dewan's office to receive their instructions for the carrying out of the mission.

In writing the Raja of Karowlee for the decoits, Dewan Sewlal had not stated that the mission was for the purpose of bringing home in a bag the head of the Pindar Chief. As the wily Hindu had said to Sirdar Baptiste: "We will get them here before speaking of this dangerous errand. Once here, and Karowlee's hopes raised over getting territory, if they then go back without accomplishing the task, that rapacious old man will cast them into prison."

So when the Bagree leaders, closeted with Baptiste and the Dewan in a room of the latter's bungalow, learned what was expected of them they, to put it mildly, received a shock. They had thought that it was to be a decoity of treasure, perhaps of British treasure, and in their proficient hands such an affair did not run into much danger generally.

The jamadars drew to one side and discussed the matter; then Ajeet said: "Dewan Sahib, what is asked of us should have been in the written message to our Raja. We be decoits, that is true, it is our profession, but the mission that is spoken of is not thus. Hunsa has ridden with Amir Khan upon a foray into Hyderabad, and he knows that the Chief is always well guarded, and that to try for his head in the midst of his troops would be like the folly of children."

The Dewan's fat neck swelled with indignation; his big ox-like eyes bulged from their holding in anger:

"Phut-t-t!" he spat in derision. "Bagrees!" he sneered; "descendants of Rajputs—bah! Have you brought women with you that will lead this force? And danger!" he snarled—he turned on Sookdee: "You are Sookdee, son of Bhart, so it was signed."

"Yes, Dewan, it is true."

"*You* are the son of your mother, not Bhart," the Dewan raved; "he was a brave man, but *you* speak of danger—bah!"

The Dewan's teeth, stained red at the edges from the chewing of *pan*, showed in a sneering grin like a hyena's as he added: "Bah! Ye are but thieves who steal from those who are helpless."

Ajeet spoke: "Dewan Sahib, we be men as brave as Bhart—we are of the same caste, but there is a difference between such an one as he took the head of and a Pindari Chief. The Pindaris are the wild dogs of Hind, they are wolves, and is it easy to trap a wolf?"

But the Dewan had worked himself into a frenzy at their questioning of the possibilities; he waved his fat hands in a gesture of dismissal crying: "Go, go!"

As the jamadars stood hesitatingly, Sewlal swung to the Frenchman: "Sirdar Sahib, make the order that I cease payment of the thousand rupees a day to these rebels, cowards. Go!" and he looked at Ajeet; "talk it over amongst yourselves, and send to me one of your wives that will lead a company—lend your women your tulwars."

Ajeet's black eyes flashed anger, and his brows were drawn into a knot just above his thin, hawk-like nose; suppressed passion at the Dewan's deadly insult was in the even, snarling tone of his voice:

"Dewan Sahib, harsh words are profitless—" his eyes, glittering, were fixed on the bulbous orbs of the man of the quill—"and the talk of women in the affairs of men is not in keeping with caste. If you pass the order that we are not to have rations now that we are far from home, what are we to do? Think you that Raja Karowlee—"

"Do! do! if you serve not Sindhia what care I what you do. Go back to your honourable trade of thieving. And as to Raja Karowlee, a man who keeps a colony of cowards—what care I for him. Go, go!"

The jamadars with glowering eyes turned from the Dewan, even the harsh salaam they uttered in going sounded like a curse.

And when they had gone, Baptiste was startled by a gurgling laugh bubbling up from the Dewan's fat throat.

"Sirdar," he chuckled, "I've given that posing Rajput a poem to commit to memory. Ha-ha! They have two strong reasons now for going—their shame and lean stomachs."

"They won't go," Baptiste declared. "When a man is afraid of anything he can find a thousand reasons for not making the endeavour. If Sindhia will give me the troops I will make an end of Amir Khan."

"And make enemies of the Pindaris: that we do not want; we want them to fight with us, not against us. The great struggle is about to take place; Holkar and Bhonsla and Sindhia, perhaps even the King of Oudh, leagued together, the accursed English will be driven from India. But even now they are trying to win over Amir Khan and his hundred thousand horsemen by promises of territory and gold. With the Chief out of the way they would disband; he is a great leader, and they flock to his flag. You saw the Englishman, Captain Barlow?"

"Yes, Dewani. Good soldier, I should say."

"Well, Sirdar, we think that he waits here to undertake some mission to Amir Khan. You see, no office can be conducted without clerks, and sometimes clerks talk."

The Frenchman twisted nervously at his slim grey moustache. "I comprehend, Dewani," he said presently; "it is expedient that Amir Khan be eliminated."

"It would be a merciful thing," Sewlal added—"it would save bloodshed."

"Well, Dewani, I must depart now. It will be interesting to see what your Bagrees do, especially when they become hungry."

# CHAPTER V

For two days the Bagrees sat nursing their wrath at the reproaches of Dewan Sewlal.

And the Dewan, in spite of his bold denunciation of the decoits, was uneasy. If they went back to Karowlee with a story of ill treatment, of broken promises, that hot-headed old Rajput would turn against Sindhia. And the present policy of the Mahratta Confederacy was to secure allies in the revolt against the British which was being secretly planned. The Dewan was also afraid of Nana Sahib. He saw in that young man a coming force. The Peshwa was actually the ruler of Mahrattaland; he had a commanding influence because he was the head of the Brahmins—the Brahmins were the real power—and his adopted son, his inborn subtle nature developed by his residence in England, now had great influence over him. The Dewan knew that; and if he failed to carry out this mission of removing the dangerous one from Nana Sahib's path it might cost him his place as Minister.

In his perplexity the Dewan asked Baptiste to formulate some excuse for getting Nana Sahib up to Chunda—some matter affecting the troops, so that he might casually get a sustaining suggestion from the wily Prince.

It so happened that when Nana Sahib swung up the gravelled drive to the Sirdar's bungalow on a golden chestnut Arab, Sewlal was there. But when, presently, Baptiste's *durwan* came in to say that Jamadar Hunsa of the new troops was sending his salaams to the Dewan, the latter gasped. He would have told the Bagree to wait, but Nana Sahib, catching the name Hunsa, commanded:

"By all means, my dear Baptiste, have that living embodiment of murder in. His face is a delight. You know"—and he smiled at the General—"that that frightfulness of expression is the very reason why the genial Kali has such a hold upon our people. You've seen her, Baptiste; four arms, one holding a platter to catch the blood that drips from a head she suspends above it by another arm; the third hand clasps a sword, and the fourth has the palm spread out as much as to say, 'That is what will happen to you.'"

The Frenchman shivered. He was snapping a finger and thumb in mental torture.

But Nana Sahib chuckled: "Her tongue protrudes thirsting for more blood—"

But the Sirdar protested: "Prince—pardon, but—"

"My dear Baptiste, when the Hunsa comes in observe if these things are not all stamped by Brahm on his frontispiece; he fascinates me."

The Dewan, devout Brahmin, had been running his fingers along a string of lacquered beads that hung about his neck, muttering a prayer against this that was like sacrilege.

When the jamadar was shown into the room his face took on a look of uneasiness. It but added to the ferocity of the square scowling massive head. His huge shoulders, stooped forward as he salaamed, suggested the half-crouch of a tiger—even the eyes, the mouth, induced thoughts of that jungle killer.

Nana Sahib, a sneer on his lips, turned to the Minister: "Play him, Dewani, as you love us. There is some rare deviltry afloat."

"Why have you come, Jamadar?" the Dewan asked.

Hunsa's pig eyes shifted from Sewlal's face to roam over the other two, and then returned a question in them.

"Tell him," Nana Sahib suggested, "that he has nothing to fear from us."

The jamadar was troubled by the English exchange, but the Dewan explained: "The Prince says you are to speak what is on your mind."

"It is this, Sahib Bahadur," Hunsa began, "there is a way that the head of Amir Khan might be obtained as a gift for Maharaja Sindhia. Then Raja Karowlee would be pleased for he would receive his commission and we would be given a reward."

"What is the way?" Sewlal queried.

"The Chief of the Pindaris, after the habit of Moslems, is one whose heart softens toward a woman who is beautiful and is pleasing to his eye."

"Ancient history," Nana Sahib commented in English, "and not confined to Musselmen."

"Speak on," the Dewan commanded curtly.

"When I rode with Amir Khan," Hunsa resumed, "in loot there fell to the Chief's share a dancing girl, and Amir Khan, perhaps out of respect to his two wives, would visit her at night quietly in the tent that was given her as a place of residing."

"Amir Khan seems to be less a Pindari and more a human than I thought him," Nana Sahib commented drily.

"The world is a very small place, Prince," Baptiste added.

"But why has Hunsa brought this tale to men of affairs?" Sewlal queried.

Hunsa cast a furtive look over his shoulder toward the verandah, and his coarse voice dropped a full octave. "The Presence has observed Bootea, the one called Gulab Begum, who is with Ajeet Singh?"

"Ah-ha!" It was Nana Sahib's exclamation.

"Yes," the Dewan answered drily.

"If a party of Bagrees were to go to the Pindari camp disguised as players and wrestlers, and the Gulab as a *nautchni*, Amir Khan might be enticed to her tent for she causes men to become drunk when she dances. Once she danced for Raja Karowlee, and, though he is old and fat and has more of wives than other possessions he became covetous of the girl. It is because of these things, that Ajeet keeps her within the length of his eye. Thus the Gulab would hold Amir Khan in her hand, and some night as he slept in her tent I would crawl neath the canvas and accomplish that which is desired."

"By Jove!" Nana Sahib exclaimed, "this jungle man has got the right idea. But if Ajeet goes on that trip he'll never come back—Hunsa will see to that."

Then the son of the Peshwa took a quick turn to the door and gazed out as if he had his Arab in mind—something wrong; but a sweet bit of deviltry had suddenly occurred to him. He had noticed the young Englishman's interest in Bootea; had known that the girl's eyes had shown admiration for the handsome sahib. A woman—by Jove! yes. If he could bring the two of them together; have the Gulab get Barlow sensually interested she might act as a spy, get Barlow to talk. No instrument like a woman for that purpose. Nana Sahib turned back to where the Dewan had been questioning Hunsa.

"That description of the Gulab as a *nautch* girl tickles my fancy, Dewani," he said. "Between ourselves I think the Resident's jackal, the impressionable young Captain, was rather taken with her. I'm giving a *nautch* this week, and the presence of Miss Gulab is desired—commanded."

"But Ajeet—"

Nana Sahib smiled sardonically. "You and Hunsa are planning to send her on a more difficult mission, so I have no doubt that this can be accomplished. The Ajeet should esteem it an honour."

The Dewan, also speaking in English, said, "I doubt if Ajeet would consent to the girl's going to the Pindari camp."

Nana Sahib swung on his heel to face Baptiste. "Sirdar, when you give an order to a soldier and he refuses to obey, what do you do?"

"Pouf, *mon* Prince," and Jean Baptiste snapped a thumb and finger expressively.

"See, Dewani?" Nana Sahib queried; "I like Hunsa's idea; and you've heard what the Commandant says."

The Dewan turned to the Bagree, "Will Ajeet consent to the Gulab acting thus?"

Hunsa's answer was illuminating: "The Chief will agree to it if he can't help himself."

There was a lull, each one turning this momentous thing over in his mind.

It was the jamadar who broke the silence; somewhat at a tangent he said: "As to a decoity, Your Honour said that we being of that profession should undertake one."

The Dewan roared; the burden of his expostulation was the word liar.

But Nana Sahib laughed tolerantly. "Don't mind me, Dewani; fancy all the petty rajas and officials stand in with these decoits for a share of the loot—I don't blame you, old chap."

Hunsa, taking the accusation of being a liar as a pure matter of course, ignored it, and now was drooling along, wedded to the one big idea that was in his mind:

"If a decoity were made perhaps it might even happen that one was killed—"

"Lovely! the 'One' will be, and his name is Ajeet," Nana Sahib cried gleefully.

But Hunsa plodded steadily on. "In that case Ajeet as Chief would be in the hands of the Dewan; then it could be mentioned to him that the Gulab was desired for this mission."

"That might be," the Dewan said quietly. "I will demand that Ajeet takes the Gulab to help secure Amir Khan and if he refuses I will give them no rations so that he will go on the decoity."

"No, Dewan Sahib," Hunsa objected; "say nothing of the Gulab, because Ajeet will refuse, and then he will not go on a decoity, fearing a trap. If you will refuse the rations now, I will say that you have promised that we will not be taken up if we make a decoity; then Ajeet will agree, because it is our profession."

"I must go," Nana Sahib declared; "this Hunsa seems to have brains as well as ferocity." He continued in English: "If you do go through with this, Dewan, tell Hunsa if anything happens when they make the decoity—and if I'm any reader of what is in a man's heart, I think something will happen the Ajeet—tell Hunsa to bring the Gulab to me. I like his idea, and we can't afford to let the girl get away. Don't forget to arrange for the Gulab at my *nautch*."

When Nana Sahib had gone Baptiste diplomatically withdrew, saying in English to the Minister: "Dewan Sahib, possibly this simple child of the jungle would feel embarrassment in opening his heart fully before a sahib, so you will excuse me."

This elimination of individuals gave the Dewan a fine opportunity; promises made without witnesses were sure to be of a richer texture; also surely the word of a Dewan was of higher value than the word of a decoit if, at a future time, their evidences clashed.

Then Hunsa was entrusted with a private matter that filled his ugly soul with delight. He assured Sewlal Sookdee, if he were promised, as he had been, full protection, would join in the enmeshing of Ajeet Singh.

Sewlal pledged his word to the jamadar that no matter if an outcry were raised over a decoity they would be protected—the matter would be hushed up.

Hunsa knew that this was no new thing; he had been engaged in many a decoity where men of authority had a share of the loot, and had effectually side-tracked investigation. In fact decoits always lived in the protection of some petty raja; they were an adjunct to the state, a source of revenue.

The Dewan had intimated that Hunsa and his men were to wait until a messenger brought them word where and when to make the decoity. Also if he betrayed them, failed to keep his compact with them, it would cause him the loss of his ugly head.

The jamadar quite believed this; it would be an easy matter, surrounded as they were by Mahratta troops.

So then for the next few days Hunsa and Sookdee cautiously developed a spirit of desire for action amongst the decoits, and a feeling of resentment against Ajeet who was opposed to engaging in a punishable crime so far from their refuge.

The Dewan sent for Ajeet and explained to him, as if it were a very great honour, that Nana Sahib, having heard of Bootea's wonderful grace, had asked her to appear at a *nautch* he was giving to the Sahibs and Hindu princes at his palace. No doubt Bootea would receive a handsome present for this, also it would incline the heart of the Prince to the Bagrees.

Ajeet was suspicious, but to refuse permission he knew would anger the Dewan; and he was in the Minister's hands. His position was none too secure; there was treachery in his own camp. He asked for a day to consult Bootea over the matter; in reality he wanted to consider it more fully before giving an answer.

Of course Hunsa knew about it, and he told Sookdee; and when the matter came up in camp they professed indignation at Ajeet's stupidity in not appreciating the honour; dancers were only too glad to appear before such people as the Prince and the Resident at a palace dance, they explained.

Of course the matter of Bootea's mission to the Pindari Chief had not been conveyed to Ajeet as yet; and Hunsa felt that this affair of the *nautch* was a propitious thing—an inserting of the thin edge of the wedge.

Somewhat grudgingly Ajeet consented, for Bootea, strangely enough, was quite eager over it. As Nana Sahib had fancied the girl had taken an unexplainable liking for Captain Barlow. Of course that, the call, is rarely explainable on reasonable grounds—it is a matter of a higher dispensation; just two pairs of eyes settle the whole business; one look and the thing is done.

The Sahib would see her in a new light—in an appealing light. In her thoughts there was nothing of a serious intent; just that to look upon him, perhaps to see in his eyes a friendly pleasure, would be intoxication.

So Ajeet took her to the palace to dance, but, of course, he had to cool his heels without the *durbar* chamber—smoke the hooka and chat with other natives while the one of desire was within.

The girl had an exquisite sense of the beauty of simplicity—both in dress and manner, and in her art; it was as if a lotus flower had been animated—given life. Her dancing was a floaty rhythm, an undulating drifting to the soft call of the *sitar*; and her voice, when she sang the *ghazal*, the love-song, was soft, holding the compelling power of subdued passion—it thrilled Barlow with an emotion that, when she had finished, caused him to take himself to task. It was as if he had said, "By Jove! fancy I've had a bit too much of that champagne—better look out."

Nana Sahib and the Captain were sitting side by side, and the Gulab, when she had finished the song, had swept her sinuous lithe form back in a graceful curtsy in front of the two, and, as if by accident, a red rose had floated to the feet of Captain Barlow. Surely her soft, dark, languorous eyes had said: "For thee."

With a cynical smile Nana Sahib picked up the rose and presented it to Barlow saying: "My dear Captain, you receive the golden apple—beauty will out."

Barlow's fingers trembled with suppressed emotion as he took the flower and carefully slipped it into a buttonhole.

Elizabeth, who sat next him, saw this by-play, and her voice was cold as she commented: "Homage is a delightful thing, but it spoils children."

Nana Sahib leaned across Barlow: "My dear Miss Hodson, these dancers always play to the gods—it is their trade. But there is safety in caste—in *varna*, which is the old Brahmin name for caste, meaning colour. When the Aryans came down into Hind they were olive-skinned and the aborigines here were quite black, so, to draw the line, they created caste and called it *varna*, meaning that they of the light skin were of a higher order than the aborigines—which they were. A white skin is like a shirt-of-mail, it protects morally, socially, in India."

"Ultimately, no doubt, Prince. And, of course, a dance-girl is one of the fourth caste, practically an outcast—an 'untouchable,'" Elizabeth commented.

Barlow knew this as a devilish arraignment of himself, for he had felt a strong attraction. He said nothing; but he was aware of a feeling of repulsion toward Elizabeth; her harshness, on so slight a provocation, suggested vindictiveness—a narrow exaction.

Nana Sahib was filled with delight—his evil soul revelled in this discord. Then and there, if he could have managed it, he would have suggested to the Captain that he would arrange for the Gulab to meet him—might even have her sent to his bungalow. But he had the waiting subtlety of a tiger that crouches by a pool for hours waiting for a kill; so, somewhat reluctantly, he let the opportunity pass. While he considered Barlow to be an Englishman possessed of rather slow perception, he knew that the Captain had a quixotic sense of honour, and possibly such a proposal might destroy his influence.

And Bootea went back to the camp with Ajeet, suffused to silence by the strange thing that had happened, the strange infatuation—for it was that—that had so suddenly filled her heart for the handsome sahib whose soft, brave eyes had looked through hers into her very soul.

# CHAPTER VI

Nana Sahib had assumed a gracious manner toward Ajeet Singh when Bootea had been brought to the *nautch*. He had bestowed a handsome gift upon the Chief, ten gold *mohrs*; and for Bootea there had been the gift of a ruby, also ten gold *mohrs*.

This munificence,—for Hunsa and Sookdee declared it to be a rare extravagance,—was not so much as reward for Bootea's *nautch* as a desire on the part of the astute Prince to prepare for the greater service required.

The Dewan also was very gracious to Ajeet over his compliance; but, at the same time, declared that an order had been passed by Baptiste that if the Bagrees would not obey the command to go after Amir Khan he would not pay them a thousand rupees a day out of the treasury. He put all this very affably; raised his two fat hands toward heaven declaring that he was helpless in the matter— Baptiste was the commander, and he was but a dewan. With a curious furtive look in his ox-eyes he advised Ajeet to consult with Hunsa over a method of obtaining money for the decoits. He would not commit himself as to making a decoity, for when they had seized upon the Chief for the crime Ajeet could not then say that the Dewan had instigated it; there would be only Hunsa's word for this, and, of course, he would deny that the Minister was the father of the scheme.

And in the camp Hunsa and Sookdee were clamouring at Ajeet to undertake a decoity for they were all in need, and to be idle was not their way of life.

Hunsa went the length of telling Ajeet that the Dewan would even send them word where a decoity of much loot could be made and in a safe way, too, for the Dewan would take care that neither sepoys nor police would be in the way.

And then one day there came to the Bagree camp a mysterious message. A yogi, his hair matted with filth till it stood twisted and writhed on his head like the serpent tresses of Medusa, his lean skeleton ash-daubed body clothed in yellow, on his forehead the crescent of Eklinga, in his hand a pair of clanking iron tongs, crawled wearily to the tents where were the decoits, and bleared out of blood-shot blobs of faded brown at Ajeet Singh.

He had a message for the Chief from the god Bhyroo who galloped at night on a black horse, and the message had to do with the decoits, for if they were successful they could make offering to the priests at the temple of Bhowanee, for in her service decoity was an honourable occupation and of great antiquity.

Hunsa and Sookdee had come to sit on their heels, and as they listened they knew that the wily old Dewan had sent the *yogi* so that it could not be said that he, the Minister, had told them this thing.

A rich jewel merchant of Delhi was then at Poona on his way to the Nizam's court. He had a wealth of jewels—pearls the size of a bird's egg, emeralds the size of a betel nut, and diamonds that were like stars. This was true for the merchant had paid the duty as he passed the border into Mahrattaland.

Ajeet gave the yogi two rupees for food, though, viewing the animated skeleton, it seemed a touch of irony.

Then the jamadars considered the message so deeply wrapped in mysticism. Hunsa unhesitatingly declared that the yogi was a messenger from the Dewan, and if they did not take advantage of it they would perhaps have to fare forth on lean stomachs and in disgrace—perhaps would be beaten by the Mahratta sepoys—undoubtedly they would.

Sookdee backed up the jamadar.

"Very well," declared Ajeet, "we will go on this mission. But remember this, Hunsa, that if there is treachery, if we are cast into the hands of the Dewan, I swear by Bhowanee that I will have your life."

"Treachery!" It was the snarl of an enraged animal, and Hunsa sprang to his feet. He whirled, and facing Sookdee, said: "Let Bhowanee decide who is traitor—let Ajeet and me take the ordeal."

"That is but fair," Sookdee declared. "The ordeal of the heated cannon ball will surely burn the hand of the traitor if there is one," and he looked at Ajeet; and though suspicious that this was still another trap, Ajeet without cowardice could not decline.

"I will take the ordeal," he declared.

"We will take the ordeal tonight," Hunsa said; "and we should prepare with haste the method of the decoity, for the merchant may pass, and we must take the road in a proper disguise. There is the village to be decided upon where he will rest in his journey, and many things."

Even Ajeet was forced to acquiesce in this.

Boastfully Hunsa declared: "The ordeal will prove that I am thinking only of our success. This method of livelihood has been our profession for generations, and yet when we are in the protection of the powerful Dewan Ajeet says I am a traitor to our salt."

For an hour they discussed the best manner of sallying forth in a way that would leave them unsuspected of robbing. One of their favourite methods was adopted; to go in a party of twenty or thirty as mendicants and bearers of the bones of relatives to the waters of the sacred Ganges. No doubt the yogi would accompany them as their priest, especially if well paid for the service.

The plot was elaborated on, or rather adapted from past expeditions. Ajeet would be represented as a petty raja, with his retinue of servants and his guard. The Gulab Begum would be convincing as a princess, the wife of the raja. The wife of Sookdee could be a lady-in-waiting.

As a respectable strong party of holy men, and a prince, they would gain the confidence of the merchant, even of the *patil* of the village where he would rest for a night.

They would send spies into Poona to obtain knowledge of the jewel merchant's movements. The spies, two men who were happy in the art of ingratiating themselves into the good graces of prospective victims, would attach themselves to the merchant's party, and at night slip away and join the robber band so that they might judge where he would camp next night; at some village that would be a day's march.

When questioned, the *yogi* told them where they would find the merchant; he was stopping with a friend in Poona. So the two set off, and the Bagrees prepared for their journey.

For the ordeal a cannon ball was needed and a blacksmith to heat it. And as Hunsa had been the father of the scheme, Sookdee declared that he must procure these from the Mahratta camp.

Hunsa agreed to this.

The Bagrees were encamped to one side of the Mahratta troops in a small jungle of *dhak* and slim-growing bamboos that afforded them privacy.

In negotiating for the loan of a blacksmith Hunsa had impressed upon a sergeant his sincerity by the gift of two rupees; and two rupees more to the blacksmith made it certain that the heating of the cannon ball would not make the test unfair to Hunsa.

A peacock perched high in the feathery top of a giant *sal* tree was crying "miaow, miaow!" to the dipping sun when, in the centre of the Bagree camp the blacksmith, sitting on his haunches in front of a charcoal fire in which nested the iron cannon ball, fanned the flames with his pair of goat-skin hand-bellows.

Lots were cast as to which of the two would take the ordeal first, and it fell to Ajeet. First seven paces were marked off, and Ajeet was told that he must not run, but take the seven steps as in a walk, carrying the hot iron on a pipal leaf on his palm.

"This food of the cannon is now hot," the blacksmith declared, dropping his bellows and grasping a pair of iron tongs.

As Sookdee placed a broad pipal leaf upon the jamadar's palm, Ajeet repeated in a firm voice: "I take the ordeal. If I am guilty, Maha Kali, may the sign of thy judgment appear upon my flesh!"

"We are ready," Sookdee declared, and the waiting blacksmith swung the instrument of justice from its heat in the glowing charcoal to the outstretched hand of the jamadar.

Hunsa's hungry eyes glowed in pleased viciousness, for the blacksmith had indeed heated the metal; the green pipal leaf squirmed beneath its heat like a worm, as Ajeet Singh, with the military stride of a soldier, took the seven paces.

Then dropping the thing of torture he extended his slim small hand to Sookdee for inspection.

Hunsa's villainy had worked out. A white rime, like a hoar frost, fretting the deep red of the scorched skin, that was as delicate as that on a woman's palm.

Sookdee muttered a pitying cry, and Hunsa declared boastfully: "When men have evil in their hearts it is known to Bhowanee; behold her sign!"

But Ajeet laughed, saying: "Let Hunsa have the iron; he, too, will know of its heat."

"Put it again in the fire," declared Sookdee, "for it is an ordeal in which only the guilty is punished; but the ball must be of the same heat."

And once more the shot was returned to the charcoal.

Gulab Begum pushed her way rapidly to where the jamadars stood; but Sookdee objected, saying: "When men appeal to Bhowanee it is not proper that women should be of the ceremony; it will indeed anger our mother goddess."

"Thou art a fool, Sookdee," Bootea declared. "The hand of your chief is in pain though he shows it not in his face. Shall a brave man suffer because you are without feeling!"

She turned to the Chief. "Here I have cocoanut oil and a bandage of soft muslin. Hold to me your hand, Ajeet."

"It is not needed, Gulab, star-flower," the Chief declared proudly.

The Gulab had poured from a ram's horn cool soothing cocoanut oil upon the burns, and then she wrapped about the hand a bandage of shimmering muslin, bound in a wide strip of silk-like plantain leaf, saying: "This will keep the oil cool to your wound, Chief; it will not let it dry out to increase the heat."

There was another band of muslin passed around the leaf, and as the Gulab turned away, she said: "Think you, Sookdee, that Bhowanee will be offended because of mercy. Some day, Jamadar, fire will be put upon your face, when the head has been lopped from your body, to hide the features of a decoit that it may not bear witness against the tribe."

"You have delayed the ordeal," Sookdee answered surlily, "and because of that Bhowanee will have anger."

The blacksmith, though pumping with both hands at his pair of bellows, had felt the impress of the two silver coins in his loin cloth, and, true to the bribe from Hunsa, had adroitly doctored his fire by dusting sand here and there so that the shot had lost, instead of gained heat. Now he cried out: "This kabob of the cannon is cooked, and my arms are tired whilst you have talked."

Rising he seized his tongs asking, "Who now will have it placed upon his palm?"

"Put it here," Sookdee said, as he laid a pipal leaf of twice the thickness he had given Ajeet upon the palm of Hunsa.

Then Hunsa, having repeated the appeal to Bhowanee, strode toward the goal, and reaching it, cast the iron shot to the ground, holding up his hand in triumph. His was the hand of a gorilla, thick skinned, rough and hard like that of a workman, and now it showed no sign of a burning.

"What say you, Ajeet Singh?" Sookdee asked.

"As to the ordeal," the Chief answered, "according to our faith Bhowanee has spoken. But know you this, though the scar is in my palm, in my heart is no treachery. As to Hunsa, the ordeal has cleared him in your minds, and perhaps it is true. We will go forth to the decoity and what is to be will be. We are but servants of Bhowanee, and if we make vow to sacrifice a buffalo at her temple perhaps she will keep us in her protection."

Ajeet knew that he had been tricked somehow, but to dispute the ordeal, the judgment of the black goddess, would be like an apostacy—it would turn every Bagree against him—it would be a shatterment of their tenets. So he said nothing but accepted mutely the decree.

But Bootea's sharp eyes had been busy. She had watched the blacksmith, to whom Ajeet had paid little attention. In the faces of Hunsa and Sookdee she had caught flitting expressions of treachery. She knew that Ajeet had been guiltless of treason to the others, for she had been close to him. Besides she had, when roused, an imperious temper. The Bagree women were allowed greater freedom than other women of Hindustan, even greater freedom than the Mahratta females who, though they appeared in public unveiled, in the homes were treated as children, almost as slaves. The Bagree women at times even led gangs of decoits. Her anger had been roused by Sookdee earlier, and now rising from where she sat, she strode imperiously forward till she faced the jamadars:

"Your Chief is too proud to deny this trick that you, Sookdee and Hunsa, and that accursed labourer of another caste, the blacksmith, that shoer of Mahratta horses whom Hunsa has bribed, have put upon him in the name of Bhowanee."

Sookdee stared in affrighted silence, and Hunsa's bellow of rage was stilled by Ajeet, who whirling upon him, the jade-handled knife in his grip, commanded: "Still your clamour! The Gulab has but seen the truth. I, also, know that, but a soldier may not speak as may one of his women-kind."

There was a sudden hush. A tremor of apprehension had vibrated from Bagree to Bagree; the jamadars felt it. A spark, one lunge with a knife, and they would be at each other's throats; the men of Alwar against the men of Karowlee; even caste against caste, for the Bagrees from Alwar were of the Solunkee caste, while the Karowlee men were of Kolee caste.

And there the slim girl form of Bootea stood outlined, a delicate bit of statuary, like something of marble that had come from the hand of Praxiteles, the white muslin sari in its gentle clinging folds showing against the now darkening wall of bamboo jungle. There was something about the Gulab, magnetic, omnipotent, that subdued men, that enslaved them; an indescribable subtlety of gentle strength, like the bronze-blue temper in steel. And her eyes—no one can describe the compelling eyes of the world, the awful eyes that in their fierce magnetism act on a man like *bhang* on a Ghazi or, like the eyes of Christ, smother him in love and goodness. The *karait* of India has a dull red eye without pupil, of which it is the belief that if a man gaze into it for a time he will go mad. To say that Bootea's eyes were beautiful was to say nothing, and to describe their compelling force was impossible.

So as they rested on the sullen eyes of Sookdee he quivered; and the others stood in silence as Ajeet took Bootea by the arm saying, "Come, my lotus flower," led her to the tent.

There the jamadar put his sinewy arms about the slender girl, and bent his handsome face to implant a kiss on her red lips, but she thrust his arms from her and drew back saying, "No, Ajeet!"

"Why, lotus—why, Gulab? Often from thy lips I have heard that there is no love in thy heart for any man even for me, but is it not a lie, the curious lie of a woman who resents a master?"

Ajeet in a mingling of awe and anger had dropped into the formal "thou" pronoun instead of the familiar "you."

"No, Ajeet, it is the truth; I do not tell lies."

"But out there thou denounced those sons of depraved parents in defence of Ajeet; thou bound up his hand as a mother dresses the wounds of a child in her love—even mocked Bhowanee and the ordeal; then sayest thou there is no love in thy heart for Ajeet."

"There is not; just the tie such as is between us, that is all. I never learned love—I was but a pawn, a prize. Seest that, Ajeet?" and Bootea laid a finger upon the iron bracelet on her arm—the badge of a widow.

Ajeet Singh sneered: "A metal lie, a—"

"Stop!" The girl's voice was almost a scream of expostulation. "To speak of that means death, thou fool. And thou hast sworn—"

Ajeet's face had blanched. Then a surge of anger re-flushed it.

"Gulab," he said presently, "take care that the love thou say'st is dead—but which is not, for it never dies in the heart of a woman, it is but a smouldering fire—take care that it springs not into flame at the words of some other man, the touch of his hands, or the light of his eyes, because then, by Bhowanee, I will kill thee."

The Gulab stamped a foot upon the earth floor of the tent: "Coward! now I hate thee! Only the weak, the cowards, threaten women. When thou art brave and strong I do not hate if I do not love. 'Tis thou, Ajeet, who art to take care."

Outside Guru Lal was casting holy oil upon the troubled waters of a disputed ordeal. The wily old priest knew well how omens and ordeals could be manipulated. Besides, unity among the Bagree leaders, leading to much loot, would bring him tribute for the gods.

"It may be," he was saying to Sookdee, "that the blacksmith, who is not of our tribe, nor of our nine castes, but is of the Sumar caste, has sought to put shame upon our gods by a trick. At best he was a surly rascal of little thought. It may be that the iron shot was made too hot for the hand of the Chief. An ordeal is a fair test when its observance is equal between men; it is then that the goddess judges and gives the verdict—her way is always just. Have not we many times read wrongly her omens, and have misjudged the signs, and have suffered. And Ajeet acted like one who is not guilty."

"And think you, Guru, that Ajeet will give you a present of rupees for this talk that is like the braying of an ass?" Hunsa growled.

But Sookdee objected, saying: "Guru Lal is a holy man of age, and his blood runs without heat, therefore if he speaks, the words are not a matter for passion, but to be considered. We will go upon a decoity, which is our duty, and leave the ordeal and all else in the hands of Bhowanee."

# CHAPTER VII

Perhaps it was the customs official that told Dewan Sewlal about the *Akbar Ka Diwa*, the Lamp of Akbar, the ruby that was so called because of its gorgeous blood-red fire, as being in the iron box of the merchant.

This ruby had been an eye in one of the two gorgeous jewelled peacocks that surmounted the "Peacock Throne" at Delhi in the time of Akbar to the time when the Persian conqueror, Nadir Shah, sacked Delhi and took the Peacock Throne and the Kohinoor, and everything else of value back to Persia. But he didn't get the ruby for the Vizier of the King of Delhi stole it. Then Alam, the eunuch, stole it from the Vizier. Its possession was desirable, not only because of its great value as a jewel, but because it held in its satanic glitter an unearthly power, either of preservation to its holder or malignant evil against his enemies.

At any rate Sewlal sent for Hunsa the night of the ordeal and explained to him, somewhat casually, that a jewel merchant passing through Mahrattaland had in his collection a ruby of no great value, but a stone that he would like to become possessed of because a ruby was his lucky gem. The Dewan intimated that Hunsa would get a nice private reward for this particular gem, if by chance he could, quite secretly, procure it for him.

Next day was a busy one in the Bagree camp.

Having followed the profession of decoits and thugs for generations it was with them a fine art; unlimited pains were taken over every detail. As it had been decided that they would go as a party of mendicants and bearers of family bones to Mother Ganges, there were many things to provide to carry out the masquerade—stage properties, as it were; red bags for the bones of females, and white bags for those of the males.

In two days one of the spies came with word that Ragganath, the merchant, had started on his journey, riding in a covered cart drawn by two of the slim, silk-skinned trotting bullocks, and was accompanied by six men, servants and guards; on the second night he would encamp at Sarorra. So a start was made the next morning.

Sookdee, Ajeet Singh, and Hunsa, accompanied by twenty men, and Gulab Begum took the road, the Gulab travelling in an enclosed cart as befitted the favourite of a raja, and with her rode the wife of Sookdee as her maid.

Ajeet rode a Marwari stallion, a black, roach-crested brute, with bad hocks and an evil eye. The Ajeet sat his horse a convincing figure, a Rajput Raja.

Beneath a rich purple coat gleamed, like silver tracery, his steel shirt-of-mail; through his sash of red silk was thrust a straight-bladed sword, and from the top of his turban of blue-and-gold-thread, peeped a red cap with dangling tassel of gold.

In the afternoon of the second day the Bagrees came to the village of Sarorra.

"We will camp here," the leader commanded, "close to the mango *tope* through which we have just passed, then we will summon the headman, and if he is as such accursed officials are, the holy one, the yogi, will cast upon him and his people a curse; also I will threaten him with the loss of his ears."

"The one who is to be destroyed has not yet come," Hunsa declared, "for here is what these dogs of villagers call a place of rest though it is but an open field."

Ajeet turned upon the jamadar: "The one who is to be destroyed, say you, Hunsa? Who spoke in council that the merchant was to be killed? We are men of decoity, we rob these fat pirates who rob the poor, but we take life only when it is necessary to save our own."

"And when a robbed one who has power, such as rich merchants have, make complaint and give names, the powers take from us our profit and cast us into jail," Hunsa retorted.

"And forget not, Ajeet, that we are here among the Mahrattas far from our own forests that we can escape into if there is outcry," Sookdee interjected. "If the voices are hushed and the bodies buried beneath where we cook our food, there will be only silence till we are safe back in Karowlee. The Dewan will not protect us if there is an outcry—he will deny that he has promised protection."

The Bagrees were already busy preparing the camp, the camp of a supposed party of men on a sacred mission.

It was like the locating of a circus. The tents they had brought stood gaudily in the hot sun, some white and some of cotton cloth dyed in brilliant colours, red, and blue, and yellow. In front of Ajeet's tent a bamboo pole was planted, from the top of which floated a red flag carrying a figure of the monkey god, Hanuman, embroidered in green and yellow.

The red and white bags carrying bones, which were supposed to be the bones of defunct relatives, were suspended from tripods of bamboo to preserve them from the pollution of the soil.

And presently three big drums, Nakaras, were arranged in front of the yogi's tent, and were being beaten by strong-armed drummers, while a conch shell blared forth a discordant note that was supposed to be pleasing to the gods.

Some of the Bagrees issued from their tents having suddenly become canonised, metamorphosed from highwaymen to devout yogis, their bodies, looking curiously lean and ascetic, now clothed largely in ashes and paint.

"Go you, Hunsa," Ajeet commanded, "into this depraved village and summon the *patil* to come forth and pay to the sainted yogi the usual gift of one rupee four annas, and make his salaams. Also he is to provide fowl and fruits for us who are on this sacred mission. He may be a son of swine, such as the lord of a village is, so speak, Jamadar, of the swords the Raja's guards carry. Say nothing as to the expected one, but let your eyes do all the questioning."

Hunsa departed on his mission, and even then the villagers could be seen assembled between the Bagrees and the mud huts, watching curiously the encampment.

"Sookdee," Ajeet said, "if we can rouse the anger of the *patil*—"

The Jamadar laughed. "If you insist upon the payment of silver you will accomplish that, Ajeet."

Ajeet touched his slim fingers to Sookdee's arm: "Do not forget, Jamadar—call me Raja. But as to the village; if we anger them they will not entertain the merchant; they will not let him rest in the village. And also if they are of an evil temper we will warn the merchant that they are thieves who will cut his throat and rob him. We will give him the protection of our numbers."

"If the merchant is fat—and when they attain wealth they always become fat—he will be happy with us, Raja, thinking perhaps that he will escape a gift of money the *patil* would exact."

"Yes," Ajeet Singh answered, "we will ask him for nothing when he departs."

After a time Hunsa was seen approaching, and with him the grey-whiskered *patil*.

The latter was a commoner. He suggested a black-faced, grey-whiskered monkey of the jungles. Indeed the pair were an anthropoid couple, Hunsa the gorilla, and the headman an ape. Behind them straggled a dozen villagers, men armed with long ironwood sticks of combat.

The headman salaamed the yogi and Ajeet, saying, "This is but a poor place for holy men and the Raja to rest, for the water is bad and famine is upon us."

"A liar, and the son of a wild ass," declared Ajeet promptly. "Give to this saint the gift of silver, lest he put the anger of Kali upon you, and call upon her of the fiery furnace in the sacred hills to destroy your houses. Also send fowl and grain, and think yourself favoured of Kali that you make offering to such a holy one, and to a Raja who is in favour with Sindhia."

But the villager had no intention of parting with worldly goods if he could get out of it. He expostulated, enlarged upon his poverty, rubbed dust upon his forehead, and called upon the gods to destroy him if he had a breakfast in the whole village for himself and people, declaring solemnly; "By my Junwa!"—though he wore no sacred thread,—"there is no food for man or horse in the village." Then he waxed angry, asking indignantly, who were these stragglers upon the road that they should come to him, an official of the Peshwa, to demand tribute; he would have them destroyed. Beyond, not two *kos* away, were a thousand soldiers,—which was a gorgeous lie,—who if he but sent a messenger would come and behead the lot, would cast the sacred bones in the gaudy bags upon the dunghill of the village bullocks.

"Tomorrow, monkey-man, the gift will be doubled," Ajeet answered calmly, "for that is the law, and you know it."

But the *patil*, thinking there would be little fight in a party of pilgrims and mendicants, called to his stickmen to bring help and they would beat these insolent ones and drive them on their way.

"Take the yogi, Hunsa," Ajeet said, "and the men that have the fire-powder and throw it upon the thatched roof of a hut in the way of a visitation from the gods, because this ape will not leave us in peace for our mission until he is subdued."

In obedience as Hunsa and the yogi moved toward the village, the *patil* cried. "Where go you?"

"We go with a message from the gods to you who offer insult to a holy one."

The villagers armed with sticks, retreated slowly before the yogi, dreading to offer harm to the sainted one. Muttering his curses, his iron tongs clanking at every step, the yogi strode to the first mud-wall huts, and there raising his voice cried aloud: "Maha Kalil consume the houses of these men of an evil heart who would deny the offering to Thee."

Then at a wave of his skeleton arm the two men threw upon the thatched roof of a hut a grey preparation of gunpowder which was but a pyrotechnical trick, and immediately the thatch burst into flames.

"There, accursed ones—unbelievers! Kali has spoken!" the yogi declared solemnly, and turning on his heels went back to the camp.

The headman and his men, with howls of dismay, rushed back to stop the conflagration. And just then the jewel merchant arrived in his cart. The curtains of the canopy were thrown back and the fat Hindu sat blinking his owl eyes in consternation. At sight of Ajeet he descended, salaamed, and asked:

"Has there been a decoity in the village—is it war and bloodshed?"

Ajeet assumed the haughty condescending manner of a Rajput prince, and explained, with a fair scope of imagination that the *patil* was a man of ungovernable temper who gave protection to thieves and outlaws, that the village itself was a nest for them. That two of his servants, having gone into the village to purchase food, had been set upon, beaten and robbed; that the conflagration had been caused by the fire from a gun that one of the debased villagers had poked through a hole in the roof to shoot his servants.

"As my name is Ragganath, it is a visitation upon these scoundrels," the merchant declared.

"It is indeed, Sethjee."

Ajeet had diplomatically used the "Sethjee," which was a friendly rendering of the name "Seth," meaning "a merchant," and the wily Hindu, not to be outdone in courtesy, promoted Ajeet.

"Such an outrage, Maharaja, on the part of these low-caste people in the presence of the sainted one, and the pilgrims upon such a sacred mission to Mother Gunga, has brought upon them the wrath of the gods. May the village be destroyed; and the *patil* when he dies come back to earth a snake, to crawl upon his belly."

"The headman even refused to give the holy one the gift of silver—tendering instead threats," Ajeet added.

The merchant spat his contempt: "Wretches!" he declared; "debased associates of skinners of dead animals, and scrapers of skulls; Bah!" and he spat again. "And to think but for the Presence having arrived here first I most assuredly would have gone into the village, and perhaps have been slain for my—"

He stopped and rolled his eyes apprehensively. He had been on the point of mentioning his jewels, but, though he was amongst saints and kings, he suddenly remembered the danger.

"We would not have camped here," Ajeet declared, "had we not been a strong party, because this village has an evil reputation. You have been favoured by the gods in finding honest men in the way of protection, and, no doubt, it is because you are one who makes offerings to the deity."

"And if the Maharaja will suffer the presence of a poor merchant, who is but a shopkeeper, I will rest here in his protection."

Ajeet Singh graciously consented to this, and the merchant commanded his men to erect his small tent beneath the limbs of the deep green mango trees.

The decoits watched closely the transport of the merchant's effects from the cart to the tent. When a strong iron box, that was an evident weight for its two carriers, was borne first their eyes glistened. Therein was the wealth of jewels the flying horsemen of the night had whispered to the yogi about.

# CHAPTER VIII

When the merchant's tent had been erected, and he had gone to its shelter, the jamadars, sitting well beyond the reach of his ears, held a council of war. Ajeet was opposed to the killing of Ragganath and his men, but Hunsa pointed out that it was the only way: they were either decoits or they were men of toil, men of peace. Dead men were not given to carrying tales, and if no stir were made about the decoity until they were safely back in Karowlee they could enjoy the fruits Of their spoils, which would be, undoubtedly, great. By the use of the strangling cloth there would be no outcry, no din of battle; they of the village would think that the camp was one of sleep. Then when the bodies had been buried in a pit, the earth tramped down flat and solid, and cooking fires built over it to obliterate all traces of a grave, they would strike camp and go back the way they had come.

Ajeet was forced to admit that it was the one thorough way, but he persisted that they were decoits and not thugs.

At this Sookdee laughed: "Jamadar," he said, "what matters to a dead man the manner of his killing? Indeed it is a merciful way. Such as Bhowanee herself decreed—in a second it is over. But with the spear, or the sword—ah! I have seen men writhe in agony and die ten times before it was an end."

"But a caste is a caste," Ajeet objected, "and the manner of the caste. We are decoits, and we only slay when there is no other way."

Hunsa tipped his gorilla body forward from where it rested on his heels as he sat, and his lowering eyes were sullen with impatience:

"Chief Ajeet," he snarled, "think you that we can rob the *seth* of his treasure without an outcry—and if there is an outcry, that he will not go back to those of his caste in Poona, and when trouble is made, think you that the Dewan will thank us for the bungling of this? And as to the matter of a thug or a decoit, half our men have been taught the art of the strangler. With these,"—and extending his massive arms he closed his coarse hands in a gnarled grip,— "with these I would, with one sharp in-turn on the *roomal*, crack the neck of the merchant and he would be dead in the taking of a breath. And, Ajeet, if this that is the manner of men causes you fear—"

"Hunsa," and Ajeet's voice was constrained in its deadliness, "that ass's voice of yours will yet bring you to grief."

But Sookdee interposed:

"Let us not quarrel," he said. "Ajeet no doubt has in his mind Bootea as I have Meena. And it would be well if the two were sent on the road in the cart, and when our work is completed we will follow. Indeed they may know nothing but that there is some jewel, such as women love, to be given them."

"Look you," cried Hunsa thrusting his coarse hand out toward the road, "even Bhowanee is in favour. See you not the jackal?"

Turning their eyes in the direction Hunsa indicated, a jackal was seen slinking across the road from right to left.

"Indeed it is an omen," Sookdee corroborated; "if on our journeys to commit a decoity that is always a good omen."

"And there is the voice!" Hunsa exclaimed, as the tremulous lowing of a cow issued from the village.

He waved a beckoning hand to Guru Lal, for they had brought with them their tribal priest as an interpreter of omens chiefly. "Is not the voice of the cow heard at sunset a good omen, Guru?" he demanded.

"Indeed it is," the priest affirmed. "If the voice of a cow is heard issuing at twilight from a village at which decoits are to profit, it is surely a promise from Bhowanee that a large store of silver will be obtained."

"Take thee to thy prayers, Guru," Ajeet commanded, "for we have matters to settle." He turned to Sookdee. "Your omens will avail little if there is prosecution over the disappearance of the merchant. I am supposed to be in command, the leader, but I am the led. But I will not withdraw, and it is not the place of the chief to handle the *roomal*. We will eat our food, and after the evening prayers will sit about the fire and amuse this merchant with stories such as honest men and holy ones converse in, that he may be at peace in his mind. As Sookdee says, the women will be sent to the grove of trees we came through on the road."

"We will gather about the fire of the merchant," Sookdee declared, "for it is in the mango grove and hidden from sight of the villagers. Also a guard will be placed between here and the village, and one upon the roadway."

"And while we hold the merchant in amusement," Hunsa added, "men will dig the pits here, two of them, each within a tent so that they will not be seen at work."

"Yes, Ajeet," Sookdee said with a suspicion of a sneer, "we will give the merchant the consideration of a decent burial, and not leave him to be eaten by jackals and hyenas as were the two soldiers you finished with your sword when we robbed the camel transport that carried the British gold in Oudh."

"If it is to be, cease to chatter like jays," Ajeet answered crossly.

In keeping with their assumed characters, the evening meal was ushered in with a peace-shattering clamour from the drums and a raucous blare from conch-shell horns. Then the devout murderers offered up prayers of fervency to the great god, beseeching their more immediate branch of the deity, Bhowanee, to protect them.

And at the same time, just within the mud walls of Sarorra, its people were placing flowers and cocoanuts and sweetmeats upon the shrine of the god of their village.

Just without the village gate the elephant-nosed Ganesh sat looking in whimsical good nature across his huge paunch toward the place of crime, the deep shadow that lay beneath the green-leafed mango trees.

In the hearts of the Bagrees there was unholy joy, an eager anticipation, a gladsome feeling toward Bhowanee who had certainly guided this rapacious merchant with his iron box full of jewels to their camp.

Indeed they would sacrifice a buffalo at her temple of Kajuria, for that was the habit of their clan when the booty was great. The taking of life was but an incident. In Hindustan humans came up like flies, returning over and over to again encumber the crowded earth. In the vicissitudes of life before long the merchant would pass for a reincorporation of his soul, and probably, because of his sins as an oppressor of the poor, come back as a turtle or a jackass; certainly not as a revered cow—he was too unholy. In the gradation of humans he was but a merchant of the caste of the third dimension in the great quartette of castes. It would not be like killing a Brahmin, a sin in the sight of the great god.

This philosophy was as subtle as the perfume of a rose, unspoken, even at the moment a floaty thought. Like their small hands and their erect air of free-men, the Rajput atmosphere, it had grown into their created being, like the hunting instinct of a Rampore hound.

The merchant, smoking his *hookah*, having eaten, observed with keen satisfaction the evening devotions of the supposed mendicants. As it grew dark their guru was offering up a prayer to the Holy Cow, for she was to be worshipped at night. The merchant's appreciation was largely a worldly one, a business sense of insurance—safety for his jewels and nothing to pay for security—men so devout would have the gods in their mind and not robbery. When the jamadars, and some of the Bagrees who were good story tellers, and one a singer, did him the honour of coming to sit at his camp-fire he was pleased.

"Sit you here at my right," he said to Hunsa, for he conceived him to be captain of the Raja's guard.

Sookdee and the others, without apparent motive, contrived it so that a Bagree or two sat between each of the merchant's men, engaging them in pleasant speech, tendering tobacco. And, as if in modesty, some of the Bagrees sat behind the retainers.

"This is indeed a courtesy," the merchant assured Hunsa; "a poor trader feels honoured by a visit from so brave a soldier as the captain of the Raja's guard."

He noticed, too, with inward satisfaction, that the jamadars had left their weapons behind, which they had done in a way of not arousing their victim's fears.

"Would not it be deemed a courtesy," the merchant asked, "if one like myself, who is a poor trader, should go to pay his respects to the Raja ere he retires, for of course it would be beneath his dignity to come to his servant?"

"No, indeed," declared Hunsa quickly, thinking of the graves that were even then being dug; "he is a man of a haughty temper, and when he is in the society of the beautiful dancing girl who is with him, he cares not to be disturbed. Even now he is about to escort her in the cart down the road to where there is a shrine that women of that caste make offering to."

It had been arranged that Ajeet would escort Bootea, with two Bagrees as attendants, to the grove of trees half a mile down the road. He had insisted on this in the way of a negative support to the murder. As there would be no fighting this did not reflect on his courage as a leader. And as to complicity, Hunsa knew that as the leader of the party, Ajeet would be held the chief culprit. It was always the leader of a gang of decoits who was beheaded when captured, the others perhaps escaping with years of jail. And Hunsa himself, even Sookdee, would be safe, for they were in league with the Dewan.

There was an hour of social talk; many times Hunsa fingered the *roomal* that was about his waist; the yellow-and-white strangling cloth with which Bhowanee had commanded her disciples, the thugs, to kill their victims. In one corner of it was tied a silver rupee for luck. The natural ferocity of his mind threw him into an eager anticipation: he took pride in his proficiency as a strangler; his coarse heavy hands, like those of a Punjabi wrestler, were suited to the task. Grasping the cloth at the base of a victim's skull, tight to the throat, a side-twist inward and the trick was done, the spine snapped like a pipe-stem. And he had been somewhat out of practice—he had regretted that; he was fearful of losing the art, the knack.

About the fat paunch of the merchant was a silver-studded belt. Hunsa eyed this speculatively. Beyond doubt in its neighbourhood would be the key to the iron box; and when its owner lay on his back, his bulbous eyes glaring upward to where the moon trickled through the thick foliage of the mango tree beneath which they sat, he would seize the keys and be first to dabble his grimy fingers in the glittering gems.

Beyond, the village had hushed—the strident call of voices had ceased. Somewhere a woman was pounding grain in a wooden mortar—a dull monotonous "thud, thud, swish, thud" carrying on the dead air. Night-jars were circling above the trees, their plaintive call, "chy-eece, chy-e-ece!" filtering downward like the weird cry of spirits. Once the deep sonorous bugling note of a *saurus*, like the bass pipe of an organ, smote the stillness as the giant crane winged his way up the river that lay beyond, a mighty ribbon of silver in the moonlight. A jackal from the far side of the village, in the fields, raised a tremulous moan.

Sookdee looked into the eyes of Hunsa and he understood. It was the *tibao*, the happiest augury of success, for it came over the right shoulder of the victim.

Hunsa, feeling that the moment to strike had come, rose carelessly, saying: "Give me tobacco."

That was a universal signal amongst thugs, the command to strike.

Even as he uttered the words Hunsa had slipped behind the merchant and his towel was about the victim's neck. Each man who had been assigned as a strangler, had pounced upon his individual victim; while Sookdee stood erect, a knife in his hand, ready to plunge it into the heart of any one who was likely to overcome his assailant.

Hunsa had thrown the helpless merchant upon his face, and with one knee between his shoulder-blades had broken the neck; no sound beyond a gurgling breath of strangulation had passed the Hindu's lips. There had been no clamour, no outcry; nothing but a few smothered words, gasps, the scuffle of feet upon the earth; it was like a horrible nightmare, a fantastic orgy of murderous fiends. The flame of the campfire flickered sneers, drawn torture, red and green shadows in the staring faces of the men who lay upon the ground, and the figures of the stranglers glowed red in its light, like devils who danced in hell.

Hunsa had turned the merchant upon his back and his evil gorilla face was thrust into the face of his victim. No breath passed the thick protruding lips upon which was a froth of death.

As the Jamadar tore the keys from the waist-band, snapping a silver chain that was about the body, he said: "Sookdee, be quick. Have the bodies carried to the pits. Do not forget to drive a spear through each belly lest they swell up and burst open the earth."

"You have the keys to the chest, Hunsa?" Sookdee said, with suspicion in his voice.

"Yes, Jamadar; I will open it. We will empty it, and place the iron box on top of the bodies in a pit, for it is too heavy to carry, and if we are stopped it might be observed."

"Take the dead," Sookdee commanded the Bagrees; "lay them out; take down the tents that are over the pits, and by that time I will be there to count these dead things in the way of surety that not one has escaped with the tale.

"Come," he said to Hunsa, "together we will go to the iron box and open it; then there can be no suspicion that the men of Alwar have been defrauded."

Hunsa turned malignant eyes upon Sookdee, but, keys in hand, strode toward the tent.

Sookdee, thrusting in the fire a torch made from the feathery bark of the *kujoor* tree, followed.

Hunsa kneeling before the iron box was fitting the keys into the double locks. Then he drew the lids backward, and the two gasped at a glitter of precious stones that lay beneath a black velvet cloth Hunsa stripped from the gems.

Sookdee cried out in wonderment; and Hunsa, slobbering gutturals of avarice, patted the gems with his gorilla paws. He lifted a large square emerald entwined in a tracery of gold, delicate as the criss-cross of a spider's web, and held it to his thick lips.

"A bribe for a princess!" he gloated. "Take you this, Sookdee, and hide it as you would your life, for a gift to the son of the Peshwa, who, methinks, is behind the Dewan in this, we will be men of honour. And this"—a gleaming diamond in a circlet of gold—"for Sirdar Baptiste," and he rolled it in his loin cloth. "And this,"—a string of pearls, that as he laid it on the black velvet was like the tears of angels,—"This for the fat pig of a Dewan to set his four wives at each other's throats. Let not the others know of these, Sookdee, of these that we have taken for the account."

Suddenly there was a clamour of voices, cries, the clang of swords, the sharp crash of a shot, and the two jamadars, startled, eyes staring, stood with ears cocked toward the tumult.

"Soldiers!" Sookdee gasped. His hand brushed Hunsa's bare arm as he thrust it into the chest and brought it forth clasping jewels, which he tied in a knot of his waistcloth. "Take you something, Hunsa, and lock the box till we see," he said darting from the tent.

Hunsa filled a pocket of his brocaded Jacket, but he was looking for the Akbar Lamp, the ruby. He lifted out a tray and ran his grimy hands through the maze of gold and silver wrought ornaments below. His fingers touched, at the very bottom, a bag of leather. He tore it open, and a blaze of blood-red light glinted at him evilly where a ruby caught the flame of the torch that Sookdee had thrown to the earth floor as he fled.

With a snarl of gloating he rolled the ruby in a fold of his turban, locked the box, and darted after Sookdee.

He all but fell over the seven dead bodies of the merchant and his men as he raced to where a group was standing beyond. And there three more bodies lay upon the ground, and beside them, held, were two horses.

"It is Ajeet Singh," Sookdee said pointing to where the Chief lay with his head in the lap of a decoit. "These two native soldiers of the English came riding in with swiftness, for behind them raced Ajeet who must have seen them pass."

"And here," another added, "as the riders checked at sight of the dead, Ajeet pulled one from his horse and killed him, but the other, with a pistol, shot Ajeet and he is dead."

"The Chief is not dead," said the one who held his head in his lap; "he is but shot in the shoulder, and I have stopped the blood with my hand."

"And we have killed the other soldier," another said, "for, having seen the bodies, we could not let him live."

From Sookdee's hand dangled a coat of one of the dead.

"This that is a leather purse," he said, "contains letters; the red thing on them I have looked upon before—it is the seal of the Englay. It was here in the coat of that one who is a sergeant—the other being a soldier."

He put the leather case within the bosom of his shirt, adding: "This may even be of value to the Dewan. Beyond that, there was little of loot upon these dogs of the Englay—eight rupees. The coats and the turbans we will burn."

Hunsa stooped down and slipped the sandals from the feet of the one Sookdee had pointed out as the officer.

"The footwear is of little value, but we will take the brass cooking pots of the merchant," Sookdee said, eyeing this performance; there was suspicion in his eyes lighted from the flare of their camp fires.

"Sookdee," Hunsa said, "you have the Englay leather packet, but they do not send *sowars* through the land of the Mahratta with the real message written on the back of the messenger. In quiet

I will rip apart the soles of this footwear. Do you that with the saddles; therein is often hidden the true writing. In the slaying of these two we have acquired a powerful enemy, the English, and the message, if there be one, might be traded for our lives. Here are the keys to the box, for it is heavy."

Into Hunsa's mind had flashed the thought that the gods had opened the way, for he had plotted to do this thing—the destruction of Ajeet.

"Have all the bodies thrown into the pit, Sookdee," he advised; "make perfect the covering of the fire and ash, and while you prepare for flight I will go and bring Bootea's cart to carry Ajeet."

Then Hunsa was swallowed up in the gloom of the night, melting like a shadow into the white haze of the road as he raced like a grey wolf toward the Gulab, who now had certainly been delivered into his hands.

Soon his heart pumped and the choke of exertion slowed him to a fast walk. The sandals, bulky with their turned-up toes, worried him. He drew a knife from his sash and slit the tops off, muttering: "If it is here, the message of value, it will be between the two skins of the soles."

Now they lay flat and snug in his hand as he quickened his pace.

# CHAPTER IX

The Gulab heard the shot at the Bagree camp, and Hunsa found her trembling from apprehension.

"What has happened, Jamadar?" she cried. "Ajeet heard the beat of iron-shod hoofs upon the road, and seeing in the moonlight the two riders knew from the manner they sat the saddles that they were of the Englay service; when he called to them they heeded him not. Then Ajeet followed the two. Why was the shot, Hunsa?"

"They have killed Ajeet," Hunsa declared; "but also they are dead, and I have the leader's leather sandals for a purpose. The shot has roused the village, and even now our people are preparing for flight. Get you into the cart that I may take you to safety." He took the ruby from his turban, saying: "And here is the most beautiful ruby in Hind; the fat pig of a Dewan wants it, but I have taken it for you."

But Bootea pushed his hand away: "I take no present from you, Hunsa."

Hunsa put the jewel back in his turban and commanded the two men, who stood waiting, "Make fast the bullocks to the cart quickly lest we be captured, because other soldiers are coming behind."

The two Bagrees turned to where the slim pink-and-grey coated trotting bullocks were tethered by their short horns to a tree and leading them to the cart made fast the bamboo yoke across their necks.

"Get into the cart, Bootea," Hunsa commanded, for the girl had not moved.

"I will not!" she declared. "I'm going back to Ajeet; he is not dead—it is a trick."

"He *is* dead," Hunsa snarled, seizing her by arm.

The Gulab screamed words of denunciation. "Take your hands off me, son of a pig, accursed man of low caste! Ajeet will kill you for this, dog!"

At this the wife of Sookdee fled, racing back toward the camp. One of the men darted forward to follow, but Hunsa stayed him, saying, "Let her go—it is better; I war not upon Sookdee."

He had the Gulab now in the grasp of both his huge paws, and holding her tight, said rapidly: "Be still you she-devil, accursed fool! You are going to a palace to be a queen. The son of the Peshwa desires you. True, I, also, have desire, but fear not for, by Bhowanee! it is a life of glory, of jewels and rich attire that I take you to; so get into the cart."

But Bootea wrenched free an arm and struck Hunsa full upon his ugly face, screaming her rebellion.

"To be struck by a woman!" Hunsa blared; "not a woman, but the spawn of a she-leopard! why should not I beat your beautiful face into ugliness with one of these sandals of a dead pig!"

He lifted her bodily, calling to the man upon the ground, the other having mounted behind the bullocks. "Put back the leather wall of the cart that I may hurl this outcast widow of a dead Hindu within."

Bootea clawed at his face; she kicked and fought; her voice screaming a call to Ajeet.

There was a heavy rolling thump of hoofs upon the roadway, unheard of Hunsa because of the vociferous struggle. Then from the shimmer of moonlight thrust the white form of a big Turcoman horse that was thrown almost to his haunches, his breast striking the back of the decoit.

The bullocks, nervous little brutes, startled by the huge white animal, swerved, and before the man who sat a-straddle of the one shaft gathered tight the cord to their nostrils, whisked the cart to the roadside where it toppled over the bank for a fall of fifteen feet into a ravine, carrying bullocks and driver with it.

The moonlight fell full upon the face of the horseman, its light making still whiter the face of Captain Barlow.

And Bootea recognised him. It was the face that had been in her vision night and day since the *nautch*.

"Save me, Sahib!" she cried; "these men are thieves; save me, Sahib!"

The hunting crop in Barlow's hand crashed upon the thick head of Hunsa in ready answer to the appeal. And as the sahib threw himself from the saddle the jamadar, with a snarl like a wounded tiger, dropped the girl and, whirling, grappled with the Englishman.

Barlow was strong; few men in the force, certainly none in the officers' mess, could put him on his back; and he was lithe, supple as a leopard; and in combat cool, his mind working like the mind of a chess player: but he realised that the arms about him were the arms of a gorilla, the chest against which he was being crushed was the chest of a trained wrestler; a smaller man would have heard his bones cracking in that clutch.

He raised a knee and drove it into the groin of the jamadar; then in the slight slackening of the holding arms as the Bagree shrank from the blow, he struck at the bearded chin; it was the clean, trained short-arm jab of a boxer.

But even as the gorilla wavered staggeringly under the blow, a soft something slipped about Barlow's throat and tightened like the coils of a python. And behind something was pressing him to his death. The other Bagree springing to the assistance of Hunsa had looped his *roomal* about the Sahib's throat with the art of a thug.

Barlow's senses were going; his brain swam; in his fancy he had been shot from a cliff and was hurtling through space in which there was no air—his lungs had closed; in his brain a hammer was beating him into unconsciousness.

Then suddenly the pressure on his throat ceased, it fell away; the air rushed to the parched lungs. With a wrench his brain cleared, and he went down; but now with power in his arms, the arms that still clung about the dazed Hunsa, and he was on top.

Scarce aware of the action, out of a fighting instinct, he dragged from its holster his heavy pistol, and beat with its butt the ugly head beneath, beat it till it was still. Then he staggered to his feet and looked wonderingly at the form of the Bagree behind who lay sprawled on the road, a great red splash across the white jacket on his breast.

In the Gulab's hand was still clutched the dagger she had drawn from her girdle and driven home to save the sahib who had sat like a god in her heart. With the other hand she held out from contact with her limbs the muslin *sari* that was crimsoned where the blood of the Bagree had fountained when she drew forth her knife.

Barlow darted forward as Bootea reeled and caught her with an arm. Close, the face, fair as that of a memsahib in the pallor of fright and the paling moonlight, sweet, of finer mould, more spiritual than the Mona Lisa's, puritanically simple, the mass of black hair drawn straight back from the low broad brow—for the rich turban had fallen in her fight for freedom—woke memory in the sahib; and as the blood ebbed back through the girl's veins, the pale cheeks flushed with rose, her eyelids quivered and drew back their shutters from eyes that were like those of an antelope.

"You—you, Gulab, the giver of the red rose, the singer of the love song!" Barlow gasped.

"Yes, Captain Sahib, you who are like a god—" Bootea checked, her head drooped.

But Barlow putting his fingers under her chin and gently lifting the face asked, "And what—what?"

"You came like one in a dream. Also, Sahib, I am but one who danced before you and you have saved me."

"And, little girl, you saved my life."

He felt a shudder run through the girl's form, and then she pushed him from her crying, "Sahib—Hunsa! Quick!"

For the jamadar, recovering his senses, had risen to his knees fumbling at his belt groggily for his knife.

Barlow swung the pistol from its holster and rushed toward Hunsa, but the latter, at sight of the dreaded weapon, fled, pursued for a few paces by the Captain.

The girl saw the sandal soles lying upon the ground where Hunsa had dropped them in the struggle, and slipped them beneath her breast-belt, a quick thought coming to her that if the Captain saw them he might recognise them as the footwear of the soldiers. Also Hunsa had said they were for a purpose.

Barlow followed the fleeing shadow for a dozen strides, then his pistol barked, and swinging on his heel he came back, saying, with a little laugh, "That was just to frighten the beggar so he wouldn't come back."

But Bootea's eyes went wide now with a new fear; the sound of the shot would travel faster even than the fleeing Hunsa: and if the decoits came—for already they would be making ready for the road—this beautiful god, with eyes like stars and a voice of music, would be killed, would be no more than the Bagree lying on the road who was but carrion. In her heart was a new thing. The struggle with Hunsa, the fright, even the horribleness of the blood upon her knife, was washed away by a hot surging flood of exquisite happiness. The Hindu name for love—"a pain in the heart"—was veritably hers in its intensity; the sahib's arm about her when she had closed her eyes had caused her to feel as if she were being lifted to heaven.

She laid a hand on Barlow's arm and her eyes were lifted pleadingly to his: "You must go, Sahib—mount your horse and go, because—"

"Because of what?"

"There are many, and you will be killed. Hunsa will bring others."

"Others—who are they?"

But the Gulab had turned from him and was listening, her eyes turned to the road up which floated from beyond upon the hushed silence that was about them,—that seemed deeper because of the dead man lying in the moonlight,—the beat of Hunsa's feet on the road. Once there was the whining note of wheels that claimed a protest from a dry axle; once there was a clang as if steel had struck steel; and on the droning through the night-hush was a rasping hum as if voices clamoured in the distance. This was the bee-hive stirring of the startled village.

"What is it, Bootea?" Barlow asked.

The eyes raised to his face were full of fright, a pleading fright. "Sahib," she answered, "do not ask—just go, because—"

"Yes, girl, why?"

"That this is dead (and her hand gestured toward the slain Bagree) and that others are dead, is; but you,—will you mount the horse and go back the way you came, Sahib?"

Her small fingers clutched the sleeve of the coat he wore—it was of hunting cloth, red-and-green: "Others are dead yonder, and evil is in the hearts of those that live. Go, Sahib—please go."

Barlow's mind was racing fast, in more materialistic grooves than the Gulab's. There was something about it he didn't understand; something the girl did not want to tell him; some horrible thing that she was afraid of—her face was full of suppressed dread.

Suddenly, through no sequence of reasoning, in fact there was no data to go upon, nothing except that a girl—the Gulab was just that—stood there afraid—through him she had just escaped from a man who was little more than an ape—stood quivering in the moonlight alone, except for himself. So, suddenly, he acted as if energised by logic, as if mental deduction made plain the way.

"You are right," he said: "we must go."

He laid a hand upon the bridle-rein of the grey, that had stood there with the submission of a cavalry horse, saying, "Come, Bootea."

Foot in stirrup he swung to the saddle; and as the grey turned, he reached down both hands saying: "Come, I'll take you wherever you want to go."

But the girl drew back and shook her beautifully-modelled head,—the delicate head with the black hair smoothed back to simplicity, and her voice was half sob: "It can't be, Sahib, I am but—" She checked; to speak of the decoits even, might lead to talk that would cause the Sahib to go to their camp, and he would be killed; and she would be a witness to testify against her own people, the slayers of the sepoys.

Barlow laughed, "Because you are a girl who dances you are not to be saved, eh?" he said. "But listen, the Sahibs do not leave women at the mercy of villains; you must come," and his strong sun-browned hands were held out.

Bootea, wonderingly, as if some god had called to her, put her hands in Barlow's, and with a twist of his strong arms she was swung across his knees.

"Put your arms about my waist, Gulab," he said, as the grey, to the tickle of a spur, turned to the road. "Don't lean away from me," he said, presently, "because we have a long way to go and that tires. That's better, girl," as her warm breast pressed against his body.

The big grey, with a deep breath, and a sniffle of satisfaction, scenting that his head was turned homeward, paced along the ghost-strip of roadway in long free strides. Even when a jackal, or it might have been a honey-badger, slipped across the road in front, a drifting shadow, the Turcoman only rattled the snaffle-bit in his teeth, cocked his ears, and then blew a breath of disdain from his big nostrils.

In the easy swinging cradle of the horse's smooth stride the minds of both Barlow and the Gulab relaxed into restfulness; her arms about the strong body, Bootea felt as if she clung to a tower of strength—that she was part of a magnetic power; and the nightmare that had been, so short a time since, had floated into a dream of content, of glorious peace.

Barlow was troubling over the problem of the gorilla-faced man, and thinking how close he had been to death—all but gone out except for that figure in his arms that was so like a lotus; and the death would have meant not just the forfeit of his life, but that his duty, the mission he was upon for his own people, the British government, had been jeopardised by his participation in some native affair of strife, something he had nothing to do with. He had ridden along that road hoping to overtake the two riders that now lay dead in the pit with the other victims of the thugs—of which he knew nothing. They were bearing to him a secret message from his government, and he had ridden to Manabad to there take it from them lest in approaching the city of the Peshwa, full of seditious spies and cutthroats, the paper might be stolen. But at Manabad he had learned that the two had passed, had ridden on; and then, perhaps because of converging different roads, he had missed them.

But most extraordinarily, just one of the curious, tangented ways of Fate, the written order lay against his chest sewn between the double sole of a sandal. Once or twice the hard leather caused him to turn slightly the girl's body, and he thought it some case in which she carried jewels.

# CHAPTER X

They had gone perhaps an eighth of a mile when the road they followed joined another, joined in an arrowhead. The grey turned to the left, to the west, the homing instinct telling him that that way lay his stall in the city of the Peshwa.

"This was the way of my journey, Bootea," Barlow said; "I rode from yonder," and he nodded back toward the highway into which the two roads wedged. "It was here that I heard your call, the call of a woman in dread. Also it might have been a business that interested me if it were a matter of waylaying travellers. Did you see two riders of large horses, such as Arabs or of the breed I ride, men who rode as do *sowars*?"

"No, Sahib, I did not see them."

This was not a lie for it was Ajeet who had seen them, and because of the Sahib's interest she knew the two men must have been of his command; and if she spoke of them undoubtedly he would go back and be killed.

"Were they servants of yours, Sahib—these men who rode?"

Barlow gave off but a little sliver of truth: "No," he answered; "but at Manabad men spoke of them passing this way, journeying to Poona, and if they were strangers to this district, it might be that they had taken the wrong road at the fork. But if you did not see them they will be ahead."

"And meaning, Sahib, it would not be right if they saw you bearing on your horse one who is not a memsahib?"

"As to that, Gulab, what might be thought by men of low rank is of no consequence."

"But if the Sahib wishes to overtake them my burden upon the horse will be an evil, and he will be sorry that Bootea had not shame sufficient to refuse his help."

She felt the strong arm press her body closer, and heard him laugh. But still he did not answer, did not say why he was interested in the two horsemen. If it were vital, and she believed it was, for him to know that they lay dead at the Bagree camp, it was wrong for her to not tell him this, he who was a preserver. But to tell him would send him to his death. She knew, as all the people of that land knew, that the sahibs went where their Raja told them was their mission, and laughed at death; and the face of this one spoke of strength, and the eyes of placid fearlessness; so she said nothing.

The sandal soles that pinched her soft flesh she felt were a reproach—they had something to do with the thing that was between the Sahib and the dead soldiers. There were tears in her eyes and she shivered.

Barlow, feeling this, said: "You're cold, Gulab, the night-wind that comes up from the black muck of the cotton fields and across the river is raw. Hang on for a minute," he added, as he slipped his arm from about her shoulders and fumbled at the back of his saddle. A couple of buckles were unclasped, and he swung loose a warm military cloak and wrapped it about her, as he did so his cheek brushing hers.

Then she was like a bird lying against his chest, closed in from everything but just this Sahib who was like a god.

A faint perfume lingered in Barlow's nostrils from the contact; it was the perfume of attar, of the true oil of rose, such as only princes use because of its costliness, and he wondered a little.

She saw his eyes looking down into hers, and asked, "What is it, Sahib—what disturbs you? If it is a question, ask me."

His white teeth gleamed in the moonlight. "Just nothing that a man should bother over—that he should ask a woman about."

But almost involuntarily he brushed his face across her black hair and said, "Just that, Gulab—that it's like burying one's nose in a rose."

"The attar, Sahib? I love it because it's gentle."

"Ah, that's why you wore the rose that I came by at the *nautch*?"

"Yes, Sahib. Though I am Bootea, because of a passion for the rose I am called Gulab."

"Lovely—the Rose! that's just what you are, Gulab. But the attar is so costly! Are you a princess in disguise?"

"No, Sahib, but one brought me many bottles of it, the slim, long bottles like a finger; and a drop of it lasts for a moon."

"Ah, I see," and Barlow smiled; "you have for lover a raja, the one who brought the attar."

The figure in the cloak shivered again, but the girl said nothing. And Barlow, rather to hear her voice, for it was sweet like flute music, chaffed: "What is he like, the one that you love? A swaggering tall black-whiskered Rajput, no doubt, with a purple vest embroidered in gold, clanking with *tulwar*, and a voice like a Brahmini bull—full of demand."

The slim arms about his waist tightened a little—that was all.

"Confess, Gulab, it will pass the time; a love story is sweet, and Brahm, who creates all things, creates flowers beautiful and sweet to stir love," and he shook the small body reassuringly.

"Sahib, when a girl dances before the great ones to please, it is permitted that she may play at being a princess to win the favour of a raja, and sing the love song to the music of the *sitar* (guitar), but it is a matter of shame to speak it alone to the Presence."

"Tell me, Gulab," and his strong fingers swept the smooth black hair.

The girl unclasped her arms from about Barlow's waist and led his finger to a harsh iron bracelet upon her arm.

At the touch of the cold metal, iron emblem of a child marriage, a shackle never to be removed, he knew that she was a widow, accounted by Brahminical caste an offence to the gods, an outcast, because if the husband still lived she would be in a *zenanna* of gloomy walls, and not one who danced as she had at Nana Sahib's.

"And the man to whom you were bound by your parents died?" he asked.

"I am a widow, Sahib, as the iron bracelet testifies with cold bitterness; it is the badge of one who is outcast, of one who has not become *sati*, has not sat on the wood to find death in its devouring flame."

Barlow knew all the false logic, the metaphysical Machiavellians, the Brahmins, advanced to thin out the undesirable females,— women considered at all times in that land of overpopulation of less value than men,—by the simple expedient of self-destruction. He knew the Brahmins' thesis culled from their Word of God, the

Vedas or the Puranas, calculated to make the widow a voluntary, willing suicide. They would tell Bootea that owing to having been evil in former incarnations her sins had been visited upon her husband, had caused his death; that in a former life she had been a snake, or a rat.

The dead husband's mother, had Bootea come of an age to live with him, though yet but a child of twelve years, would, on the slightest provocation, beat her—even brand her with a hot iron; he had known of it having been done. She would be given but one meal a day—rice and chillies. Even if she had not yet left her father's house he would look upon her as a shameful thing, an undesirable member of the family, one not to be rid of again in the way of marriage; for if a Hindu married her it would break his caste—he would be a veritable pariah. No servant would serve him; no man would sell him anything; if he kept a shop no one would buy of him; no one would sit and speak with him—he would be ostracised.

The only life possible for the girl would be that of a prostitute. She might be married by the temple priests to the god Khandoka, as thousands of widows had been, and thus become a nun of the temple, a prostitute to the celibate priests. Knowing all this, and that Bootea was what she was, her face and eyes holding all that sweetness and cleanness, that she lived in the guardianship of Ajeet Singh, very much a man, Barlow admired her the more in that she had escaped moral destruction. Her face was the face of one of high caste; she was not like the ordinary *nautch* girl of the fourth caste. Everything about Bootea suggested breeding, quality. The iron bracelet, indicated why she had socially passed down the scale—there was no doubt about it.

"I understand, Gulab," he said; "the Sahibs all understand, and know that widowhood is not a reproach."

"But the Sahib questioned of love; and how can one such know of love? The heart starves and does not grow for it feeds upon love—what we of Hind call the sweet pain in the heart."

"But have none been kind, Gulab—pleased by your flower face, has no one warmed your heart?"

The slim arms that gripped Barlow in a new tightening trembled, the face that fled from the betraying moonlight was buried against his tunic, and the warm body quivered from sobs.

Barlow turned her face up, and the moonlight showed vagrant pearls that lay against the olive cheeks, now tinted like the petals of a rose. Then from a service point of view, and as a matter of caste, Barlow went *ghazi*. He drooped his head and let his lips linger against the girl's eyes, and uttered a superb common-place: "Don't cry, little girl," he said; "I am seven kinds of a brute to bother you!"

And Bootea thought it would have been better if he had driven a knife into her heart, and sobbed with increased bitterness. Once her fingers wandered up searchingly and touched his throat.

Barlow casting about for the wherefore of his madness, discovered the moonlight, and heard the soft night-air whispering through the harp chords of trees that threw a tracery of black lines across the white road; and from a grove of mango trees came the gentle scent of their blossoms; and he remembered that statistics had it that there was but one memsahib to so many square miles in that land of expatriation; and he knew that he was young and full of the joy of life; that a British soldier was not like a man of Hind who looked upon women as cattle.

There did not obtrude into his mental retrospect as an accusation against this unwarrantable tenderness the vision of the Resident's daughter—almost his fiancée. Indeed Elizabeth was the antithesis in physical appeal of the gentle Gulab; the drawing-room perhaps; repartee of Damascus steel fineness; tutored polish, class, cold integrity—these things associated admirably with the unsensuous Elizabeth. Thoughts of her, remembrances, had no place in glamorous perfumed moonlight.

So he set his teeth and admonished the grey Turcoman, called him the decrepit son of a donkey, being without speed; and to punish him stroked his neck gently: even this forced diversion bringing him closer to the torturing sweetness of the girl.

But now he was aware of a throbbing on the night wind, and a faint shrill note that lay deep in the shadows beyond. It was a curious rumbling noise, as though ghosts of the hills on the right were playing bowls with rounded rocks. And the shrilling skirl grew louder as if men marched behind bagpipes.

The Gulab heard it, too, and her body stiffened, her head thrust from the enveloping cloak, and her eyes showed like darkened sapphires.

"Carts carrying cotton perhaps," he said. But presently he knew that small cotton carts but rattled, the volume of rumbling was as if an army moved.

From up the road floated the staccato note of a staff beating its surface, and the clanking tinkle of an iron ring against the wooden staff.

"A mail-carrier," Barlow said.

And then to the monotonous pat-pat-pat of trotting feet the mail-carrier emerged from the grey wall of night.

"Here, you, what comes?" the Captain queried, checking the grey.

The postie stopped in terror at the English voice.

"Salaam, Bahadur Sahib; it is war."

"Thou art a tree owl," and Barlow laughed. "A war does not spring up like a drift of driven dust. Is it some raja's elephants and carts with his harem going to a *durbar*?"

"Sahib, it is, as I have said, war. The big brass cannon that is called 'The Humbler of Cities,' goes forth to speak its order, and with it are sepoys to feed it the food of destruction. Beyond that I know not, Sahib, for I am a man of peace, being but a runner of the post."

Then he salaamed and sifted into the night gloom like a thrown handful of white sand, echoing back the clamp-clamp-clamp of his staff's iron ring, which was a signal to all cobras to move from the path of him who ran, slip their chilled folds from the warm dust of the road.

And on in front what had been sounds of mystery was now a turmoil of noises. The hissing screech, the wails, were the expostulations of tortured axles; the rumbling boom was unexplainable; but the jungle of the hillside was possessed of screaming devils. Black-faced, white-whiskered monkeys roused by the din, screamed cries of hate and alarm as they scurried in volplaning leaps from tree to tree. And peacocks, awakened when they should have slept, called with their harsh voices from lofty perches.

A party of villagers hurried by, shifting their cheap turbans to hide faces as they scurried along.

The Gulab was trembling; perhaps the decoits, led by Hunsa, had come by a shorter way; for they were like beasts of the jungle in this art of silent, swift travel.

"Sahib," she pleaded, "go from the road."

"Why, Bootea?"

"The one with the staff spoke of soldiers."

He laughed and patted her shoulder. "Don't fear, little lady," he said, "an army doesn't make war upon one, even if they are soldiers. It will be but a wedding party who now take the wife to the village of her husband."

"Not at night; and a Sahib who carries a woman upon his saddle will hear words of offence."

Though Barlow laughed he was troubled. What if the smouldering fire of sedition had flared up, and that even now men of Sindhia's were slipping on a night march toward some massing of rebels. The resonant, heavy moaning of massive wheels was like the rumble of a gun carriage. And, too, there was the drumming of many hoofs upon the road. Barlow's ear told him it was the rhythmic beat of cavalry horses, not the erratic rat-a-tat, rat-a-tat of native ponies.

With a pressure upon the rein he edged the grey from the white road to a fringe of bamboo and date palms, saying; "If you will wait here, Gulab, I'll see what this is all about."

He slipped from the saddle and lifted her gently to the ground saying, "Don't move; of a certainty it is nothing but the passing of some raja. But, if by any chance I don't return, wait until all is still, until all have gone, and then some well-disposed driver of a bullock cart will take you on your way." Putting his hand in his pocket, and drawing it forth, he added: "Here is the compeller of friendship—silver; for a bribe even an enemy will become a friend."

But the Gulab with her slim fingers closed his hand over the rupees, and pressed the back of it against her lips saying, "If I die it is nothing. But stay here, Sahib, they may be—"

She stopped, and he asked, "May be who, Gulab?"

"Men who will harm thee."

But Barlow lifting to the saddle passed to the road, and Bootea crumpled down in a little desolate heap of misery, her fingers thrust within her bodice, pleading with an amulet for protection for the Sahib. She prayed to her own village god to breathe mercy into the hearts of those who marched in war, and if it were the Bagrees, that Bhowanee would vouchsafe them an omen that to harm the one on a white horse would bring her wrath upon their families and their villages.

Captain Barlow reined in the grey on the roadside, for those that marched were close. Now he could see, two abreast, horses that carried cavalry men. Ten couples of the troop rode by with low-voiced exchanges of words amongst themselves. A petty officer rode at their heels, and behind him, on a bay Arab, whose sweated skin glistened like red wine in the moonlight, came a *risiladar*, the commander of the troop. A little down the road Barlow could see an undulating, swaying huge ribbon of white-and-pink bullocks, twenty-four yoke of the tall lean-flanked powerful *Amrit Mahal*, the breed that Hyder Ali long ago had brought on his conquering way to the land of the Mahrattas. And beyond the ghost-like line of white creatures was some huge thing that they drew.

The commander reined his Arab to a stand beside Barlow and saluted, saying, "Salaam, Major Sahib—you ride alone?"

Barlow said: "My salaams, Risiladar, and I am but a captain. I ride at night because the days are hot. My two men have gone before me because my horse dropped a shoe which had to be replaced. Did the Risiladar see my two servants that were mounted?"

"I met none such," the commander answered. "Perhaps in some village they have rested for a drink of liquor; they of the army are given to such practices when their Captain's eye is not upon them. I go with this"—and he waved a gauntleted hand back toward the thing that loomed beyond the bullocks that had now come to a halt. "It is the brass cannon, the like of which there is no other. We go to the camp of the Amil, who commands the Sindhia troops, taking him the brass cannon that it may compel a Musselman zemindar to pay the tax that is long past due. Why the barbarian should not pay I know not for a tax of one-fourth is not much for a foreigner, a debased follower of Mahomet, to render unto the ruler of this land that is the garden of the world. He has shut himself and men up in his mud fort, but when this brass mother of destruction spits into his stronghold a ball or two that is not opium he will come forth or we will enter by the gate the cannon has made."

"Then there will be bloodshed, Risiladar," Barlow declared.

"True, Captain Sahib; but that is, after a manner, the method of collecting just dues in this land where those who till the soil now, were, but a generation or two since, men of the sword,—they can't forget the traditions. In the land of the British Raj six inches of a paper, with a big seal duly affixed, would do the business. That I know, for I have travelled far, Sahib. As to the bloodshed, worse will be the trampling of crops, for in the district of this worshipper of Mahomet the wheat grows like wild scrub in the jungle, taller than up to the belly of my horse. That is the whyfore of the cannon, in a way of speaking, because from a hill we can send to this man a slaying message, and leave the wheat standing to fill the bellies of those who are in his hands as a tyrant. Sirdar Baptiste was for sending a thousand sepoys to put the fear of destruction in the debtor; but the Dewan with his eye on revenue from crops, hit upon this plan of the loud-voiced one of brass."

Then the commander ordered the advance, and saluting, said: "Salaam, Captain Sahib, and if I meet with your servants I will give them news that you desire their presence."

When the huge cannon had rumbled by, and behind it had passed a company of sepoys on foot, Barlow turned his horse into the jungle for Gulab.

# CHAPTER XI

Bootea's eyes glistened like stars when, lowering a hand, Barlow said: "Put a foot upon mine, Gulab, and I'll swing you up."

When they were on the road she said; "I saw them. It is as the runner said, war—is it so, Sahib?"

"The Captain says that he goes to collect revenue, but it may be that he spoke a lie, for it is said that a man of the land of the Five Rivers, which is the Punjaub, has five ways of telling a tale, and but one of them is the truth and comes last."

The girl pondered over this for a little, and then asked; "Does the Sahib think perhaps it is war against his people?"

That was just what was in Barlow's mind since he had seen the big gun going forth at night; that perhaps the plot that was just a whisper, fainter than the hum of a humming bird's wing, was moving with swift silent velocity.

"Why do you ask that question? Have you heard from lips—perhaps loosened by wine or desire—aught of this?"

When she remained without answer, Barlow tapped his fingers lightly upon her shoulder, saying, "Tell me, girl."

"I have heard nothing of war," she said. "There was a something though that men whispered in the dark."

"What was it?"

"It was of the Chief of the Pindaris."

She felt the quivering start that ran through Barlow's body; but he said quietly: "With the Pindaris there is always trouble. Something of robbery—of a raid, was it?"

"I will listen again to those that whisper in the dark," she answered, "and perhaps if it concerns you, for your protection, I will tell."

"I hope those men didn't fall in with my two chaps," Barlow said, rather voicing his thoughts than in the way of speaking to the girl.

"The two who rode—they were the Captain Sahib's servants?"

Barlow started. "Yes, they were: I suppose I can trust you."

"And the Sahib is troubled? Perhaps it was a message for the Sahib that they carried."

"I don't know," he answered, evasively. "I was thinking that perhaps they might be messengers, for our sepoys are not stationed here, and come but on such errands."

"And if they were lulled, and the message stolen, it would cause trouble?"

She felt him tremble as he looked down into her eyes.

"I don't know. But the messages of a Raj are not for the ears of men to whom they have not been sent."

Barlow had an intuition that the girl's words were not prompted by idle curiosity. He was possessed of a sudden gloomy impression that she knew something of the two men who rode. And it was strange that they had not been seen upon either of the roads. The officer spoke of them frankly, and not as a man hiding something.

Suddenly he took a firm resolve, perhaps a dangerous one; not dangerous though if his men had really gone through.

"Gulab," he said,—and with his hand he turned her face up by the chin till their eyes were close together,—"if the two bore a message for me, and it was stolen, I would be like that one you loved was lost."

The beautiful face swung from his palm and he could hear her gasping.

"You know something?" he said, and he caressed the smooth black tresses.

"I did not see them, Sahib."

They rode in silence for half a mile and then she said, "Perhaps, Sahib, Bootea can help you—if the message is lost."

"And you will, girl?"

"I will, Sahib; even if I die for doing it, I will."

His arm tightened about her with a shrug of assuring thankfulness, and she knew that this man trusted her and was not sorry of her burden. Little child-dreams floated through her mind that the silver-faced moon would hang there above and light the world forever,—for the moon was the soul of the god Purusha whose sacrificed body had created the world,—and that she would ride forever in the arms of this fair-faced god, and that they were both of one caste, the caste that had as mark the sweet pain in the heart.

And Barlow was sometimes dropping the troubled thought of the missing order and the turmoil that would be in the Council of the Governor General when it became known, to mutter inwardly: "By Jove! if the chaps get wind of this, that I carried the Gulab throughout a moonlit night, there'll be nothing for me but to send in my papers. I'll be drawn;—my leg'll be pulled." And he reflected bitterly that nothing on earth, no protestation, no swearing by the gods, would make it believed as being what it was. He chuckled once, picturing the face of the immaculate Elizabeth while she thrust into him a bodkin of moral autopsy, should she come to know of it.

Bootea thought he had sighed, and laying her slim fingers against his neck said, "The Sahib is troubled."

"I don't care a damn!" he declared in English, his mind still on the personal trail.

Seeing that she, not understanding, had taken the sharp tone as a rebuke, he said, "If I had been alone, Gulab, I'd have been troubled sorely, but perhaps the gods have sent you to help out."

"Ah, yes, God pulled our paths together. And if Bootea is but a sacrifice that will be a favour, she is happy."

If the girl had been of a white race, in her abandon of love she would have laid her lips against his, but the women of Hind do not kiss.

The big plate of burnished silver slid, as if pushed by celestial fingers, across the azure dome toward the loomed walls of the Ghats that it would cross to dip into the sea, the Indian Ocean, and mile upon mile was picked from the front and laid behind by the grey as he strode with untiring swing toward his bed that waited on the high plateau of Poona.

The night-jars, even the bats, had stilled their wings and slept in the limbs of the neem or the pipal, and the air that had borne the soft perfume of blossoms, and the pungent breath of jasmine, had chilled and grown heavy from the pressure of advancing night.

The two on the grey rode sleepily; the Gulab warm and happy, cuddled in the protecting cloak, and Barlow grim, oppressed by fatigue and the mental strain of feared disaster. Now the muscles of the horse rippled in heavier toil, and his hoofs beat the earth in shorted stride; the way was rising from the plain as it approached the plateau that was like an immense shelf let into the wall of the world above the lowland; a shelf that held jewels, topaz and diamonds, that glinted their red and yellow lights, and upon which rested giant pearls, the moonlight silvering the domes and minarets of white palaces and mosques of Poona. The dark hill upon which rested the Temple of Parvati threw its black outline against the sky, and like a burnished helmet glowed the golden dome beneath which sat the alabaster goddess. At their feet, strung out between forbidding banks of clay and sand, ran a molten stream of silver, the sleepy waters of the Muta.

"By Jove!" and Barlow, suddenly cognisant that he had practically arrived at the end of his ride, that the windmill of Don Quixote stood yonder on the hill, realised that in a sense, so far as Bootea was concerned, he had just drifted. Now he asked: "I'm afraid, little girl, your Sahib is somewhat of a fool, for I have not asked where you want me to take you."

"Yonder, Sahib," and her eyes were turned toward the jewelled hill.

As they rose to the hilltop that was a slab of rock and sand carrying a city, he asked: "Where shall I put you down that will be near your place of rest, your friends?"

"Is there a memsahib in the home of the Sahib?" she asked.

"No, Bootea, not so lucky—nobody but servants."

"Then I will go to the bungalow of the Sahib."

"Confusion!" he exclaimed in moral trepidation.

Bootea's hand touched his arm, and she turned her face inward to hide the hot flush that lay upon it. "No, Sahib, not because of Bootea; one does not sleep in the lap of a god."

"All right, girl," he answered—"sorry."

As the grey plodded tiredly down the avenue of trees, a smooth road bordered by a hedge of cactus and lanten, Barlow turned him to the right up a drive of broken stone, and dropping to the ground at the verandah of a white-waited bungalow, lifted the girl down, saying: "Within it can be arranged for a rest place for you."

A *chowkidar*, lean, like a mummified mendicant, rose up from a squeaking, roped *charpoy* and salaamed.

"Take the horse to the stable, Jungwa, and tell the *syce* to undress him. Remember to keep that monkey tongue of yours between your teeth for in my room hangs a bitter whip. It is a lie that I have not ridden home alone," Barlow commanded.

# CHAPTER XII

As Barlow led the Gulab within the bungalow she drew, as a veil, a light silk scarf across her face.

Upon the floor of the front room a bearer, head buried in yards of pink cotton cloth, his *puggri*, lay fast asleep.

As Barlow raised a foot to touch the sleeper in the ribs the girl drew him back, put the tips of her finger to her lips, and pointed toward the bedroom door.

Barlow shook his head, the flickering flame of the wick in an iron oil-lamp that rested in a niche of the wall exaggerating to ferocity the frown that topped his eyes.

But Bootea pleaded with a mute salaam, and raising her lips to his ear whispered, "Not because of what is not permitted—not because of Bootea—please."

With an arm he swept back the beaded tendrils of a hanging door-curtain, the girl glided to the darkness of the room, and Barlow, lifting from its niche the iron lamp, followed. Within, she pointed to the door that lay open and Barlow, half in rebellion, softly closed it. As he turned he saw that she had dropped from their holding cords the heavy brocaded silk curtains of the window.

His limbs were numb from the long ride with the weight of the girl's body across his thighs; he was tired; he was mentally distressed over the messengers he had failed to locate, and this, the almost forced intrusion of Bootea into his bedroom, the closed door and the curtained windows, her doing, was just another turn of the kaleidoscope with its bits of broken glass of a nightmare. He dropped wearily into a big cane-bottomed Hindu chair, saying; "Little wilted rose, cuddle up on that divan among the cushions and rest, while you tell me why we sit in *purdah*."

The girl dragged a cushion from the divan, and placing it on the floor beside his chair, sat on it, curling her feet beneath her knees.

Barlow groaned inwardly. If his mind had not been so lethargic because of the things that weighted it, like the leaden soles upon a diver's boots, he would have roused himself to say, "Look here, a chap can't pull a girl who is as sweet as a flower and as trusting as a babe, out of trouble and then make bazaar love to her; he can't do it if he's any sort of a chap." All this was casually in his mind, but he let his tired eyes droop, and his hand that hung over the teak-wood arm of the chair rested upon the girl's shoulder.

"Bootea will soon go so that the Sahib may sleep, for he is tired," she said; "but first there is something to be said, and I have come close to the Sahib because men not alone whisper in the dark but they listen."

The hand that rested on Bootea's shoulder lifted to her cheek, and strong fingers caressed its oval.

"Would the Sahib sleep, and would his mind rest if he knew where the two who rode are?"

Barlow sat bolt upright in the chair, roused, the lethargy gone, as if he had poured raw whisky down his throat. And he was glad, the closed door and the drawn curtains were not now things of debasement. Curious that he should care what this little Hindu maid was like, but he did. His hand now clasped the girl's wrist, it almost hurt in its tenseness.

"Yes, Gulab,"—and he subdued his voice,—"tell me if you know."

"They are dead upon the road beyond where you saved Bootea."

"Why didn't you tell me this before?"

"It was too late, Sahib; and if you had gone there they would have killed you."

"Who?"

"That, I cannot tell."

"You must, Gulab."

"No, Bootea will not."

Barlow stared angrily into the big eyes that were lifted to his, that though they lingered in soft loving upon his face, told him that she would not tell, that she would die first; even as he would have given his life if he had been captured by tribesmen and asked to betray his fellow men as the price of liberty.

He threw himself back wearily in the chair. "Why tell me this now,—to mock me, to exult?" he said, reproach in his voice.

"But it is the message, Sahib, that is more than the life of a *sepoy*, is it not?"

Again he sat up: "Why do you say this—do you know where it is?"

She drew from beneath her bodice the sandal soles, saying: "These are from the feet of the messenger who is dead. The one the Sahib beat over the head with his pistol dropped them,—and he was carrying them for a purpose. The Sahib knows, perhaps, the secret way of this land."

In the girl's hand was clasped the knife from her girdle, and she tendered it, hilt first: "Bootea knows not if they are of value, the leather soles, but if the Sahib would open them, then if there are eyes that watch the curtains are drawn."

Barlow revivified, stimulated by hope, seized the knife and ran its sharp point around the stitching of the soles. Between the double leather of one lay a thin, strong parchment-like paper.

He gave a cry of exultation as, unfolding it, he saw the seal of his Raj. His cry was a gasp of relief. Almost the shatterment of his career had lain in that worn discoloured sole, and disaster to his Raj if it had fallen into the hands of the conspirators.

In an ecstasy of relief he sprang to his feet, and lifting Bootea, clasped her in his arms, smothering her face in kisses, whispering: "Gulab, you are my preserver; you are the sweetest rose that ever bloomed!"

He felt the pound of her heart against his breast, and her eyes mirrored a happiness that caused him to realise that he was going too far—drifting into troubled waters that threatened destruction. The girl's soul had risen to her eyes and looked out as though he were a god.

As if Bootea sensed the same impending evil she pushed Barlow from her and sank back to the cushion, her face shedding its radiancy.

Cursing himself for the impetuous outburst Barlow slumped into the chair.

"Gulab," he said presently, "my government gives reward for loyalty and service."

"Bootea has had full reward," the girl answered.

He continued: "We had talk on the road about the Pindaris; what did they who whisper in the dark say?"

"That the chief, Amir Khan, has gathered an army, and they fear that because of an English bribe he will attack the Mahrattas; so the Dewan has brought men from Karowlee to go into the camp of the Pindaris in disguise and slay the chief for a reward."

This information coming from Bootea was astounding. Neither Resident Hodson nor Captain Barlow had suspected that there had been a leak.

"And was there talk of this message from the British to—?" Barlow checked.

"To the Sahib?" Bootea asked. "Not of the message; but it was whispered that one would go to the Pindari camp to talk with Amir Khan, and perhaps it was the Sahib they meant. And perhaps they knew he waited for orders from the government."

Then suddenly it flashed upon Barlow that because of this he had been marked. The foul riding in the game of polo that so nearly put him out of commission—it had been deliberately foul, he knew that, but he had attributed it to a personal anger on the part of the Mahratta officer, bred of rivalry in the game and the fanatical hate of an individual Hindu for an Englishman.

"Now that a message has come will the Sahib go to the Pindari camp?" Bootea persisted.

"Why do you ask, Gulab?"

"Not in the way of treachery, but because the Sahib is now like a god; and because I may again be of service, for those who will slay Amir Khan will also slay the Sahib."

"Gulab,—"

Barlow's voice was drowned by yells of terror in the outer room.

"Thieves! Thieves have broken in to rob, and they have stolen my lamp! *Chowkidar, chowkidar!* wake, son of a pig!"

It was the bearer, who, suddenly wakened by some noise, had in the dark groped for his lamp and found it missing.

"Heavens!" the Captain exclaimed. "Now the cook house will be empty—the servants will come!" He rubbed a hand perplexedly over his forehead. "Quick, Gulab, you must hide!"

He swung open a wooden door between his room and a bedroom next. Within he said: "There's a bed, and you must sleep here till daylight, then I will have the *chowkidar* take you to where you wish to go. You couldn't go in the dark anyway. Bar the door; you will be quite safe; don't be frightened." He touched her cheek with his fingers: "Salaam, little girl." Then, going out, he opened the door leading to the room of clamour, exclaiming angrily, "You fool, why do you scream in your dreams?"

"God be thanked! it is the Sahib." The bearer flopped to his knees and put his hands in abasement upon his master's feet.

Jungwa had rushed into the room, staff in hand, at the outcry. Now he stood glowering indignantly upon the grovelling bearer.

"It is the opium, Sahib," he declared; "this fool spends all his time in the bazaar smoking with people of ill repute. If the Presence will but admonish him with the whip our slumbers will not again be disturbed."

The bearer, running true to the tenets of native servants, put up the universal alibi—a flat denial.

"Sahib, you who are my father and my mother, be not angry, for I have not slept. I observed the Sahib pass, but as he spoke not, I thought he had matters of import upon his mind and wished not to be disturbed."

"A liar—by Mother Gunga!" The *chowkidar* prodded him in the ribs with the end of his staff, and turning in disgust, passed out.

"Come, you fool!" Barlow commanded, returning to his room, and, sitting down wearily upon the bed, held up a leg.

The bearer knelt and in silence stripped the *putties* from his master's limbs, unlaced the shoes, and pulled off the breeches.

When Barlow had slipped on the pyjamas handed him, he said: "Tell the *chowkidar* to come to me at his waking from the first call of the crows."

# CHAPTER XIII

An omen of dire import all thugs believe is to hear the cry of a kite between midnight and dawn; to hear it before midnight does not matter, for the sleeper in turning over smothers the impending disaster beneath his body. But Captain Barlow had put up no such defence if evil hung over him, for when the *chowkidar* stood outside the door calling softly, "Captain Sahib! Captain Sahib!" Barlow lay just as he had flopped on the bed, his tiredness having held him as one dead.

Gently the soft voice of the *chowkidar* pulled him back out of his Nirvana of non-existence, and he called sleepily, "What is it?"

"It is Jungwa," the watchman answered, "and I have received the Sahib's order to come at this hour."

Then Barlow remembered. He swung his feet to the floor, saying, "Come!"

When the watchman had walked out of his sandals to approach in his bare feet, the Captain said, "Is your tongue still to remain in your mouth, Jungwa, or has it been made sacrifice to the knife for the sin of telling in the cookhouse tales of your Sahib and last night?"

"No, Sahib, I have not spoken. I am a Meena of the Ossary *jat*. In Jaipur we guard the treasury and the zenanna of the Raja, and it is our chief who puts the *tika* upon the forehead of the Maharaja when he ascends to the throne. Think you, then, Sahib, that an Ossary would betray a trust?"

Barlow fixed the lean saffron-hued face with a searching look, and muttered, "Damned if I don't believe the old chap is straight!" "I think it is true," he said. "Shut the door." Then he continued: "The one who came last night is in the next room and you must take her out through the bathroom door, for there is cover of the crotons and oleanders, and then to the road. Acquire a *gharry* and go with her to where she directs you."

"Salaam, Sahib! your servant will obey. And as to the *chota hazri*, Sahib?"

"By Jove! right you are, Jungwa"; for Barlow had forgotten that—the little breakfast, as it was called.

Then he ran his fingers through his hair. To send the Gulab off without even a cup of tea was one thing; to admit the bearer to know of her presence was another.

The wily old watchman sensed what was passing in his master's mind, and he hazarded, diplomatically, "If the One is of high caste she will not eat what is brought by the bearer who is of the Sudra caste, but from the hands of a Meena none but the Brahmin *pundits* refuse food."

Barlow laughed; indeed the grizzled one had perception—he was an accomplice in the plot of secrecy.

"Good! Eggs and toast and tea. Demand plenty—say your Sahib is hungry because of a long ride and nothing to eat. But hurry, I hear the 'seven sisters' (crows) calling to sleepers that the sun is here with its warmth."

Then the bearer entered, but Barlow ordered him away, saying, "Sit without till I call."

As he slipped into breeches and brown riding boots he cursed softly the entanglement that had thrust upon him this thing of ill flavour. Of course the watchman, even if he did keep his mouth shut, which would be a miracle in that land of bazaar gossip, would have but one opinion of why Bootea had spent the night in the bungalow. But if Barlow squared this by speaking of a secret mission, that would be a knowledge that could be exchanged for gold. Perhaps not all servants were spies, but there were always spies among servants.

"Damn the thing!" he muttered; but he was helpless. The old man would give no sign of what, no doubt, was in his mind; he would hold that leathery face in placid acquiescence in prevalent moral vagary.

Then he tapped lightly on the wooden door, calling softly, "Bootea—Bootea!"

When it was opened he said: "Food is coming, Gulab. A man of caste brings it, and it is but eggs from which no life has been taken, so you may eat. Then the *chowkidar* will go with you."

Jungwa brought the breakfast and put it down, saying, "I will wait, Sahib, outside the bathroom door."

"Here is money—ten rupees for whatever is needed. Be courteous to the lady, for she is not a *nautchni*."

"The Sahib would entertain none such," the *chowkidar* answered with a grave salaam.

"Damn the thing!" Barlow groaned.

# CHAPTER XIV

An hour later Barlow, mounted on a stalky Cabuli polo-pony, rode to the Residency, happy over the papers in his pocket, but troubling over how he could explain their possession and keep the girl out of it. To even mention the Gulab, unless he fabricated a story, would let escape the night-ride, and, no doubt, in the perversity of things, Resident Hodson would want to know where she was and where he had taken her, and insist on having her produced for an official inquisition. The Resident, a machine, would sacrifice a native woman without a tremor to the official gods.

Barlow could formulate no plausible method; he could not hide the death of the two native messengers, and would simply have to take the stand of, "Here is this message from His Excellency and as to how I came by it is of as little importance as an order from the War Office regulating the colour of thread that attaches buttons to a tunic."

He turned the Cabuli up the wide drive that led to the Residency, the big white walled bungalow in which Hodson lived, and shook his riding crop toward Elizabeth who was reading upon the verandah. He swung from the saddle, and held out his hand to the girl, saying cheerily, "Hello, Beth! Didn't you ride this morning, or are you back early?"

The novel seemed to require support of the girl's hand, or she had not observed that of the caller. Her face, always emotionless, was repellent in its composure as she said; "Father is just inside in his office with a native, and I fancy it's one of the usual dark things of mystery, for he asked me to sit here by the window that he might have both air and privacy; I'm to warn off all who might stand here against the wall with an open ear."

"I'll pull a chair up and chat to you till he's—"

"No, Captain Barlow—" Barlow winced at this formality—
"Father, I'm sure, wants you in this matter; in fact, I think a *chuprassi*
is on his way now to your bungalow with the Resident's salaams."

Barlow laid his fingers on the girl's shoulder: "I'm ghastly
tired, Beth. I'll come back to you."

"Yes, India is enervating," she commented in a flat tone.

Barlow had a curious impression that the girl's grey eyes had
turned yellow as she made this observation.

"Ah, Captain, glad you've come," Hodson said, rising and
extending a hand across a flat-topped desk. "I'm—I'm—well—pull
a chair. This is one Ajeet Singh," and he drooped slightly his thin,
lean, bald head toward the Bagree Chief, who stood stiff and erect,
one arm in a sling.

At this, Ajeet, knowing it for an informal introduction, put his
hand to his forehead, and said, "Salaam, Sahib."

"*Tulwar* play, sir, and an appeal for protection to the British,
eh?" and Barlow indicated the arm in the sling.

Still speaking in English Hodson said: "As to that,—" he
pursed his thin lips,—"something dreadful has happened; this man
has been mixed up in a decoity and has come for protection; he
wants to turn Approver."

"The usual thing; when these cut-throats are likely to be
caught they turn Judas; to save their own necks they offer a sacrifice
of their comrades."

"Yes," the Resident affirmed, "but I'm glad he came. Perhaps
we had better just sit tight and let him go on—he's only nicely
started. I've practically promised him that if what he confesses
is of service to His Excellency's government I will give him our
conditional pardon, and use what influence I have with the Peshwa.
But I fancy that old Baji Rao is mixed up in it himself."

He turned to the decoit: "Commence again, and tell the truth;
and if I believe, you may be given protection from the British; but
as to Sindhia I have no power to protect his criminals."

The decoit cleared his throat and began: "I, Ajeet Singh, hold
allegiance to the Raja of Karowlee, and am Chief of the Bagrees,
who are decoits."

The Resident held up his hand: "Have patience." He rose, and
took from a little cabinet a small alabaster figure of *Kali* which he
placed upon the table, saying in English to Barlow, "When these

decoits confess to be made Approvers, half of the confession is lies, for to swear them on our Bible is as little use as playing a tin whistle. If he's a Bagree this is his goddess."

In Hindi he said: "Ajeet Singh, if you are a Bagree decoit you are in the protection of Bhowanee, and you make oath to her."

"Yes, Sahib."

"This is Bhowanee,—that is your name for Kali,—and with obeisance to her make oath that you will tell the truth."

"Yes, Sahib, it is the proper way."

"Proceed."

The jamadar with the fingers of his two hands clasped to his forehead in obeisance, declared: "If I, Ajeet Singh, tell that which is not true, Mother *Kali*, may thy wrath fall upon me and my family."

Then Hodson shifted the black goddess and let it remain upon a corner of his table, surmising that the sight of it would help.

"Speak, now," the Resident commanded; and the Jamadar proceeded.

"Dewan Sewlal sent to Raja Karowlee for men for a mission, and whether it was in the letter he sent that *thugs* should come I know not, but in our party were thugs, and that led to why I am here."

"What is the difference, Ajeet," Hodson asked sharply. "You are a decoit who robs and kills, and thugs kill and rob; you are both disciples of this murderous creature, Kali."

"We who are decoits, while we make offerings to Kali, are not thugs. They have a chief mission of murder, while we have but desire to gain for our families from the rich. The thugs came in this wise, sahib. Bhowanee created them from the sweat of her arms, and gave to them her tooth for a pick-axe, which is their emblem, a rib for a knife, and the hem of her garment for a noose to strangle. The hem of her sacred garment was yellow-and-white, and the *roomal* that they strangle with is yellow-and-white. They are thugs, Sahib, and we are decoits."

"A fine distinction, sir," and Barlow laughed.

"Proceed," Hodson commanded.

"We were told by the Dewan to go to the camp of the Pindaris and bring back the head of Amir Khan."

"Lovely!" Barlow muttered softly; but Hodson started,—a slight rouge crept over his pale face and he said, "By Gad! this grows interesting, my dear Captain."

"Absolutely Oriental," Barlow added.

Then when their voices had stilled Ajeet continued: "But Hunsa had ridden with the Pindari Chief and he knew that he was well guarded, and that it would be impossible to bring his head in a basket, so we refused to go on this mission. The Dewan was angry and would not give us food or pay. Through Hunsa the Dewan sent word that we must obtain our living in the way of our profession, which is decoity."

"I wonder," Barlow queried.

But Hodson, nodding his head said: "Quite possible; and also quite probable that the dear avaricious Dewan would claim a share of the loot if it were of value, jewels especially." He addressed Ajeet, "I have nothing to do with this; I am not Sindhia."

"True, Sahib Bahadur, but a decoity was made upon a merchant on the road and he and his men were killed, but also two English *sowars* were slain."

"By heavens!" The cool, trained, bloodless machine, that was a British Resident at a court of intrigue, was startled out of his composure; his eyes flashed to those of Barlow.

But the Captain, knowing all this beforehand, had an advantage, and he showed no sign of trepidation.

Then the thin drawn face of the Resident was flattened out by control, and he commanded the decoit to talk on.

"I tried to save the two sepoys, and one was a sergeant, but I was stricken down with a wound and it was in the way of treachery."

Ajeet laid a hand upon his wounded shoulder, saying, "When the two *sepoys* rode suddenly out of the night into our camp, where there in the moonlight lay the bodies of the merchant and his men, the Bagrees were afraid lest the two should make report. They rushed upon the two riders, and it was then that I was wounded. I would have been killed but for this protection," and Ajeet rubbed affectionately the beautiful strong shirt-of-mail that enwrapped his torso.

"And observe, Sahib, the wound is from behind, which is a wound of treachery. As I rushed to the two and cried to them to be gone, a ball from a short gun in the hands of some Bagree smote me upon the shoulder, and this,—" he again touched the shirt-of-mail,—"and my shoulder-blade turned it from my heart. Even then Hunsa thought I was dead. And he was in league with the Dewan to obtain for Nana Sahib a girl of my household, who is called the Gulab because she is as beautiful as the moon."

At this statement Barlow knew why the man he had beaten with his pistol had tried to seize the Gulab. It was startling. The leg that had rested across a knee clamped noisily to the floor, and a smothered "Damn!" escaped from his lips. What a devilish complicated thing it was.

Ajeet resumed: "Hunsa rushed to where the Gulab was in hiding and helped the men who had been sent by Nana Sahib to steal her. Then he came back to our camp saying that many men had beaten him, and that he had been forced to flee."

At this vagary Barlow chuckled inwardly.

"What of the two soldiers?" Hodson asked; "why were they here in this land and at the camp of the Bagrees?"

"I know not, Sahib."

"Were the bodies robbed by your men—they would be—did they find papers that would indicate the two were messengers?" and the Resident's bloodless fingers that clasped a pen were trembling with the suppression of the awful interest he strove to hide, for he knew, as well as Barlow, what their mission was.

"Yes, Sahib, they were stripped and the bodies thrown in the pit with the others. Eight rupees were taken, but as to papers I know nothing."

"Where is the woman you call the Gulab?"

"She will be in the hands of Nana Sahib," Ajeet answered; "and because of that I have come to confess so your Honour will save my life from him for he will make accusation that I was Chief of those who killed the soldiers of the British; and that the Sahib will cause to have returned to me the Gulab."

The Resident took from a drawer a form, and his pen scratched irritably at blanks here and there. He tossed it over to Barlow saying, "I'm going to give this decoit this provisional pardon; perhaps it will nail him. What he has confessed is of value. You translate this to him while I think; I can't make mistakes—I must not."

Captain Barlow read to Ajeet the pardon, which was the form adopted by the British government to be issued to certain thugs and decoits who became spies, called Approvers, for the British.

"You, Ajeet Singh, are promised exemption from the punishment of death and transportation beyond seas for all past offences, and such reasonable indulgence as your services may seem to merit, and may be compatible with your safe custody on condition:—1st, that you make full confession of all the decoities in which you have been engaged; 2nd, that you mention truly the names of all your associates in these crimes, and assist to the utmost of your power in their arrest and conviction. If you act contrary to these conditions—conceal any of the circumstances of the decoities in which you have been engaged—screen any of your friends—attempt to escape—or accuse any innocent person—you shall be considered to have forfeited thereby all claims to such exemption and indulgence."

When the Captain had finished interpreting this the Resident passed it to the decoit, saying: "This will protect you from the British. You are now bound to the British; and I want you to bring me any papers that may have been found upon the two soldiers. Bring here this woman, the Gulab, if you can find her. Go now."

When Ajeet, with a deep salaam, had gone from the room Hodson threw himself back in his chair wearily and sighed. Then he said: "A woman! the jamadar was lying—all that stuff about Nana Sahib. There's been some deviltry; they've used this woman to trap the messengers; that's India. It's the papers they were after; they must have known they were coming; and they've hidden the woman. We've got to lay hands upon her, Captain—she's the key-note."

# CHAPTER XV

Barlow had waited until the decoit would have gone before showing the papers that were in his pocket because it was an advantage that the enemy should think them lost. He was checked now as he put a hand in his pocket to produce them by the entrance of Elizabeth, and he fancied there was a sneer on her thin lips.

"Father," she said, as she leaned against the desk, one hand on its teak-wood top, "I've been listening to the handsome leader of thieves; I couldn't help hearing him. I fancy that Captain Barlow could tell you just where this woman, the Gulab, who is as beautiful as the moon, is. I'm sure he could bring her here—if he *would*."

The Captain's fingers unclasped from the papers in his pocket, and now were beating a tattoo on his knee.

"Elizabeth!" the father gasped, "do you know what you are saying?" His cold grey eyes were wide with astonishment. "Did you hear all of Ajeet Singh's story?"

"Yes, all of it."

"It's your friend, Nana Sahib, whom you treat as if he were an Englishman and to be trusted, that knows where this woman is, Elizabeth."

A cynical laugh issued from the girl's lips that were so like her father's in their unsympathetic contour: "Yes, one may trust men, but a woman's eyes are given her to prevent disaster from this trust which is so natural to the deceivable sex."

"Elizabeth! you do not know what you are saying—what the inference would be."

"Ask Captain Barlow if he doesn't know all about the Gulab's movements."

The Resident pushed irritably some papers on his desk, and turning in his chair, asked, "Can you explain this, Captain—what it is all about?"

There were ripples of low temperature chilling the base of Barlow's skull. "I can't explain it—it's beyond me," he answered doggedly.

The girl turned upon him with ferocity. "Don't lie, Captain Barlow; a British officer does not lie to his superior."

"Hush, Beth," the father pleaded.

"Don't you know, Captain Barlow," the girl demanded, "that this woman, the Gulab, is one who uses her beauty to betray men, even Sahibs?"

"No, I don't know that, Miss Hodson. I saw her dance at Nana Sahib's and I've heard Ajeet's statement. I don't know anything evil of the girl, and I don't believe it."

"A man's sense of honour where a woman is concerned—lie to protect her. I have no illusions about the Sahibs in India," she continued, in a tone that was devilish in its cynicism, "but I did think that a British officer would put his duty to his King above the shielding of a *nautch* girl."

"Elizabeth!" Hodson rose and put a hand upon the girl's arm; "do you realise that you are doing a dreadful thing—that you are impeaching Captain Barlow's honour as a soldier?"

Barlow's face was white, and Hodson was trembling, but the girl stood, a merciless cold triumph in her face: "I do realise that, father. For the girl I care nothing, nor for Captain Barlow's intrigue with such, but I am the daughter of the man who represents the British Raj here."

Barlow, knowing the full deviltry of this high protestation, knowing that Elizabeth, imperious, dominating, cold-blooded, was knifing a supposed rival—a rival not in love, for he fancied Elizabeth was incapable of love—felt a surge of indignation.

"For God's sake, Elizabeth, what impossible thing has led you to believe that Captain Barlow has anything to do with this girl?" the father asked.

"I'll tell you; the matter is too grave for me to remain silent. This morning I rode early—earlier than usual, for I wanted to pick up the Captain before he had started. As I turned my mount in to his compound I saw, coming from the back of the bungalow, this native woman, and she was being taken away by his *chowkidar*. She had just come out some back door of the bungalow, for from the drive I could see the open space that lay between the bungalow and the servants' quarters."

Hodson dropped a hand to the teak-wood desk; it looked inadequate, thin, bloodless; blue veins mapped its white back. "You are mistaken, Elizabeth, I'm sure. Some other girl—"

"No, father, I was not mistaken. There are not many native girls like the Gulab, I'll admit. As she turned a clump of crotons she saw me sitting my horse and drew a gauze scarf across her face to hide it. I waited, and asked the *chowkidar* if it were his daughter, and the old fool said it was the wife of his son; and the girl that he claimed was his son's wife had the iron bracelet of a Hindu widow on her arm. And the Gulab wears one—I saw it the night she danced."

A ghastly hush fell upon the three. Barlow was moaning inwardly, "Poor Bootea!"; Hodson, fingers pressed to both temples, was trying to think this was all the mistaken outburst of an angry woman. The strong-faced, honest, fearless soldier sitting in the chair could not be a traitor—*could not be*.

Suddenly something went awry in the inflamed chambers of Elizabeth's mind—as if an electric current had been abruptly shut off. She hesitated; she had meant to say more; but there was a staggering vacuity.

With an effort she grasped a wavering thing of tangibility, and said: "I'm going now, father—to give the keys to the butler for breakfast. You can question Captain Barlow."

Elizabeth turned and left the room; her feet were like dependents, servants that she had to direct to carry her on her way. She did not call to the butler, but went to her room, closed the door, flung herself on the bed, face downward, and sobbed; tears that scalded splashed her cheeks, and she beat passionately with clenched fist at the pillow, beating, as she knew, at her heart. It was incredible, this thing, her feelings.

"I don't care—I don't care—I never did!" she gasped.

But she did, and only now knew it.

"I was right—I'm glad—I'd say it again!"

But she would not, and she knew it. She knew that Barlow could not be a traitor; she knew it; it was just a battered new love asserting itself.

And below in the room the two men for a little sat not speaking of the ghoulish thing. Barlow had drawn the papers from his pocket; he passed them silently across the table.

Hodson, almost mechanically, had stretched a hand for them, and when they were opened, and he saw the seal, and realised what they were, some curious guttural sound issued from his lips as if he had waked in affright from a nightmare. He pulled a drawer of the desk open, took out a cheroot—and lighted it. Then he commenced to speak, slowly, droppingly, as one speaks who has suddenly been detected in a crime. He put a flat hand on the papers, holding them to the desk. And it was Elizabeth he spoke of at first, as if the thing under his palm, that meant danger to an empire, was subservient.

"Barlow, my boy," he said, "I'm old, I'm tired."

The Captain, looking into the drawn face, had a curious feeling that Hodson was at least a hundred. There was a floaty wonderment in his mind why the fifty-five-years'-service retirement rule had not been enforced in the Colonel's case. Then he heard the other's words.

"I've had but two gods, Barlow, the British Raj and Elizabeth; that's since her mother died. In a little, a few years more, I will retire with just enough to live on plus my pension—perhaps in France, where it's cheap. And then I'll still have two gods, Elizabeth and the one God. And, Captain, somehow I had hoped that you and Elizabeth would hit it off, but I'm afraid she's made a mistake."

Barlow had been following this with half his receptivity, for, though he fought against it, the memory of Bootea—gentle, trusting, radiating love, warmth—cried out against the bitter unfemininity of the girl who had stabbed his honour and his cleanness. The black figure of Kali still rested on the table, and somehow the evil lines in the face of the goddess suggested the vindictiveness that had played about the thin lips of his accuser.

And the very plea the father was making was reacting. It was this, that he, Barlow, was rich, that a chance death or two would make him Lord Barradean, was the attraction, not love. A girl couldn't be in love with a man and strive to break him.

Hodson had taken up the papers, and was again scanning them mistily.

"They were on the murdered messenger—he was killed, wasn't he, Barlow?"

"Yes."

"And has any native seen these papers, Captain?"

"No, I cut them from the soles of the sandals the messenger wore, myself, Sir."

"That is all then, Captain; we have them back—I may say, thank God!" He stood up and holding out his hand added, "Thank you, Captain. I don't want to know anything about the matter—I'm too much machine now to measure rainbows—fancy I should wear a strip of red-tape as a tie."

"If you will listen, Sir—there is another that I want to put right. Your daughter did see the Gulab, but because she had brought me the sandals. And you can take an officer's word for it that the Gulab is not what Elizabeth believes."

"Captain, I have lived a long time in India, too long to be led away by quick impressions, as unfortunately Elizabeth was. I've outlived my prejudices. When the *mhowa* tree blooms I can take glorious pleasure from its gorgeous fragrant flowers and not quarrel with its leafless limbs. When the pipal and the neem glisten with star flowers and sweeten the foetid night-air, it matters nothing to me that the natives believe evil gods home in the branches. I know that even a cobra tries to get out of my way if I'll let him, and I know that the natives have beauty in their natures—one gets to almost love them as children. So, my dear Captain, when you tell me that the Gulab rendered you and me and the British Raj this tremendous service, and add, quite unnecessarily, that she's a good girl, I believe it all; we need never bring it up again. Elizabeth has just made a mistake. And, Barlow, men are always forgiving the mistakes of women where their feelings are concerned—they must—that is one of the proofs of their strength. But these"—and he patted the papers lovingly—"well, they're rather like a reprieve brought at the eleventh hour to a man who is to be executed. We're put in a difficult position, though. To pass over in silence the killing of two soldiers would end only in the House of Commons; somebody would rise in his place and want to know why it had been hushed up. But to take action, to create a stir, would give rise to a suspicion of the existence of this."

Hodson rose from his chair and paced the floor, one hand clasped to his forehead, his small grey eyes carrying a dream-look as though he were seeking an occult enlightenment; then he sat down wearily, and spoke as if interpreting something that had been whispered him.

"Yes, Barlow, this decoit has been seized by the Nana Sahib lot. His life was forfeit, and they've offered him his life back to come here and turn Approver—to become a spy, not *for* us but as a spy *on* us for them. Ajeet would know that information of his coming to me would be carried to them by spies—the spies are always with me—and his life wouldn't be worth two annas. I gave him that pardon because we have no power to seize him here, but it will make them think that we have fallen into the trap. They might even believe—wily and suspicious as they are—that what he gleans here is the truth.

"There's a curious efficacy, Barlow, in what I might call an affectation of simplicity. You know those stupid heavy-headed crocodiles in that big pool of the Nerbudda below the marble gorge, and how they'll take nearly an hour wallowing and sidling up to a mud-bank before they crawl out to bask in the sun; but just show the tip of your helmet above the rock and they're gone. That's perhaps what I mean. As we might say back in dear old London, this wily Rajput thinks he has pulled my leg."

"I think, Colonel, that you are dead onto his wicket."

"Well, then, the thing to do is to emulate the mugger. But this"—Hodson lifted the paper and he grew crisp, incisive, his grey eyes blued like temper purpling polished steel—"we've got to act: they've got to be delivered, and soon."

"I am ready, Sir."

"It's a dangerous mission—most dangerous."

"Pardon, Sir?"

"Sorry, Captain. I was just thinking aloud—musing; forgive me. Perhaps when one likes a young man he lets the paternal spirit come in where it doesn't belong. I'm sorry. There's a trusty Patan here who could go with you," Hodson continued, "and this side of his own border he is absolutely to be trusted; I have my doubts if any Patan can be relied upon by us across the border."

"I will go alone," Barlow said quietly. Then his strong white teeth showed in a smile. "You know the Moslem saying, Colonel, that ten Dervishes can sleep on one blanket, but a kingdom can only hold one king. I don't mean about the honour of it, but it will be easier for me. I went alone through the Maris tribe when we wanted to know what the trouble was that threatened up above the Bolan, and I had no difficulty. You know, Sir, the playful name the chaps have given me for years?"

"Yes—the 'Patan'—I've heard it."

"I make a good Musselman—scarce need any make-up, I'm so dark; I can rattle off the *namaz* (daily prayer), and sing the *moonakib*, the hymn of the followers of the Prophet."

"Yes," Hodson said, his words coming slowly out of a deep think, "there will be Patans in the Pindari camp; in fact Pindari is an all-embracing name, having little of nationality about it. Rajputs, Bundoolas, Patans, men of Oudh, Sindies—men who have the lust of battle and loot, all flock to the Pindari Chief. Yes, it's a good idea, Captain, the disguise; not only for an unnoticed entrance to the camp, but to escape a waylaying by Nana Sahib's cut-throats."

"Yes, Colonel, from what I have learned—from the Gulab it was, Sir—the Dewan has an inkling that I am going on a mission; and if I rode as myself the King might lose an officer, and officers cost pounds in the making."

The Resident toyed with the papers on his desk, his brow wrinkled from a debate going on behind it; he rose, and grasping the black Kali carried it back to the cabinet, saying: "That devilish thing, so suggestive of what we are always up against here, makes me shiver."

Then he sat down, adding, "Captain, there is another important matter connected with this. The Rana of Udaipur is being stripped of every rupee by Holkar and Sindhia; they take turn about at him. Holkar is up there now, where we have chased him—threatened to sack Udaipur unless he were paid seventy lakhs, seven million rupees—the accursed thief! We have managed to get an envoy to the Rana with a view to having him, and the other smaller rulers of Mewar, join forces with us to crush forever the Mahratta power— drive them out of Mewar for all time. The Rajputs are a brave lot— men of high thought, and it is too bad to have these accursed cut-throats bleeding to death such a race. If the Rana would sign this paper also as an assurance of friendship, to be shown the Pindari Chief, it would help greatly."

"I understand, Colonel. You wish me to get that from the Rana?"

"Yes, Captain; and I may say that if you can get through with all this there will be no question about your Majority; you might even go higher up than Major."

"By Jove! as to that, my dear Colonel, this trip is just good sport—I love it: less danger than playing polo with these rotters. I'll swing over to Udaipur first—it's just west of the Pindari camp,—been there once before on a little pow-wow—then I'll switch back to Amir Khan."

"I wish you luck, Captain; but be careful. If we can feel sure that this horde of Pindaris are not hovering on our army's flank, like the Russians hovered on Napoleon's in the Moscow affair, it will be a great thing—you will have accomplished a wonderful thing."

"Right you are, Sir," Barlow exclaimed blithely. The stupendous task, for it was that, tonicked him; he was like a sportsman that had received news of a tiger within killing distance. He rose, and stretched out his hand for the paper, saying: "I've got a job of cobbling to do—I'll put this between the soles of my sandal, as it was carried before—it's the safest place, really. Tomorrow I'll become an apostate, an Afghan; and I'll be busy, for I've got to do it all myself. I can trust no one with a dark skin."

"Not even the Gulab, I fear, Captain; one never knows when a woman will be swayed by some mental transition." He was thinking of Elizabeth.

"You're right, Colonel," Barlow answered. "I fancy I could trust the Gulab—but I won't."

# CHAPTER XVI

Captain Barlow had been through a busy day. The very fact that all he did in preparation for his journey to the Pindari camp had been done with his own hands, held under water, out of sight, had increased the strain upon him.

In India in the usual routine of matters, a staff of ten servants form a composite second self to a Sahib: to hand him his boots, and lace them; to lay out his clothes, and hold them while slipped into; to bring a cheroot or a peg of whiskey; a *syce* to bring the horse and rub a towel over the saddle—to hold the stirrup, even, for the lifted foot, and trotting behind, guard the horse when the Sahib makes a call; a man to go here and there with a note or to post a letter; a servant to whisk away a plate and replenish the crystal glass with pearl-beaded wine without sign from the drinker, and appear like a bidden ghost, clad in speckless white, silent and impassive of face, behind his master's chair at the table when he dines out; everything in fact beyond the mental whirl of the brain to be arranged by one or other of the ten.

But this day Barlow had been like a man throwing detectives off his trail. Not one of his servants must suspect that he contemplated a trip—no, not just that, for the Captain had intimated casually to the butler that he would go soon to Satara.

Thus it had to be arranged secretly that he would ride from his bungalow as Captain Barlow and leave the city as Ayub Alli, an Afghan.

Perhaps Barlow was over tired, that curious knotted condition of the nerves through overstrain that rasps a man's mental fibre beyond the narcotic of sleep, and yet holds him in a hectic state of half unconsciousness. He counted camels—long strings of soured, complaining beasts, short-legged, stout, shaggy desert-ships, such as merchants of Kabul used to carry their dried fruits,—figs and dates and pomegranates, and the wondrous flavoured Sirdar melon,—wending across the Sind Desert of floating white sand to Rajasthan.

Once a male, tickled to frenzy by the caress of a female's velvet lips upon his rump, with a hoarse bubbling scream, wheeled suddenly, snapping the thin lead-cord that reached from the tail of the camel in front to the button in his nostril, and charged the lady in an exuberance of affection with a full broadside—thrust from his chest that bowled her over, where she lay among the fragments of two huge broken burnt-clay *gumlas*, that, filled with water, had been lashed to her sides.

Barlow sat up at this startling tumult that was the outcome of his slipping a little into slumber. He threw his head back on the pillow with a smothered, "Damn!"

His bed had creaked, and an answering echo as if something had slipped or slid, perhaps the sole of a bare foot on the fibrous floor matting, at the window, fell upon his senses. Turning his face toward the sound he waited, eyes trying to pierce the gloom, and ear attuned. He almost cried out in alarm as something floated through the dark from the window and fell with a soft thud upon his face. He brushed at the something—perhaps a bat, or a lizard, or a snake—with his hand and received a sharp prick, a little dart of pain in a thumb. He sprang from the bed, lighted the wick that floated in the iron lamp, and discovered that the thing of dread was a rose, its petals red against the white sheet.

He knew who must have thrown the rose, and almost wished that it had been a chance missil, even a snake, but he put the lamp down, passed into the bathroom, and unbarring the wooden door, called softly, "Who is there?"

From the cover of an oleander a slight girlish form rose up and came to the door saying, "It is Bootea, Sahib; do not be angry,—there is something to be said."

By the arm he led her within and bidding her wait, passed to the bedroom and drew the heavy curtains of the windows. Then he went through the drawing-room and out to the verandah, where the watchman lay asleep on his roped charpoy. Barlow woke him: "There's a thief prowling about the bungalow. Do not sleep till I give you permission. See that no one enters," he commanded.

He went back to his room, closed and barred the door, and told Bootea to come.

When the girl entered he said: "You should not have come here; there are eyes, and ears, and evil tongues."

"That is true, Sahib, but also death is evil—sometimes."

"I have brought this to the Sahib," Bootea said as she drew a paper from her breast and passed it to the Captain. It was the pardon the Resident had given that morning to Ajeet Singh.

Barlow, though startled, schooled his voice to an even tone as he asked: "Where did you get this—where is Ajeet?"

"As to the paper, Sahib, what matters how Bootea came by it; as to Ajeet, he is in the grasp of the Dewan who learned that he had been to the Resident in the way of treachery."

"Ajeet thought Nana Sahib had stolen you, Bootea."

"Yes, Sahib, for he did not find me when he went to the camp, and I did not go there. But now he would betray the Sahibs, that is why I have brought back the paper of protection."

"Will they kill Ajeet?" Barlow asked.

"I will tell the Sahib what is," the girl answered, drawing her *sari* over her curled-in feet, and leaning one arm on Barlow's chair. "The decoity that was committed last night was, as Ajeet feared, because of treachery on the part of the Dewan. I will tell it all, though it might be thought a treachery to the decoits. As to being false to one's own clan Ajeet is, because he is a Bagree—but I am not."

Barlow pondered over this statement. The girl had mystified him—that is as to her breeding. Sometimes she spoke in the first person and again in the third person, like so many natives, as if her language had been picked up colloquially. But then the use of the third person when she used Bootea instead of a nominative pronoun might be due to a cultured deference toward a Sahib.

"I thought you were not of these people—you are of high caste, Bootea," he said presently.

He heard the girl gasp, and looking quickly into her eyes saw that they were staring as if in fright.

For a space of a few seconds she did not answer; then she said, and Barlow felt her voice was being held under control by force of will: "I am Bootea, one in the care of Ajeet Singh. That is the present, Sahib, and the past—" She touched the iron bracelet on her arm, and looked into Barlow's eyes as if she asked him to bury the past.

"Sorry, girl—forgive me," he said.

"Ajeet has told why the men were brought—for what purpose?"

"Yes, Gulab; to kill Amir Khan."

"And when they refused to go on this mission, the Dewan, to get them in his power, connived with Hunsa to make the decoity so that their lives would be forfeit, then if the Dewan punished them for not going the Raja of Karowlee could not make trouble. Hunsa told the Dewan that if I were sent to dance before Amir Khan, some of the men going as musicians and actors, the Chief would fall in love with me, and that I could betray him to those who would kill him; that he would come to my tent at night unobserved— because he has a wife with him—and that Hunsa would creep into the tent and kill him as he slept; then we would escape."

Barlow sprang to his feet and paced the floor; then he plumped into the chair again, saying: "What an unholy scheme, even for India. Gad! how I wish I'd killed the brute when I had the chance."

"I did not know that Hunsa had proposed this—neither did Ajeet; for they wanted to get him in their power through the decoity so that if he refused permission he might be killed. And now Ajeet is trapped through the decoity and Bootea is going to the Pindari camp."

"You're not going to betray Amir Khan, have him murdered!" Barlow cried, aghast at the villainy, at the thought that one so sweet could be forced to complicity in such a ghastly crime.

"No, Sahib, to *save* his life, for if I do not go now Ajeet will be killed, and all the others put in prison because of the decoity. Worse will happen Bootea,—she will be placed in the seraglio of Nana Sahib."

"Damn it! they can't do that!" Barlow exclaimed angrily. "I'll stop that."

"No, the Sahib can't; and he has a mission, he is not of the service of protecting Bootea."

"You can't save Amir Khan's life unless you betray the Bagrees to him?"

"Yes, Sahib, I can. Perhaps the Chief will like Bootea, and will listen to what she says. Men such as brave warriors always treat

Bootea not as a *nautchni* so I will ask him not to come to the tent at night because of ill repute. Hunsa will not be able to slay him unless it is a trap on my part to get him from the watching eyes of his men. If Hunsa becomes suspicious, and there is real danger, I will threaten that I will expose him to the Chief. If we come back because we have failed in our mission, having tried to succeed, it will not be like refusing to go; and perhaps there will be mercy shown."

"Mercy!" Barlow sneered; "Nana Sahib knows nothing of mercy, he's a tiger."

"But if I refuse to go another *nautchni* will be sent, perhaps more beautiful than I am, and she would betray the Chief, and perhaps all would be killed."

"By Jove! you're some woman, you're magnificent—you're like a Rajputni princess."

A slim hand was placed on Barlow's wrist and the girl said, "Sahib, I am just Bootea,—please, please!"

"And that's your reason for taking this awful chance, to save Ajeet and the others—is it?"

"There is another reason, Sahib." The girl dropped her eyes and turning a gold bangle on her wrist gazed upon a ruby that had the contour of a serpent's head. Presently she asked, "Will the Sahib go to Khureyra and have a knife thrust between his ribs?"

Barlow was startled by this query. "Why should I go to Khureyra, Gulab?"

"To see Amir Khan."

"What makes you say that?"

"Because it is known. But the Chief is not now there—he has taken his horsemen to Saugor."

Again this was startling. Also the information was of great value. If the Pindari horde had left the territory of Sindhia and crossed the border into Saugor they were closer to the British.

Barlow patted the girl's hand, saying, "My salaams to you, little girl."

He felt her slim cool fingers press his hand, but he shrank from the claiming touch, muttering, "The damned barrier!"

Suddenly Barlow remembered Bootea had spoken of another reason for going to the Pindari camp. He puzzled over this a little, hesitating to question her; she had not told him what it was, but had asked if he were going there; the reason evidently had something to do with him. It couldn't be treachery—she had done so much for him; it must be the something that looked out of her eyes when they rested on his face, the unworded greatest thing on earth in the way of fealty and devotion. Possibly this was the grand motive, the reason she had given being secondary.

"You said, Gulab, that you had another reason for this awful trip; what is it?" he asked.

The girl's eyes dropped to the ruby bracelet again; "To acquire merit in the eyes of Mahadeo, Sahib."

"To do good acts so that you may be reincarnated as a heaven-born, a Brahmini, perhaps even come back as a memsahib."

At this her big eyes rose to Barlow's face, and he could swear that there were tears misting them; and sensing that if she had fallen in love with him, what he had said about her becoming a memsahib had hurt. Perhaps she, as he did, realised that that was the barred door to happiness—that she wasn't of the white race.

"Yes, Sahib," she said presently, "a Swami told me that in a former life I had been evil."

"The Swami is an awful liar!" Barlow ejaculated.

"The holy ones speak the truth, Sahib. The Swami said that because of having been beautiful I had caused deaths through jealousy."

"Oh, the crazy fool!" Barlow declared in English; "and it's all rot! This is the reason you spoke of, Gulab—good deeds; is it the only other reason?"

The girl turned her face away, and Barlow saw her shoulders quiver.

He rose from the chair, and lifting the girl to her feet held her in his arms, saying: "Look me in the eyes, Gulab, and tell me if you are going through this devilish thing because of me."

"Bootea is going to the camp of Amir Khan because Hunsa and the others have been told to kill the Sahib; and she will see that this is not accomplished."

Barlow clasped the girl to his breast and smothered her face in kisses; "You are the sweetest little woman that ever lived," he said; "and I am a sinner, for this can only bring you misery."

"Sahib—it can't be, but it is not misery. The sweet pain has been put in the heart of Bootea by the Sahib's eyes, and she is happy. But do not go as a Sahib."

Barlow cursed softly to himself, muttering, "India! Even dreams are not unheard!" Then, "What made you say that?" he queried.

"It is known because that is the way of the Sahib. He knows that where he sleeps or eats, or plays games with the little balls, that there are always servants, and it is known that Captain Barrle is called the Patan by his friends."

"St. George and the Cross!" he ejaculated. "If I were thus would they know me?" he asked. "There would be danger, but the Sahib knowing of this, could take more care in the way of deceit. But Bootea will know—the eyes will not be hidden."

Then he thought of Hunsa, and asked, "But aren't you afraid to go with that beast, Hunsa?"

The girl laughed. "The decoits have orders from the Dewan to kill him if I complain of him; but if they do not he is promised the torture when he comes back if I make complaint. If the Sahib will but wait a few days before the journey so that Bootea has made friends with Amir Kami before he comes, it will be better. We will start in two days."

"I'll see, Gulab," he answered evasively. "You are going now?"

"Yes, Sahib—it has been said."

"I'll send the doorman with you."

"No, Bootea will be better alone," she touched the knife in her sash; "it must not be known that Bootea came to the Sahib."

Barlow took her arm leading her through the bathroom to the back door; he opened it, and listened intently for a few seconds. Then he took her oval face in his palms and kissed her, passionately, saying, "Goodbye, little girl; God be with you. You are sweet."

"The Sahib is like a god to Bootea," she whispered.

As the girl slipped away between the bushes, like something floating out of a dream, Barlow stood at the open door, a resurge of abasement flooding his soul. In the combat between his mentality and his heart the heart was making him a weakling, a dishonourable weakling, so it seemed. He pulled the door shut, and went back to his bed and finally fell asleep, a thing of tortured unrest.

# CHAPTER XVII

Barlow was up early next morning, wakened by that universal alarm clock of India, the grey-necked, small-bodied city crow whose tribe is called the Seven Sisters—noisy, impudent, clamorous, sharp-eyed thieves that throng the compounds like sparrows, that hop in through the open window and steal a slice of toast from beside the cup of tea at the bedside.

He mounted the waiting Cabuli pony and rode to the Residency. He had much to talk over with Hodson in the light of all that had transpired in the last two days, and, also, he had a hope that Elizabeth would be possessed of an after-the-storm calm, would greet him, and somehow give him a moral sustaining against his lapse in heart loyalty. Mentally he didn't label his feeling toward Elizabeth love. Toward her it had been largely a matter of drifting, undoubted giving in to suasion, more of association than what was said. She had class; she was intellectual; there was no doubt about her wit—it was like a well-cut diamond, sparkling, brilliant—no warmth. When Barlow reflected, jogging along on the Cabuli, that he probably did not love Elizabeth, picturing the passion as typified by Romeo and Juliet as instance, he suddenly asked himself: "By Jove! and does anybody except the pater love Elizabeth?" He was doubtful if anybody did. All the servants held her in esteem, for she was just, and not niggardly; but hers was certainly not a disposition to cause spontaneous affection. Perhaps the word admirable epitomised Elizabeth all round. But he felt that he needed a sort of Christian Science sustaining, as it were, in this sensuous drifting—something to make his slipping appear more obnoxious.

As he rode up to the verandah of the Residency he saw Elizabeth cutting flowers, probably to decorate the breakfast table. That was like Elizabeth; instead of leaving it to the *mahli* (gardener), with the butler to festoon the table, she was doing it herself. It was an occupation akin to water-colour painting or lace work, just the sort of thing to find Elizabeth at—typical.

Barlow was possessed of a hopeful fancy that perhaps she had not ridden expecting that he would call on the Resident; but as always with the Resident's daughter he could deduct nothing from her manner. She nodded pleasantly, looking up, a gloved hand full of roses; and, as he slipped from the saddle, relinquishing the horse to the *syce*, she fell in beside him as far as the verandah, where they stood talking desultory stuff; the morning sun on the pink and white oleanders, the curious snake-like mottling of the croton leaves, and the song of a *dhyal* that, high in a tamarind, was bubbling liquid notes of joy.

"The Indian robin red-breast makes one homesick," Elizabeth said.

"Home—", but the girl put a quick hand on his arm checking him; the action was absolutely like Elizabeth, imperious. A small, long-tailed, brown-breasted bird had darted across the compound to a mango tree from where he warbled a love song as sweet and rich toned as the evensong of a nightingale.

The *dhyal*, as if feeling defeat in the sweeter carol of his rival, hushed.

"The *shama*," Elizabeth said; "when I hear him I close my eyes and picture the downs and oaked hills of England, and fancy I'm listening to the nightingale or the lark."

Barlow turned involuntarily to look into the girl's face; it was an inquisitive look, a wondering look; gentle sentiment coming from Elizabeth was rather a reversal of form.

Also there was immediately a reversal of bird form, a shatterment of sentiment, a rasping maddening note from somewhere in the dome of a pipal tree. A Koel bird, as if in derision of the feathered songsters, sent forth his shrill plaintive, "Koe-e-el, Koe-e-el, Ko-e-e-el!"

"Ah-a-a!" Barlow exclaimed in disgust—"that's India; the fever-bird, the koel, harbinger of the hot-spell, of burning sun and stifling dust, and throbbing head."

He cursed the koel, for the gentle mood had slipped from Elizabeth. He had hoped that she would have spoken of yesterday, give him a shamed solace for the hurt she had given him. Of course

Hodson would have told her all about the Gulab. But while that, the service, was sufficient for the Resident, Elizabeth would consider the fact that Barlow knew Bootea well enough to have this service rendered; it would touch her caste—also her exacting nature.

Something like this was floating through his mind as he groped mentally for an explanation of Elizabeth's attitude, the effect of which was neutral; nothing to draw him toward her in a way of moral sustaining, but also, nothing to antagonise him.

She must know that he was leaving on a dangerous mission; but she did not bring it up. Perhaps with her usual diffident reserve she felt that it was his province to speak of that.

At any rate she called to a hovering bearer telling him to give his master Captain Barlow's salaams. Then with the flowers she passed into the bungalow. She had quite a proppy, military stride, bred of much riding.

Barlow gazed after Elizabeth ruefully, wishing she had thrown him a life belt. However, it did not matter; it was up to him to act in a sane manner, men of the Service were taught to rely on themselves. And in Barlow was the something of breeding that held him to the true thing, to the pole; the breeding might be compared to the elusive thing in the magnetic needle. It did not matter, he would probably marry Elizabeth—it seemed the proper thing to do. Devilish few of the chaps he knew babbled much about love and being batty over a girl—that is, the girls they married.

Then the bearer brought Hodson's salaams to the Captain.

And Hodson was a Civil Servant in excelsis. He took to bed with him his Form D and Form C—even the "D. O.", the Demi Official business, and worried over it when he should have slept or read himself to sleep. Duty to him was a more exacting god than the black Kali to the Brahmins; it had dried up his blood—atrophied his nerves of enjoyment. And now he was depressed though he strove to greet Barlow cheerily.

"It's a devilish shindy, this killing of our two chaps," he burst forth with; "I've pondered over it, I've worried over it; the only solace in the thing is, that the arm of the law is long."

"I think you've got it, sir," Barlow encouraged. "When we've smashed Sindhia—and we will—we'll demand these murderers, hang a few of them, and send the rest to the Andamans."

"Yes, it has simply got to wait; to stir up things now would only let the Peshwa know what you are going to do—we'd show him our hand. And I don't mind telling you, Captain, that he is an absolute traitor; and I believe that it's that damn Nana Sahib who's influencing him."

"There's no doubt about it, sir."

"No, there is not!" the Resident declared gloomily. "The two dead *sowars* must be considered as sacrifice, just as though they had fallen in battle; it's for the good of the Raj. If I get hauled over the coals for this I don't give a damn. I've pondered over it, almost prayed over it, and it's the only way. There's talk of a big loot of jewellery by these decoits, and the killing of the merchant and his men, but I've got nothing to do with that. The one wonderful thing is, that we saved the papers. That little native woman that brought them to you must be rewarded later. By the way, Barlow, I took the liberty of explaining all that to Elizabeth, and I think she's pretty badly cut up over the way she acted. But you understand, don't you, Captain? I believe that if it had been my case I'd have, well, I'd have known that it was because the girl cared. Elizabeth is undemonstrative—too much so, in fact; but I fancy—well, never mind: it's so long ago that I took notice of these things that I find I'm trying to speak in an unknown tongue."

The little man rose and bustled about, pulling out drawers from the cabinet and shoving them back again, venting little asthmatic coughs of sheer nervousness. Then coming up to Barlow he held out his hand saying: "My dear boy, God be with you; but don't take chances—will you?"

At that instant Elizabeth appeared at the doorway: "Captain Barlow will have breakfast with us, won't he, father—it's all ready, and Boodha says he has a chop-and-kidney curry that is a dream?"

"Jupiter!" Hodson exclaimed; "fancy I'm getting India head; was sending Barlow off without a word about breakfast. Of course he'll stay—thanks, Elizabeth."

The tired drawn parchment face of the Resident became revivified, it was the face of a happy boy; the grey eyes blued to youth. Inwardly he murmured: "Elizabeth is wonderful! I knew it; good girl!"

It was a curious breakfast—mentally. Elizabeth was the Elizabeth of the verandah. Perhaps it was the passionate beating of the pillow the day before, when she had realised for the first time what Barlow meant to her, that now cast her into defence; encased her in an armour of protection; caused her to assume a casualness. She would give worlds to not have said what she had said the day before, but the Captain must know that she had been roused by a knowledge of his intimacy with the Gulab. Just what had occurred did not matter—not in the least; it was his place to explain it. That was Elizabeth's way—it was her manner of thought; a subservience of impulse to propriety, to class. In the light of her feeling when she had lain, wet-eyed, beating the pillow, she knew that if he had put his arms about her and said just even stupid words—"I'm sorry, Beth, you know I love you"—she would have capitulated, perhaps even in the capitulation have said a Bethism: "It doesn't matter—we'll never mention it again."

But Barlow, very much of a boy, couldn't feel this elusive thing, and rode away after breakfast from the bungalow muttering: "By gad! Elizabeth should have said something over roasting me. Fancy she doesn't care a hang. Anyway—I'll give her credit for that—she doesn't hunt with the hounds and run with the hare. If it's the prospect of sharing a title with me, a rotter would have eaten the leek. Yes, Elizabeth is class."

# CHAPTER XVIII

Dewan Sewlal was in a shiver of apprehension over the killing of the two sepoys; there would be trouble over this if the Resident came to know of it.

But Hunsa had assured him that the soldiers and their saddles had been buried in the pit with the others, and that nobody but the decoits knew of their advent.

Then when he learned that Ajeet Singh had been to the Resident he was in a panic. But as that British official made no move, said nothing about the decoity, he fancied that perhaps Ajeet had not mentioned this, in fact he had no proof that he had made a confession at all. But Ajeet's complicity in the decoity where the merchant and his men had been killed, gave the Dewan just what he had planned for—the power of death over the Chief. As to his own complicity he had taken care to speak of the decoity to no one but Hunsa. The yogi had been inspired, of course, but the yogi would not appear as a witness against him, and Hunsa would not, because it would cost him his head.

So now, at a hint from Nana Sahib, the Dewan seized upon Ajeet, voicing a righteous indignation at his crime of decoity, and gave him the alternative of being strangled with a bow-string or forcing the Gulab to go to the camp of Amir Khan to betray him. Not only would Ajeet be killed, but Bootea would be thrust into the *seraglio*, and the other Bagrees put in prison—some might be killed. Ajeet was forced to yield to these threats. The very complicity of the Dewan made him the more hurried in this thing. Also he wanted to get the Bagrees away to the Pindari camp before the Resident made a move.

The mission to Amir Khan would be placed in the hands of Hunsa and Sookdee, Ajeet being retained as a pawn; also his wound had incapacitated him. He was nominally at liberty, though he knew well that if he sought to escape the Mahrattas would kill him.

The jewels that had been stolen from the merchant were largely retained by the Bagrees, though the Dewan found, one night, very mysteriously, a magnificent string of pearls on his pillow. He did not ask questions, and seemingly no one of his household knew anything about the pearls.

When the yogi asked Hunsa about the ruby, the Akbar Lamp, Hunsa, who had determined to keep it himself, as, perhaps, a ransom for his life in that troublous time, declared that in the turmoil of the coming of the soldiers he had not found it. Indeed this seemed reasonable, for he, having fled down the road to the Gulab, had not been there when they had opened the box and looted it.

So the Dewan sent for Ajeet, Hunsa and Sookdee, and declared that if the Bagree contingent of murder did not start at once for the Pindari camp he would have them taken up for the decoity.

It was Ajeet who answered the Dewan: "Dewan Sahib, we be men who undertake all things in the favour of Bhowanee, and we make prayer to that goddess. If the Dewan will give fifty rupees for our *pooja*, tomorrow we will make sacrifice to her, for without the feast and the sacrifice the signs that she would vouchsafe would be false. Then we will take the signs and the men will go at once."

"You shall have the money," the Dewan declared: "but do not delay."

That evening the Bagrees made their way to a mango grove for the feast, carrying cocoanuts, raw sugar, flour, butter, and a fragrant gum, goojul. A large hole was dug in the ground and filled with dry cow-dung chips which were set on fire. Sweet cakes were baked on the fire and then broken into small pieces, a portion of the fire raked to one side, and their priest sprinkled upon it the fragrant gum, calling in a loud voice: "Maha Kali, assist and guide us in our expedition. Keep calamity from us who worship Thee, and have made this feast in Thy honour. Give us the sign, that we may know if it is agreeable to Thee that we destroy the enemy of Maharaja Sindhia."

When the Bagrees had eaten much cooked rice and meatballs, which were served on plantain leaves, they drank robustly of *mhowa* spirit, first spilling some of this liquor upon the ground in the name of the goddess.

The strong rank native liquor roused an enthusiasm for their approaching interview of the sacred one. Once Ajeet laid his hand upon the pitcher that Hunsa was holding to his coarse lips, and pressing it downward, admonished:

"Hunsa, whilst Bhowanee does not prohibit, it is an offence to approach her except in devout silence."

The surly one flared up at this; his ungovernable rage drew his hand to a knife in his belt, and his eyes blazed with the ferocity of a wounded tiger.

"Ajeet," he snarled, "you are now Chief, but you are not Raja to command slaves."

With a swift twist of his wrist Ajeet snatched the pitcher from the hand of Hunsa, saying: "Jamadar, it is the liquor that is in you, therefore you have had enough."

But Hunsa sprang to his feet and his knife gleamed like the spitting of fire in the slanting rays of the setting sun, as he drove viciously at the heart of his Chief. There was a crash as the blade struck and pierced the matka which Ajeet still held by its long neck.

There was a scream of terror from the throats of the women; a cry of horror from the Guru at this sacrilege—the spilling of liquor upon the earth in anger at the feast of Bhowanee.

Ajeet's strong fingers, slim bronzed lengths of steel, had gripped the wrist of his assailant as Bootea, darting forward, laid a hand upon the arm of Hunsa, crying, "Shame! shame! You are like sweepers of low caste—eaters of carrion, they who respect not Bhowanee. Shame! you are a dog—a tapper of liquor!"

At the touch of the Gulab on his arm, and the scorn in her eyes, Hunsa shivered and drew back, his head hanging in abasement, but his face devilish in its malignity.

Ajeet, taking a brass dish, poured water upon the hand that had gripped the wrist of Hunsa, saying, "Thus I will cleanse the defilement." Then he sat down upon his heels, adding: "Guru, holy one, repeat a prayer to appease Bhowanee, then we will go into the jungle and take the auspices."

The Guru strode over to Hunsa, and holding out his thin skinny palm commanded, "Jamadar, from you a rupee; and tomorrow I will put upon the shrine of Kali cocoanuts and sweet-meats and marigolds as peace offerings."

Hunsa took from his loin cloth a silver coin and dropped it surlily in the outstretched hand, sneering: "To Bhowanee you will give four annas, and you will feast to the value of twelve annas, for that is the way of your craft. The vultures always finish the bait when the tiger has been slain."

Soon the feathery lace work of bamboos beneath which they sat were whispering to the night-wind that had roused at the dropping of the huge ball of fire in the west, and the soft radiance of a gentle moon was gilding with silver the gaunt black arms of a babool. Then the priest said: "Come, jamadars, we now will go deeper into the silent places and listen for the voice of Bhowanee."

He untangled from the posture of sitting his parchment-covered matter of bones, and carrying in one hand a brocaded bag of black velvet and in the other a staff, with bowed head and mutterings started deeper into the jungle of cactus and slim whispering bamboo, followed by Ajeet, Sookdee and Hunsa. Presently he stopped, saying, "Sit you in a line, brave chiefs, facing the great temple of Siva, which is in the mountains of the East, so that the voice of Bhowanee coming out of the silent places and from the mouth of the jackal or the jackass, shall be known to be from the right or the left, for thus will be the interpretation."

The priest took his place in front of the jamadars, sitting with his back to them, and placed upon the ground, first a white cloth of cotton, and then the velvet bag, upon which rested a silver pickaxe.

When Ajeet saw the pickaxe he said angrily: "That is the emblem of thugs; we be decoits, not stranglers, Guru."

"They are equal in honour with Bhowanee," the Guru replied: "they slay for profit, even as you do, and among you are those who are thugs, for I minister to both."

Then the Guru buried his shrivelled skull in his thin hands and drooped forward in silent listening. Ajeet objected no more, and in the new silence they could hear the shrill rasping of cicadae in the foliage of a gigantic elephant-creeper, that, like a huge python, crawled its way from branch to branch, sprawling across a dozen stately trees. From somewhere beyond was a steady "tonk! tonk! tonk!"—like the beat of wood against a hollow pipe—of the little green-plumaged coppersmith bird. A honey-badger came timorously creeping, his feet shuffling the fallen leaves, peered at the strange figures of the men, and, at the move of an arm, fled scurrying through the stillness with the noise of some great creature.

Suddenly the jungle was stilled, even from the voice of the rasping cicadae; the leaves had ceased to whisper, for the wind had hushed. The devotees could hear the beating of their hearts in the strain of waiting for a manifestation from the dread goddess. The white-robed figure of the Guru was like a shrivelled statue of alabaster where the faint moon picked it out in blotches as the light filtered through leaves above.

Sookdee gasped in terror as just above them a tiny tree owl called, "Whoo-whoo, whoo-whoo!" as if he jeered. But Ajeet knew that that, in their belief, was a sign of encouragement, meaning not overmuch, but not an evil omen. From far off floated up on the dead night air the belling note of a startled cheetal, and almost at once the harsh, grating, angry roar of a leopard, as though he had struck for the throat of the stag and missed. These were but jungle voices, not in the curriculum of their pantheistic belief, so the Guru and the Bagrees sat in silence, and no one spoke.

Then, the night carried the faint trembling moan of a jackal, as the Guru knew, a *female* jackal, coming from a distance on the left.

"Oo-oo-oo-oo-oo! Aye-aye! yi-yi-yi-yi!" the jackal wailed, the note rising to a fiendish crescendo; and then suddenly it hushed and there was only a ghastly silence in the jungle depths.

The white-clothed, ghost-like priest sprang to his feet, and with his lean left arm stretched high in suppliance, said: "Bhowanee, thou hast vouchsafed to thy devotees the *pilsao*. We will strew thy shrine with flowers and sweetmeats."

He turned to the jamadars who had risen, saying, "Bhowanee is pleased; the suspicies are favourable; had the call of the jackal been from the right it would have been the *tibao* and we should have had to wait until the sweet goddess gave us another sign. Now we may go back, and perhaps she will confirm this omen as we go."

Hunsa, always possessed of a mean disposition, and still sulky over the encounter with Ajeet, was in an evil mood as they trudged through the jungle to their camp. When Ajeet spoke of the priest's success in his appeal, he snarled: "The hangman always advises the one who is to have his neck stretched that he is better off dead."

"What do you mean by that?" Ajeet queried.

"Just that you are not going on this mission, Ajeet;" then he laughed disagreeably.

"If you are afraid to go Sookdee will be well without you," Ajeet retorted.

Before more could be said in this way, and as they approached the camp, the lowing of a cow was heard.

"Dost hear that, Guru?" Hunsa queried. "In a decoity is not the lowing of a cow in a village held to be an evil omen?"

"Not so, Hunsa," the Priest declared. "It is an evil omen if the decoity is to be made on the village in which the cow raises her voice, but we are going to our own camp in peace, and it is a voice of approval."

"As to that," Ajeet commented, "if Hunsa is right, it is written in our code of omens that hearing a cow call thus simply means that one of the party making the decoity will be killed; perhaps as he was the one to notice it, the evil will fall upon him."

"You'd like that," Hunsa growled.

"Not being given to lies, it would not displease me, for, as the hangman said, you would be better dead."

But they were now at their camp, and the jamadars, standing together for a little, settled it that the omens being favourable, and the wrath of the Dewan feared, they would take the way to the Pindari camp next day.

# CHAPTER XIX

Dewan Sewlal had warned Hunsa and Sookdee against their natural proclivities for making a decoity while travelling to the Pindari camp, as the mission was more important than loot—an enterprise that might cause them to be killed or arrested. Indeed the Gulab had made this a condition of her going with them. She was practically put in command. Both Nana Sahib and the Dewan were pleased over what they deemed her sensible acquiescence in the scheme. As has been said, the Dewan, recognising the debased ferocity of Hunsa, had promised him the torture when he returned if Bootea had any cause of complaint.

The decoit, believing that Bootea was designed for Nana Sahib's harem, knew that as one favoured in the Prince's eyes, he would surely be put to death if he offended her.

So, travelling with the almost incessant swift progress which was an art with all decoits, in a few days they arrived at Rajgar, the town to which Amir Khan had shifted. He had taken possession of a palace belonging to the Rajput Raja as his head-quarters, and his army of horsemen were encamped in tents on the vast sandy plain that extended from both sides of the river Nahal: the local name of this river was "The Stream of Blood," so named because a fierce force of Arab mercenaries in the employ of Sindhia, many years before, had butchered the entire tribe of Nahals—man, woman, and child,—higher up in the hills.

As had been planned, some of the decoits had come as recruits to the Pindari standard. This created no suspicion, because free-lance soldiers, adventurous spirits, from all over India flocked to a force that was known to be massed for the purpose of loot. It was an easy service; little discipline; a regular Moslem fighting horde, holding little in reverence but the daily prayer and the trim of a spear, or the edge of a sword. Amir Khan was the law, the army regulation, the one thing to obey. As to the matter of prayers, for those who were not followers of the Prophet, who carried no little prayer carpet to kneel upon, face to Mecca, there was, it being a Rajput town, always the shrine of Shiva and his elephant-headed son, Ganesh, to receive obeisance from the Hindus. And those who had come as players, wrestlers, were welcomed joyously, for, there being no immediate matter of a raid and throat-cutting, and little of disciplinary duties, time hung heavy on the hands of these grown-up children.

Hunsa was remembered by several of the Pindaris as having ridden with them before; and he also had suffered an apostacy of faith for he now swore by the Beard of the Prophet, and turned out at the call of the *muezzin*, and testified to the fact that there was but one god—Allah. And he had known his Amir Khan well when he had told the Dewan that the fierce Pindari was gentle enough when it came to a matter of feminine beauty, for Bootea made an impression.

Of course it would have taken a more obdurate male than Amir Khan to not appreciate the exquisite charm of the Gulab; no art could have equalled the inherent patrician simplicity and sweetness of her every thought and action. Perhaps her determination to ingratiate herself into the good graces of the Chief was intensified, brought to a finer perfection, by the motive that had really instigated her to accept this terrible mission, her love for the Englishman, Barlow.

Of course this was not an unusual thing; few women have lived who are not capable of such a sacrifice for some one; the "grand passion," when it comes, and rarely out of reasoning, smothers everything in the heart of almost every woman—once. It had come to Bootea; foolishly, impossible of an attainment, everything against its ultimate accomplished happiness, but nothing of that mattered. She was there, waiting—waiting for the service that Fate had whispered into her being.

And she danced divinely—that is the proper word for it. Her dancing was a revelation to Amir Khan who had seen *nautchnis* go through their sensuous, suggestive, voluptuous twistings of supple forms, disfigured by excessive decoration—bangles, anklets, nose rings, high-coloured swirling robes, and with voices worn to a rasping timbre that shrilled rather than sang the *ghazal* (love song) as they gyrated. But here was something different. Bootea's art was the art that was taught princesses in the palaces of the Rajput Ranas, not the bidding of a courtesan for the desire of a man. Her dress was a floating cloud of gauzy muslin: and her sole evident adornment the ruby-headed gold snake-bracelet, the iron band of widowhood being concealed higher on her arm. Some intuition had taught the girl that this mode would give rise in the warrior's heart to a feeling of respectful liking: it had always been that way with real men where she was concerned.

When Amir Kahn passed an order that Bootea was to be treated as a queen, his officers smiled in their heavy black beards and whispered that his two wives would yet be hand-maidens to a third, the favourite.

Hunsa saw all this, for he was the one that often carried a message to the Gulab that her presence was desired in the palace. But there were always others there; the players and the musicians—the ones who played the sitar (guitar) and the violin; and the officers.

Hunsa was getting impatient. Every time he looked at the handsome black-bearded head of the warrior he was like a covetous thief gazing upon a diamond necklace that is almost within his grasp. He had come there to kill him and delay was dangerous. He had been warned by the Dewan that they suspected Barlow meant to visit the Chief on behalf of the British. He might turn up any day. When he spoke to Bootea about her part in the mission, the enticing of Amir Khan to her tent so that he might be killed, she simply answered:

"Hunsa, you will wait until I give you a command to kill the Chief. If you do not, it is very likely that you will be the sacrifice, for he is not one to be driven." She vowed that if he broke this injunction she would denounce him to Amir Khan; she would have done so at first but for the idea that treachery to her people could not be justified but by dire necessity.

Every day the Gulab, as she walked through the crowded street, scanned the faces of men afoot and on horseback, looking for one clothed as a Patan, but in his eyes the something she would know, the something that would say he was the deified one. And she had told Amir Khan that there was a Patan coming with a message for him, and that when such an one asked for audience that he should say nothing, but see that he was admitted.

Then one day—it was about two weeks of waiting—Captain Barlow came. He was rather surprised at the readiness with which he was admitted for an audience with the Chief. It was in the audience hall that he was received, and the Chief was surrounded, as he sat on the Raja's dais, by officers.

Barlow had come as Ayub Alli, an Afghan, and as it was a private interview he desired, he made the visit a formal one, the paying of respects, with the usual presenting of the hilt of his sword for the Chief to touch with the tips of his fingers in the way of accepting his respects.

The Chief, knowing this was the one Bootea had spoken of, wrote on a slip of yellow paper something in Persian and tendered it to Barlow, saying, "That will be your passport when you would speak with me if there is in your heart something to be said."

Going, Barlow saw that he had written but the one word [Transcriber's note: three Afghan or Persian characters], translated, "the Afghan."

Hunsa, too, had watched for the coming of Barlow. The same whisper that had come to Bootea's ears that he would ride as a Patan had been told him by the Dewan. Knowing that when Barlow arrived he would endeavour to see the Chief in his quarters, Hunsa daily hovered near the palace and chatted with the guard at the gates; the heavy double teak-wood gates, on one side of which was painted, on a white stone-wall, a war-elephant and the other side a Rajput horseman, his spear held at the charge. This was the allegorical representation, so general all over Mewar, of Rana Pertab charging a Mogul prince mounted on an elephant.

Thus Hunsa had seen the tall Patan and heard him make the request for an audience with Amir Khan. It was the walk, the slight military precision, that caused the decoit to mutter, "No hill Afghan that."

And when Barlow had come forth the Bagree trailed him up through the chowk; and just as the man he followed came to the end of the narrow crowded way, Hunsa saw Bootea, coming from the opposite direction, suddenly stop, and her eyes go wide as they were fixed on the face of the tall Patan.

"It is the accursed Sahib," Hunsa snarled between his grinding teeth. He brooded over the advent of the messenger and racked his animal brain for some scheme to accomplish his mission of murder, and counteract the other's influence. And presently a bit of rare deviltry crept into his mind, joint partner with the murder thought. If he could but kill the Chief and have the blame of it cast upon the Sahib, who, no doubt, would have his interviews with Amir Khan alone.

During the time Hunsa had been there, several times in the palace, somewhat of a privileged character, known to be connected with the Gulab, he had familiarised himself with the plan of the marble building: the stairways that ran down to the central court; the many passages; the marble fret-work screen niches and mysterious chambers.

Either Hunsa or Sookdee was now always trailing Barlow— his every move was known. And then, as if some evil genii had taken a spirit hand in the guidance of events, Hunsa's chance came. Barlow, who had tried three times to see Amir Khan, one day received a message at the gate that he was to come back that evening, when the Chief, having said his prayers, would give him a private audience.

Hunsa had seen Barlow making his way from the *serai* where he camped with his horse toward the palace, and hurrying with the swift celerity of a jungle creature, he reached the gate first. His head wrapped in the folds of a turban so that his ugly face was all but hidden, he was talking to the guard when Barlow gave the latter his yellow slip of passport; and as the guard left his post and entered the dim entrance to call up the stairway for one to usher in the Afghan, Hunsa slipped nonchalantly through the gate and stood in the shadow of a jutting wall, his black body and drab loin-cloth merging into the gloom.

# CHAPTER XX

"Is the one alone?" Amir Khan asked when a servant had presented Barlow's yellow slip of paper.

"But for the orderly that is with him."

"Tell him to enter, and go where your ears will remain safe upon your head."

The bearer withdrew and Captain Barlow entered, preceded by the orderly, who, with a deep salaam announced:

"Sultan Amir Khan, it is Ayub Alli who would have audience." Then he stepped to one side, and stood erect against the wall.

"Salaam, Chief," Barlow said with a sweep of a hand to his forehead, and Amir Khan from his seat in a black ebony chair inlaid with pearl-shell and garnets, returned the salutation, asking: "And what favour would Ayub Alli ask?"

"A petition such as your servant would make is but for the ears of Amir Khan."

The black eyes of the Pindari, deep set under the shaggy eyebrows, hung upon the speaker's face with the fierce watchful stab of a falcon's.

Barlow saw the distrust, the suspicion. He unslung from his waist his heavy pistol, took the *tulwar* from the wide brass-studded belt about his waist, and tendered them to the orderly saying: "It is a message of peace but also it is alone for the ears of Amir Khan."

The Pindari spoke to the orderly, "Go thou and wait below."

When he had disappeared the Pindari rose from the ebon-wood chair, stretched his tall giant form, and laughed. "Thou art a seemly man, Ayub Alli, but thinkst thou that Amir Khan would have fear that thou sendst thy playthings by the orderly?"

"No, Chief, it was but proper. And you will know that the message is such that none other may hear it."

"Sit on yonder divan, Afghan, and tell this large thing that is in thy mind."

As Barlow took a seat upon the divan covered by a red-and-green Bokharan rug, lifting his eyes suddenly, he was conscious of a mocking smile on the Pindari's lips; and the fierce black eyes were watching his every move as he slipped a well-strapped sandal from a foot. Rising, he stepped to the table at one end of which the Pindari sat, and placing the sandal upon it, said: "If the Chief will slit the double sole with his knife he will find within that which I have brought."

"The matter of which you speak, Afghan, is service, and Amir Khan is not one to perform a service of the hands for any one."

"But if I asked for the Chief's knife, not having one—"

*'Inshalla*! but thou art right; if thou hadst asked for the knife thou mightst have received it, and not in the sandal," he laughed. The laugh welled up from his throat through the heavy black beard like the bubble of a bison bull.

The Pindari reached for the sandal, and as he slit at the leather thread, he commented: "Thou hast the subtlety of a true Patan; within, I take it, is something of value, and if it were in a pocket of thy jacket, or a fold at thy waist, those who might seek it with one slit of their discoverer, which is a piece of broken glass carrying an edge such as no blade would have, would take it up. But a man's sandals well strapped on are removed but after he is dead."

"Bismillah!" The Pindari had the paper spread flat upon the black table and saw the seal of the British Raj. He seemed to ponder over the document as if the writing were not within his interpretation. Then he said: "We men of the sword have not given much thought to the pen, employing scribblers for that purpose, but tomorrow a *mullah* will make this all plain."

Barlow interrupted the Chief. "Shall I read the written word?"

"What would it avail? Hereon is the seal of the *Englay* Raj, but as you read the thumb of the Raj would not be upon your lip in the way of a seal. The *mullah* will interpret this to me. Is it of an alliance?" he asked suddenly.

"It is, Chief."

The Pindari laughed: "Holker would give me a camel-load of gold rupees for this and thy head: Sindhia might add a province for the same."

"True, Chief. And has Amir Khan heard a whisper of reward and a dress of honour from Sindhia's Dewan for his head?"

"Afghan, there is always a reward for the head of Amir Khan; but a gift is of little value to a man who has lost his life in the trying. Without are guards ready to run a sword through even a shadow, and here I could kill three."

He raised his black eyes and scanned the form of Ayub Alli. There was a quizzical smile on his lips as he said:

"Go back and sit thee upon the divan."

When Barlow had taken his place, the Chief laughed aloud, saying, "Well done, Captain Sahib; thou art perfect as a Patan; even to the manner of sitting down one would have thought that, except for a saddle, thou hadst always sat upon thy heels."

Barlow smiled good humouredly, saying, "It is even so; I am Captain Barlow. And this,"—he tapped the loose baggy trousers of the Afghan hillman, and the sheepskin coat with the wool inside— "was not in the way of deceit but for protection on the road."

"It is well thought of," the Pindari declared, "for a Sahib travelling alone through Rajasthan would be robbed by a Mahratta or killed by a Rajput. But as to the deceiving of Amir Khan, dost thou suppose that he gives to a Patan the paper of admittance, or of passing, such as he gave to thee. Even at the audience I was pleased with thy manner of disguise."

Barlow was startled. "Did you know then that I was a Sahib— how did you know?"

"Because thou wert placed in my hand in the way of protection."

Then Barlow surmised that of all outside his own caste there could be but one, and he knew that she was in the camp, for he had seen her. "It was a woman."

"A rare woman; even I, Chief of the Pindaris—and we are not bred to softness—say that she is a pearl."

"They call her the Gulab," Barlow ventured.

"She is well named the Gulab; the perfume of her is in my nostrils though it mixes ill with the camel smell. Without offence to Allah I can retain her for it is in the Koran that a man may have four wives and I have but two."

"But the Gulab is of a different faith," Barlow objected and a chill hung over his heart.

The Pindari laughed. "The Sahibs have agents for the changing of faith, those who wear the black coat of honour; and a *mullah* will soon make a good Musselmani of the beautiful little infidel. Of course, Sahib, there is the other way of having a man's desire which is the way of all Pindaris; they consider women as fair loot when the sword is the passport through a land. But as to the Gulab, the flower is most too fair for a crushing. In such a matter as I have spoken of the fragrance is gone, and a man, when he crushes the weak, has conflict with himself."

"It's a topping old barbarian, this leader of cut-throats," Barlow admitted to himself; but in his mind was a horror of the fate meant for the girl. And somehow it was a sacrifice for him, he knew, an enlargement of the love that had shown in the soft brown eyes. As he listened schemes of stealing the Gulab away, of saving her were hurtling through his brain.

"And mark thee, Sahib, Amir Khan has found favour with the little flower, for when I thought of an audience with her in her own tent—for to be a leader of men, in possession of two wives, and holding strong by the faith of Mahomet, it is as well to be circumspect—the Gulab warned me that a knife might be presented as I slept. A jealous lover, perhaps, I think—it would not have been Ayub Alli by any chance?"

What Barlow was thinking, was, "A most subtle animal, this." And he now understood why the Pindari, as if he had forgotten the message, was talking of the Gulab; as an Oriental he was coming to the point in circles.

"It was not, Chief," Barlow answered. "A British officer on matters of state, would break his *izzat* (honour) if he trifled with women."

"Put thy hand upon thy beard, Afghan—though thou hast not one—and swear by it that it was not thee the woman meant when she spoke of a knife, for I like thee."

Barlow put his hand to his chin. "I swear that there was nothing of evil intent against Amir Khan in my heart," he said; "and that is the same as our oath, for it is but one God that we both worship."

The Chief again let float from his big throat his low, deep, musical laugh.

"An oath is an oath, nothing more. To trust to it and go to sleep in its guardianship, one may never wake up. Even the gods cannot bind a heart that is black with words. It was one of my own name who swore on the shrine of Eklinga at Udaipur friendship for a Prince of Marwar, and changed turbans with him, which is more binding than eating opium together, then slew him like a dog. Of my faith, an oath, 'by the Beard of the Prophet,' is more binding, I think. Too many gods, such as the men of Hind have, produce a wavering. But thou hast sworn to the truth as I am a witness. The delay of an audience was that thou mightst be well watched before much had been said, for a child at play hides nothing, and if thou hadst gone but once to the tent of the Gulab, Amir Khan would have known.

"But as to this,"—his hand tapped the document—"it has been said that the British Raj doles out the lives of its servants as one doles grain in a time of famine. If an envoy, such as a Raja sends in a way of pride, came with this, and were made a matter of sacrifice, perhaps twenty lives would have paid of the trying, but as it is, but one is the account."

Barlow shot a quick searching look into the Pindari's eyes; was it a covert threat? But he answered: "It is even so, it was spoken of as a matter for two, but—"

The Chief laughed: "I know, Sahib; thou art pleasing to me. Of the Sahibs I have little knowledge, but I have heard it said they were a race of white Rajputs, save that they did not kill a brother or a father for the love of killing. What service want they of Amir Khan?"

"There are rumours that the Mahrattas, forgetting the lessons they have received—both Holkar and Sindhia having been thoroughly beaten by the British—are secretly preparing war."

"A *johur*, a last death-rush, is it not?"

"They will be smashed forever, and their lands taken."

"But the King of Oudh has been promised a return to glory to join in this revolt. The fighting Rajputs—what of them? Backed by the English they should hold these black accursed Mahrattas in check."

Barlow rose and, the wary eyes of the Chief on every move, stepped over to the table and pointed to a signature upon the document.

"That," he said, "is the signature of the Rana of Mewar, meaning that he also passes the salt of friendship to Amir Khan."

He turned the document over, and there written upon it was the figure "74 1/2."

"Bismillah!" the Chief cried for he had not noticed this before; "it is the *tilac*, the Rana's sealing of the document; it is the mystic number that means that the contents are sacred, that the curse of the Sack of Fort Chitor be upon him who violates the seal, it is the oath of all Rajputs—*tilac*, that which is forbidden. And the Sahibs have heard a rumour that Amir Khan has a hundred thousand horsemen to cut in with. Even Sindhia is afraid of me and desires my head. The Sahibs have heard and desire my friendship."

"That is true, Chief."

"This is the right way," and the Pindari brought his palm down upon the Government message. "I have heard men say that the English were like children in the matter of knowing nothing but the speaking of truth; I have heard some laugh at this, accounting it easy to circumvent an enemy when one has knowledge of all his intentions, but truth is strength. We have faith in children because they have not yet learned the art of a lie. In two days, Captain Sahib, thou wilt be called to an audience." He rose from his chair, and, with a hand to his forehead said: "Salaam, Sahib. May the protection of Allah be upon you!"

"Salaam, Chief," Barlow answered, and he held out a hand with a boyish frankness that caused the Pindari to grasp it, and the two stood, two men looking into each other's eyes.

"Go thou now, Sahib; thou art a man. Go alone and with quiet, for I would view this message and put it in yonder strong box before others enter."

# CHAPTER XXI

When Captain Barlow had gone Amir Khan took up the message and read it. Once he chuckled, for it was in his Oriental mind that the deceiving of Barlow as to his knowledge of writing was rather a joke. Once as he read the heavy silk *purdah* of the door swayed a little at one side as if a draught of wind had shifted it and an evil face appeared in the opening.

Presently he rose from his chair, took the lamp in one hand and the paper in the other, and crossed to the iron box in a far corner of the room. He set the flickering light upon the floor, and dropping to his knees, drew from his waistband a silver chain, at the end of which were his seal and keys. His broad shoulders blanked the tiny cone of light, and behind through a marble fretwork, a delicate tracery of lotus flowers that screened the window, trickled cold shafts of moonlight that fell upon something evil that wriggled across the white and black slabs of marble from beneath the door curtain. The moonlight glistened the bronze skin of the silent, crawling thing that was a huge snake, or a giant centipede; it was even like a square-snouted, shovel-headed *mugger* that had crept up out of the slimy river that circled sluggishly the eastern wall of the palace.

Once as Amir Khan fitted a key in the lock he checked and knelt, as silent, as passive as a bronze Buddha, listening; and the creeping thing was but a blur, a shadow without movement, silent. Then he raised the lid of the box and paused, holding it with his right hand, the flickering light upon his bronze face showing a smile as his eyes dwelt lovingly upon the gold and jewels within.

And again the thing crept, or glided, not even a slipping purr, noiseless, just a drifting shadow; only where a ribbon of moonlight from between a lotus and a leaf picked it out was the brown thing of evil marked against the marble. Then the divan blurred it from sight. From behind the divan to the ebony chair, and the wide black-topped table the shadow drifted; and when Amir Khan had clanged the iron lid closed, and risen, lamp in hand, there was nothing to catch his eye.

He placed the lamp that was fashioned like a lotus upon the table, and dropping into his chair, yawned sleepily. Then he raised his voice to call his bearer:

"Abd—"

The name died on his lips, for the brown thing behind the chair had slipped upward with the silent undulation of a panther, and a deadly *roomal* (towel) had flashed over the Chief's head and was now a strangling knot about his tawny throat; the hard knuckles of Hunsa were kneading his spine at the back of the skull with a half twist of the cloth. He was pinioned to the back of the chair; he was in a vise, the jaws of which closed his throat. Just a stifled gurgle escaped from his lips as his hand clutched at a dagger hilt. The muscles of the naked brown body behind stood out in knobs of strength, and the face of the strangler, pan-reddened teeth showing in the flickering light as if they had bitten into blood, was the face of a ghoul.

The powerful Pindari struggled in smothering desperation; and Hunsa, twisting the gorilla hands, sought in vain to break the neck—it was too strong.

Then the chair careened sidewise, and the Pindari shot downward, his forehead striking a marble slab, stunning him. Hunsa, with the death-grip still on the roomal, planted a knee between the victim's shoulder-blades, and jerked the head upward—still the spine did not snap; and slowly tightening the pressure of the cloth he smothered the man beneath his knee till he felt the muscles go slack and the body lie limp—dead!

Then Hunsa crossed the *roomal* in his left hand, and stretching out his right grasped the Chief's dagger where it lay upon the floor, and drove it, from behind, through his heart. He placed the knife upon the floor where drops of blood, trickling from its curved point, lay upon the white marble like spilled rubies. He unfastened the silver chain that carried the keys and crossed the floor with the slouching crouch of a hyena. Rapidly he opened the iron box, took the paper Amir Khan had placed there, and hesitated for a second, his ghoulish eyes gloating over the jewels and gold; but he did not touch them, his animal cunning holding him to the simple plan that was now working so smoothly. He locked the box and slipped the key-chain about the dead man's waist; then seizing the right hand of his victim he smeared the thumb in blood and imprinted it upon the paper just beside the seal of the British Raj, muttering: "This will do for Nana Sahib as well as your head, Pindari, and is much easier hidden."

He placed the paper in a roll of his turban, blew out the flickering light, and with noiseless bare feet glided cautiously to the door. The *purdah* swung back and there was left just the silent room, all dark, save for little trickles of silver that dropped spots and grotesque lines upon the body of the dead Chief. It fell full upon the knife flooding its blade into a finger-like mirror, and glinted the blood drops as if in reality they had turned to rubies. Without the *purdah* Hunsa did not crouch and run, he walked swiftly, though noiselessly, as one upon a message. Ten paces of the dim-lighted hall he turned to the right to a balcony.

Here at the top of a narrow winding stone stairway Hunsa listened; no sound came from below, and he glided down. Beneath was a balcony corresponding with the one above, and just beyond was a domed cell that he had investigated. It was a cell that at one time had witnessed the quick descent of headless bodies to the river below. A teakwood beam with a round hole in the centre spanned the cell just above an opening that had all the appearance of a well. Hunsa had investigated this exit for this very purpose, for he had been somewhat of a privileged character about the palace.

He now unslung from about his waist, hidden by his baggy trousers, a strong, fine line of camel hair. Making one end fast to the teakwood sill he went down hand over hand, his strong hard palms gripping the soft line. At the end of it he still had a drop of ten or twelve feet, but bracing his shoulders to one wall and his feet to the other he let go. Hunsa was shaken by his drop of a dozen feet, but the soft sand of the river bed had broken the shock of his fall. He picked himself up, and crouching in the hiding shadow of the bank hurried along for fifty yards; then he clambered up cautiously to the waste of white sand that was studded with the tents of the Pindari horsemen. On his right, floating up the hill in terraces, its marble white in the moonlight, was the palace where Amir Khan lay dead. It still held a sombre quietude; the murder had not been discovered.

He had mapped this route out carefully in the day and knew just how to avoid the patrolling guards, and he was back in the narrow *chouk* of the town that was a struggling stream of swaggering Pindaris, and darker skinned Marwari bunnias and shopkeepers. Hunsa pushed his way through this motley crowd and continued on to the gate of the palace.

To the guard who halted him he said: "If the other who went up to see the Chief has gone, I would go now, *meer* sahib. As I have said, it is a message from the Gulab Begum."

"I looked for you when I returned from above," the guard answered, "but you had gone. The Afghan has gone but a little since—stay you here."

He called within, "Yacoub!"

It was the orderly who had conducted Barlow to Amir Khan who answered, and to him the guard said: "Go to the Chief's apartment and say that one waits here with word from the favourite."

Hunsa sat down nonchalantly upon a marble step, and drew the guard into a talk of raids, explaining that he had ridden once upon a time with Chitu, on his foray into the territory of the Nizam.

# CHAPTER XXII

Hunsa had come back to the palace in haste so that the murder of Amir Khan might be discovered soon after Captain Barlow had left, and that the crime might be fastened upon the Sahib. As he waited, chatting to the guard, there was suddenly a frenzied deep-throated call of alarm from the upper level of rooms that was answered by other voices here and there crying out; there was the hurrying scuffling of feet on the marble stairs, and Yacoub appeared, his eyes wide in fright, crying:

"The Chief has been stabbed! he's dead! he's murdered! Guard the door—let no one out—let no one in!"

"Beat the *nakara*," the guard commanded; "raise the alarm!"

He seized his long-barrelled matchlock, blew on the fuse, and pointing up toward the moonlit sky, fired. Just within, in a little court, Yacoub, with heavy drum-stick, was pounding from the huge drum a thunderous vibrant roar, and somebody at his command had seized a horn, and from its copper throat a strident shriek of alarm split the air.

The narrow street was now one surging mass of excited Pindaris. With their riding whips they slashed viciously at any one other than their own soldier caste that ventured near, driving them out, crying: "This is alone for the Pindaris!"

A powerful, whiskered jamadar pushed his way through the mob, throwing men to the right and left with sweeps of his strong arm, and, reaching the guard, was told that Amir Khan lay up in his room, murdered. Then an *hazari* (commander of five thousand) came running and pushed through the throng that the full force of the tragedy held almost silent.

The guard saluted, saying: "Commander Kassim, the Chief has been slain."

"How—who?"

"I know not, Commander."

"Who has passed the guard here?"

"But one, the Afghan, who was expected by the Chief. He went forth but lately."

"A Patan!" Kassim roared. "Trust a woman and a snake but not a Patan." He turned to the whiskered jamadar: "Quick, go you with men and bring the Afghan." To another he said, "Command to enter from there"—his hand swept the mob in front—"a dozen trusty *sowars* and flood the palace with them. Up, up; every room, every nook, every place of hiding; under everything, and above everything, and through everything, search. Not even let there be exemption of the seraglio—murder lurks close to women at all times. Seize every servant that is within and bind him; let none escape."

He swept a hand out toward the Pindaris in the street that were like a pack of wolves: "Up the hill—surround the palace! and guard every window and rat-run!"

The guard saluted, venturing: "Commander, none could have entered from outside to do the foul deed."

"Liar! lazy sleeper!"—he smashed with his foot the *hookah* that sat on the marble floor, its long stem coiled like a snake—"While you busied over such, and opium, one has slipped by."

He reached out a powerful hand and seized the shoulder of a Pindari and jerked him to the step, commanding: "Stay here with this monkey of the tall trees, and see that none pass. I go to the Chief. When the Afghan comes have him brought up."

Hunsa had stood among the Pindaris, shoved hither and thither as they surged back and forth. Once the flat of a *tulwar* had smote him across the back, but when he turned his face to the striker who recognised him as a man of privilege, one of the amusers, he was allowed to remain.

The startling cry, "The Chief has been murdered! the Sultan is dead!" swept out over the desert sand that lay white in the moonlight, and the night air droned with the hum of fifty thousand voices that was like the song of a world full of bees. And the night palpitated with the beat of horses' feet upon the hard sand and against the stony ford of the parched river as the Pindari horsemen swept to Rajgar as if they rode in the sack of a city.

Hoarse bull-throated cries calling the curse of Allah upon the murderer were like a deep-voiced hymn of hate—it was continuous.

The *bunnias*, and the oilmen, and the keepers of cookshops hid their wares and crept into dark places to hide. The flickering oil lamps were blotted out; but some of the Pindaris had fastened torches to their long spears, and the fluttering lights waved and circled like shooting stars.

Rajgar was a Shoel; it was as if from the teak forests and the jungles of wild mango had rushed its full holding of tigers, and leopards, and elephants, and screaming monkeys.

Soon a wedge of cavalry, a dozen wild-eyed horsemen, pushed their way through the struggling mob, at their head the jamadar bellowing: "Make way—make the road clean of your bodies."

"They bring the Afghan!" somebody cried and pointed to where Barlow sat strapped to the saddle of his Beluchi mare.

"It is the one who killed the Chief!" another yelped; and the cries rippled along from mouth to mouth; *tulwars* flashed in the light of the lurid torches as they swept upward at the end of long arms threateningly; but the jamadar roared: "Back, back! you're like jackals snapping and snarling. Back! if the one is killed how shall we know the truth?"

One, an old man, yelled triumphantly: "Allah be praised! a wisdom—a wisdom! The torture; the horse-bucket and the hot ashes! The jamadar will have the truth out of the Afghan. Allah be praised! it is a wisdom!"

At the gate straps were loosed and Barlow was jerked to the marble steps as if he had been a blanket stripped from the horse's back.

"It is *the* one, Jamadar," the guard declared, thrusting his face into Barlow's; "it is the Afghan. Beyond doubt there will be blood upon his clothes—look to it, Jamadar."

"We found the Afghan in the *serai*, and he was attending to his horse as if about to fly; beyond doubt he is the murderer of our Chief," one who had ridden with the jamadar said.

"Bring the murderer face to face with his foul deed," the jamadar commanded; and clasped by both arms, pinioned, Barlow was pushed through the gate and into the dim-lighted hall. In the scuffle of the passing Hunsa sought to slip through, impelled by a devilish fascination to hear all that would be said in the death-chamber. If the case against the Sahib were short and decisive—perhaps they might slice him into ribbons with their swords—Hunsa would then have nothing to fear, and need not attempt flight.

But the guard swept him back with the butt of his long smooth-bore, crying: "Dog, where go you?" Then he saw that it was Hunsa, the messenger of his Chiefs favourite—as he took the Gulab to be—and he said: "You cannot enter, Hunsa. It is a matter for the jamadars alone."

At that instant the Gulab slipped through the struggling groups in the street, the Pindaris gallantly making way for her. She had heard of the murder of the Chief, and had seen the dragging in of the Afghan.

"Let me go up, guard," she pleaded.

"It is a matter for men," he objected. "The jamadar would be angry, and my sword and gun would be taken away and I should be put to scrub the legs of horses if I let you pass."

"The jamadar will not be angry," she pleaded, "for there is something to be said which only I have knowledge of. It was spoken to me by the Chief, he had fear of this Afghan, and, please, in the name of Allah, let Hunsa by, for being alone I have need of him."

The soft dark eyes pleaded stronger than the girl's words, and the guard yielded, half reluctantly. To the young Pindari he said, "Go you with these two, and if the jamadar is for cutting off their heads, say that those in the street pulled me from the door-way, and these slipped through; I have no fancy for the compliment of a sword on my neck."

In the dim hallway two men stood guarding the door to the Chief's chamber, and when the man who had taken the Gulab up explained her mission, one of them said, "Wait you here. I will ask of Kassim his pleasure." Presently he returned; "The Commander will see the woman but if it is a matter of trifling let the penalty fall upon the guard below. The mingling of women in an affair of men is an abomination in the sight of Allah."

When Bootea entered the chamber she gave a gasping cry of horror. The Chief lay upon the floor, face downward, just as he had dropped when slain, for Kassim had said; "Amir Khan is dead, may Allah take him to his bosom, and such things as we may learn of his death may help us to avenge our Chief. Touch not the body."

Her entrance was not more than half observed, for Kassim at that moment was questioning the Afghan, who stood, a man on either side of him, and two behind.

He was just answering a question from the Commander and was saying: "I left your Chief with the Peace of Allah upon both our heads, for he gripped my hand in fellowship, and said that we were two men. Why should I slay one such who was veritably a soldier, who was a follower of Mahomet?"

The man who had brought Barlow up to Amir Khan when he came for the audience, said: "Commander, I left this one, the Afghan, here with the Chief and took with me his sword and the short gun; he had no weapons."

"Inshalla! it was but a pretence," the Commander declared; "a pretence to gain the confidence of the Chief, for he was slain with his own knife. It was a Patan trick."

The Commander turned to the Afghan: "Why hadst thou audience with the Chief alone and at night here—what was the mission?"

Barlow hesitated, a slight hope that might save his own life would be to declare himself as a Sahib, and his mission; but he felt sure that the Chief had been murdered because of this very thing, that somebody, an agent of Nana Sahib, had waited hidden, had killed the Chief and taken the paper. To speak of it would be to start a rumour that would run across India that the British had negotiated with the Pindaris, and if the paper weren't found there—which it wouldn't be—he wouldn't be believed. Better to accept the roll of the dice as they lay, that he had lost, and die as an Afghan rather than as an Englishman, a spy who had killed their Chief.

"Speak, Patan," Kassim commanded; "thou dwellest overlong upon some lie."

"There was a mission," Barlow answered; "it was from my own people, the people of Sind."

"Of Sindhia?"

"No; from the land of Sind, Afghanistan. We ride not with the Mahrattas; they are infidels, while we be followers of the true Prophet."

"Thou art a fair speaker, Afghan. And was there a sealed message?"

"There was, Commander Sahib."

"Where is it now?"

"I know not. It was left with Amir Khan."

There was a hush of three seconds. Then Kassim, whose eye had searched the room, saw the iron box. "This has a bearing upon matters," he declared; "this affair of a written message. Open the box and see if it is within," he commanded a Pindari.

"How now, woman," for the Gulab had stepped forward; "what dost thou here—ah! there was talk of a message from the Chief. It might be, it might be, because,"—his leonine face, full whiskered, the face of a wild rider, a warrior, softened as he looked at the slight figure,—"our noble Chief had spoken soft words of thee, and passed the order that thou wert Begum, that whatsoever thou desired was to be."

"Commander," Bootea said, and her voice was like her eyes, trembling, vibrant, "let me look upon the face of Amir Khan; then there are things to be said that will avenge his death in the sight of Allah."

Kassim hesitated. Then he said; "It matters not—we have the killer." And reverently, with his own hands, he turned the Chief on his back, saying, softly, "In the name of Allah, thou restest better thus."

The Gulab, kneeling, pushed back the black beard with her hand, and they thought that she was making oath upon the beard of the slain man. Then she rose to her feet, and said: "There is one without, Hunsa, bring him here, and see that there is no weapon upon him."

Kassim passed an order and Hunsa was brought, his evil eyes turning from face to face with the restless query of a caged leopard.

"There is no paper, Commander Sahib," the jamadar said, returning from his search of the iron-box.

"There was none such," Kassim growled; "it was but a Patan lie; the message is yonder," and he pointed to the smear of blood upon the marble floor.

Then he turned to Bootea: "Now, woman, speak what is in thy mind, for this is an affair of action."

"Commander Sahib," Bootea began, "yonder man,"—and she pointed a slim hand toward Barlow—"is not an Afghan, he is a Sahib."

This startling announcement filled the room with cries of astonishment and anger; *tulwars* flashed. Barlow shivered; not because of the impending danger, for he had accepted the roll of the dice, but at the thought that Bootea was betraying him, that all she had said and done before was nothing—a lie, that she was an accomplice in this murder of the Chief, and was now giving the Pindaris the final convincing proof, the reason.

To deny the revelation was useless; they would torture him, and he was to die anyway; better to die claiming to be a *messenger* from the British rather than as one sent to murder the Chief.

Kassim bellowed an order subduing the tumult; then he asked: "What art thou, a Patan, or as the woman says, an Englay?"

"I am a Sahib," Barlow answered; "a Captain in the British service, and came to your Chief with a written message of friendship."

Kassim pointed to the blood on the floor: "Thou wert a good messenger, infidel; thou hast slain a follower of the Prophet."

But Bootea raised a slim hand, and, her voice trembling with intensity, cried: "Commander, Amir Khan was not slain with the dagger, he was killed by the *towel*. Look you at his throat and you will see the mark."

"Bismillah!" came in a cry of astonishment from the Commander's throat, and the marble walls of the *Surya-Mahal* (room of audience) echoed gasps and curses. Kassim himself had knelt by the dead Chief, and now rising, said: "By Allah! it is true. That dog—" his finger was thrusting like a dagger at Barlow.

But Bootea's clear voice hushed the rising clamour: "No, Commander, the sahibs know not the thug trick of the *roomal*, and few thugs could have overcome the Chief."

"Who then killed him—speak quick, and with the truth," Kassim commanded.

He was interrupted by one of Hunsa's guards, crying: "Here, where go you—you had not leave!" And Hunsa, who had turned to slip away, was jerked back to where he had stood.

"It is that one," Bootea declared, sweeping a hand toward Hunsa. "About his waist is even now the yellow-and-white *roomal* that is the weapon of Bhowanee. With that he killed Amir Khan. Take it from him, and see if there be not black hairs from the beard of the Chief in its soft mesh."

"By the grace of Allah it is a truth!" the Commander ejaculated when the cloth passed to him had been examined. "It is a revelation such as came to Mahomet, and out of the mouth of a woman. Great is Allah!"

"Will the Commander have Hunsa searched for the paper the Sahib has spoken of?" Bootea asked.

"In his turban—" Kassim commanded—"in his turban, the nest of a thief's loot or the hiding-place of the knife of a murderer. Look ye in his turban!"

As the turban was stripped from the head of Hunsa the Pindari gave it a whirling twist that sent its many yards of blue muslin streaming out like a ribbon and the parchment message fell to the floor.

"Ah-ha!" and a man, stooping, thrust it into the hands of the Commander.

The Pindari who held the turban, threw it almost at the feet of Bootea, saying, "Methinks the slayer will need this no more."

Bootea picked up the blue cloth and rolled it into a ball, saying, "If it is permitted I will take this to those who entrusted Hunsa with this foul mission to show them that he is dead."

"A clever woman thou art—it is a wise thought; take it by all means, for indeed that dog's head will need little when they have finished with him," the soldier agreed.

Kassim had taken the written paper closer to the light. At sight of the thumb blood-stain upon the document, he gave a bellow of rage. "Look you all!" he cried holding it spread out in the light of the lamp; "here is our Chief's message to us given after he was dead; he sealed it with his thumb in his own blood, after he was dead. A miracle, calling for vengeance. Hunsa, dog, thou shalt die for hours—thou shalt die by inches, for it was thee."

Kassim held the paper at arm's length toward Barlow, asking: "Is this the message thou brought?"

"It is, Commander."

Kassim whirled on Hunsa, "Where didst thou get it, dog of an infidel?"

"Without the gate of the palace, my Lord. I found it lying there where the Sahib had dropped it in his flight."

"Allah! thou art a liar of brazenness." He spoke to a Jamadar: "Have brought the leather nosebag of a horse and hot ashes so that we may come by the truth."

Then Kassim held the parchment close to the lamp and scanned it. He rubbed a hand across his wrinkled brow and pondered. "Beside the seal here is the name, Rana Bhim," and he turned his fierce eyes on Barlow.

"Yes, Commander; the Rana has put his seal upon it that he will join his Rajputs with the British and the Pindaris to drive from Mewar Sindhia—the one whose Dewan sent Hunsa to slay your Chief."

"Thou sayest so, but how know I that Hunsa is not in thy hand, and that thou didst not prepare the way for the killing? Here beside the name of the Rana is drawn a lance; that suggests an order to kill, a secret order." He turned to a sepoy, "Bring the Rajput, Zalim."

While they waited Bootea said: "It was Nana Sahib who sent Hunsa and the decoits to slay Amir Khan, because he feared an alliance between the Chief and the British."

"And thou wert one of them?"

"I came to warn Amir Khan, and—"

"And what, woman—the decoits were your own people?"

"Yonder Sahib had saved my life—saved me from the harem of Nana Sahib, and I came to save his life and your Chief's."

Now there was an eruption into the chamber; men carrying a great pot of hot ashes, and one swinging from his hand the nosebag of a horse; and with them the Rajput.

"Here," Kassim said, addressing the Hindu, "what means this spear upon this document? Is it a hint to drive it home?"

The Rajput put his fingers reverently upon the Rana's signature. "That, Commander, is the seal, the sign. I am a Chondawat, and belong to the highest of the thirty-six tribes of Mewar, and that sign of the lance was put upon state documents by Chonda; it has been since that time—it is but a seal. Even as that,"—and Zalim proudly swung a long arm toward the wall where a huge yellow sun embossed on gypsum rested—"even that is an emblem of the Children of the Sun, the Sesodias of Mewar, the Rana."

"It is well," Kassim declared; "as to this that is in the message, tomorrow, with the aid of a mullah, we will consider it. And now as to Hunsa, we would have from him the truth."

He turned to the Gulab; "Go thou in peace, woman, for our dead Chief had high regard for thee; and Captain Sahib, even thou may go to thy abode, not thinking to leave there, however, without coming to pay salaams. Thou wouldst not get far."

# CHAPTER XXIII

When the two had gone Kassim clapped his hands together: "Now then for the ordeal, the search for truth," he declared.

Hot wood-ashes were poured into the horse-bag, and, protesting, cursing, struggling, the powerful Bagree was dragged to the centre of the room.

"Who sent thee to murder Amir Khan?" Kassim asked.

"Before Bhowanee, Prince, I did not kill him!"

At a wave of Kassim's hand upward the bag of ashes was clapped over the decoit's head, and he was pounded on the back to make him breathe in the deadly dust. Then the bag was taken off, and gasping, reeling, he was commanded to speak the truth. Once Kassim said: "Dog, this is but gentle means; torches will be bound to thy fingers and lighted. The last thing that will remain to thee will be thy tongue, for we have need of that to utter the truth."

Three times the nosebag was applied to Hunsa, like the black cap over the head of a condemned murderer, and the last time, rolling on the floor in agony, his lungs on fire, his throat choked, his eyes searing like hot coals, he gasped that he would confess if his life were spared.

"Dog!" Kassim snarled, "thy life is forfeit, but the torture will cease; it is reward enough—speak!"

But the Bagree had the obstinate courage of a bulldog; the nerves of his giant physical structure were scarce more vibrant than those of a bull; as to the torture it was but a question of a slower death. But his life was something to bargain for. Half dead from the choking of his lungs, with an animal cunning he thought of this; it was the one dominant idea in his numbed brain. As he lay, his mighty chest pumping its short staccato gasps, Commander Kassim said: "Bring the dog of an infidel water that he may tell the truth."

When water had been poured down the Bagree's throat, he rolled his bloodshot eyes beseechingly toward the Commander, and in a voice scarce beyond a hoarse whisper, said: "If you do not kill me, Prince, I will tell what I know."

"Tell it, dog, then die in peace," Kassim snarled.

But Hunsa shook his gorilla head, and answered, "Bhowanee help me, I will not tell. If I die I die with my spirit cast at thy shrine."

Kassim stamped his foot in rage; and a jamadar roared: "Tie the torches to the infidel's fingers; we will have the truth."

Half-a-dozen Pindaris darted forward, and poised in waiting for the command to bind to the fingers of the Bagree oil-soaked torches; but Kassim moved them back, and stood, his brow wrinkled in pondering, his black eyes sullenly fixed on the face of the Bagree. Then he said: "What this dog knows is of more value to our whole people, considering the message that has been brought, than his worthless life that is but the life of a swine."

He took a turn pacing the marble floor, and with his eyes called a jamadar to one side. "These thugs, when they cast themselves in the protection of Kali, die like fanatics, and this one is but an animal. Torture will not bring the truth. Mark you, Jamadar, I will make the compact with him. Do not lead an objection, but trust me."

"But the dead Chief, Commander—?"

"Yes, because of him; he loved his people. And the knowledge that yon dog has he would not have sacrificed."

"But is Amir Khan to be unavenged?" the jamadar queried.

"Allah will punish yonder infidel for the killing of one of the true faith. Go and summon the officers from below and we will decide upon this."

Soon a dozen officers were in the room, and the sowars were sent away. Then Kassim explained the situation saying: "A confession brought forth by torture is often but a lie, the concoction of a mind crazed with pain. If this dog, who has more courage than feeling, sees the chance of his life he will tell us the truth."

But they expostulated; saying that if they let him go free it would be a blot upon their name.

"The necessity is great," Kassim declared, "and this I am convinced is the only way. We may leave his punishment to Allah, for Allah is great. He will not let live one so vile."

Finally the others agreed with Kassim who said that he would take the full onus upon himself for not slaying the murderer, that if there were blame let it be upon his head. Then he spoke to Hunsa: "This has been decided upon, dog, that if thou confess, reveal to us information that is of value to our people, the torture shall cease, and no man's head in the whole Pindari camp shall be raised against thee either to wound or take thy life."

"But the gaol, Hazari Sahib?"

"No, dog, if thou but tell the truth in full, that we may profit, tomorrow thou may go free, and if any man in the camp wounds thee his life will pay for it. Till noon thou may have for the going; even food for thy start on the way back to the land of thy accursed tribe. By the Beard of the Prophet no man of all the Pindari force shall wound thee. Now speak quick, for I have given a pledge."

There were murmurs amongst the jamadars at Kassim's terms, for their hearts were full of hate for the creature who had slain their loved chief. But Kassim was a man famous for his intelligence. In all the councils Amir Khan had been swayed by the Hazari's judgment. It was an accursed price to pay, they felt, but the Chief was dead; to kill his slayer perhaps was not as great a thing as to have Hunsa's confession written and attested to. All that vast horde of fierce riding Pindaris and Bundoolas had been gathered by Amir Khan with the object of being a power in the war that was brewing—the war in which the Mahrattas were striving for ascendency, and the British massing to crush the Mahratta horde. It had been Amir Khan's policy to strike with the winning force; perhaps his big body of hard-riding *sowars* being the very power that would throw the odds to one or other of the contenders. Their reward would be loot, unlimited loot, so dear to the heart of the Pindari, and an assignment of territory. To know, beyond doubt, who had instigated the murder of the Chief was precious knowledge. It might be, as the Gulab had said, Sindhia's Dewan, but there was the English officer there at that time; and the message of friendship may have been a message of deceit and the true object the slaying of Amir Khan who was looked upon as a great leader.

Hunsa had lain watching furtively the effect of the Commander's words upon the others; now he said, "I will tell the truth, Hazari, for thou hast given a promise in the name of Allah that I am free of death at the hands of thy people."

"Wait, dog of an infidel!" Kassim commanded: "quick, call the *Mullah* to write the confession, for this is a sin to be washed out in much blood, and the proof must be at hand so the guilty will have no plea for mercy. Also it is a matter of secrecy; we here being officers will have it on our honour, and the *Mullah*, because of his priesthood, will not speak of it: also he will bear witness of its sanctity."

Soon a Pindari announced, "Commander Sahib, here is the holy one," and at a word from Kassim the priest unrolled his sheets of yellow paper, and sitting cross-legged upon a cushion with a salaam to the dead Chief, dipped his quill in a little ink-horn and held it poised.

Then Hunsa, his eyes all the time furtively watching the scowling faces about him; fear and distrust in his heart over the gift of his life, but impelled by his knowledge that it was his only chance, narrated the story of Nana Sahib and the Dewan's scheme to rid the Mahrattas of the leader they feared, Amir Khan; told that they knew that the British were sending overtures for an alliance, but that fearing to kill the messenger—unless it could be done so secretly it would never be discovered—they had determined to remove the Chief. When he spoke of the other Bagrees, Kassim realised that in the excitement of fixing the murder upon one there they had forgotten his troop associates, and a hurried order was passed for their capture.

Of course it was too late; the others, at the first alarm, had slipped away.

When the confession was finished Kassim commanded the *Mullah* to rub his cube of India ink over the thumb of the decoit and the mark was imprinted on the paper. Then he was taken to one of the cave cells cut out of the solid rock beneath the palace, and imprisoned for the night.

"Come, Jamadars," Kassim said—and his voice that had been so coarse and rough now broke, and sobs floated the words scarce articulate—"and reverently let us lay Amir Khan upon his bed. Then, though there be no call of the *muezzin*, we will kneel here; even without our prayer carpets, and pray to Allah for the repose of the soul of a true Musselman and a great warrior. May his rest be one of peace!"

He passed his hand lovingly over the face of the Chief and down his beard, and his strong fearless eyes were wet.

Then Amir Khan was lifted by the Jamadars and carried to a bed in the room that adjoined the *surya mahal.*

When they had risen from their silent prayer, Kassim said: "Go ye to your tents. I will remain here with the guard who watch."

# CHAPTER XXIV

Captain Barlow and Bootea had gone from the scene of the murder through the long dim-lighted hall, its walls broken here and there by niches of mystery, some of them closed by marble fretwork screens that might have been doors, and down the marble stairway, in silence. Barlow had slipped a hand under her arm in the way of both a physical and mental sustaining; his fingers tapped her arm in affectionate approbation. Once he muttered to himself in English, "Splendid girl!" and not comprehending, the Gulab turned her star-eyes upward to his face.

At the gate the soldier who had accompanied them spoke to the guard, and the latter, standing on a step bellowed: "Ho, ye Pindaris, here goes forth the Afghan in innocence of the foul crime! Above they have the slayer, who was Hunsa the thug; and, Praise be to Allah! they will apply the torture. Let him pass in peace, all ye. And take care that no one molest the beautiful Gulab. The peace of Allah upon the soul of the great Amir Khan!"

A rippling thunder of deep voices vibrated the thronged street, crying, "Allah Akbar! the peace of God be upon the soul of the dead Chief!"

A lane was opened up to them by the grim, wild-eyed, bandit-looking horsemen, *tulwar* over shoulder and knives in belt, who called: "Back ye! the favoured of the Commander passes. Back, make way! 'tis an order."

The faces of the soldiers that had been wreathed in revenge and blood-lust when Barlow had been brought, were now friendly, and there were cries of "Salaam, brother! salaam, Flower of the Desert!" for it had been spread that the Gulab had discovered the murderer, had denounced him.

"Brave little Gulab!" Barlow said in a low voice, bending his head to look into her eyes, for he felt the arm trembling against his hand.

She did not answer, and he knew that she was sobbing.

When they were past the turbulent crowd he said, "Bootea, your people will all have fled or been captured."

"Yes, Sahib," she gasped.

"Perhaps even your maid servant will have been taken."

"No, Sahib, they would not take her; her home is here."

By her side he travelled to where the now deserted tents of the decoits stood silent and dark, like little pagodas of sullen crime. A light flickered in one tent, and silhouetted against its canvas side they could see the form of a woman crouched with her head in her hands.

"The maid is there," Barlow said: "but it is not enough. I will bring my blankets and sleep here at the door of your tent."

"No, Sahib, it is not needed," the girl protested.

"Yes, Bootea, I will come." Then with a little laugh he added; "The gods have ordained that we take turns at protecting each other. It is now my turn; I will come soon."

She turned her small oval face up to look at this wonderful man, to discover if he were really there, that it was not some kindly god who would vanish. He clasped the face, with its soul of adoration, in his two palms and kissed her. Then fearing that she would fall, for she had closed her eyes and reeled, he took her by the arm, opened the flap of the tent, and steadied her into the arms of her handmaid.

It was a fitful night's sleep for Barlow; the beat of horses' hoofs on the streets or the white sands beyond was like the patter of rain on a roof. There were hoarse bull-throated cries of men who rode hither and thither; tremulous voices floated on the night air wild dirges, like the weird Afghan love song. Sometimes a long smooth-bore barked its sharp call. At sunrise the Captain was roused from this tiring sleep by the strident weird sing-song of the Mullah sending forth from a minaret of the palace his call to the faithful to prayer, prayer for the dead Chief. And when the voice had ceased its muezzin:

> "Allah Akbar, Allah Akbar;
> Confess that there is no God but God;
> Confess that Mohammad is the prophet of God;
> Come to Prayer, Come to Prayer,
> For Prayer is better than Sleep."

the big drums sent forth a thundering reverberation. He could hear the voices of the two women within, and called, "Bootea, Bootea!"

The Galub came shyly from the tent saying, "Salaam, Sahib." Then she stood with her eyes drooped waiting for him to speak.

"It is this, Bootea," Barlow said, "do not go away until I am ready to depart, then I will take you where you wish to go."

"If it is permitted, Sahib, I will wait," she answered as simply as a child.

Barlow put a finger under her chin, and lifting her face smiled like a great boy, saying: "Gulab, you are wonderfully sweet."

Then Barlow went to the *serai*, looked after his horse, had his breakfast, and passed back into the town. He saw a continuous stream of men moving toward the small river that swept southward, to the east of the town, and asking of one the cause was told that the *ahiria* (murderer)—for now Hunsa was known as the murderer—was being sent on his way. The speaker was a Rajput. "It is strange, Afghan," he said, "that one who has slain the Chief of these wild barbarians, who are without gods, should be allowed to depart in peace. We Rajputs worship a god that visits the sin upon the head of the sinner, but the order has been passed that no man shall harm the slayer of Amir Khan. Perhaps it is whispered in the Bazaar that Commander Kassim coveted the Chiefship."

Barlow being in the guise of a Musselman said solemnly: "Allah will punish the murderer, mark you well, man of Rajasthan."

"As to that, Afghan, one stroke of a *tulwar* would put the matter beyond doubt; as it is, let us push forward, because I see from yonder steady array of spears that the Pindaris ride toward the river, and I think the prisoner is with them. It was one Hunsa, a thug, and though the thugs worship Bhowanee, they are worse than the *mhangs* who are of no caste at all."

As Barlow came to where the town reached to the river bank he saw that the concourse of people was heading south along the river. This was rather strange, for a bridge of stone arches traversed by the aid of two islands the Nahal to the other side. A quarter of a mile lower down he came to where the river, that above wandered in three channels over a rocky bed, now glided sluggishly in one channel. It was like a ribboned lake, smooth in its slow slip over a muddy bed, and circling in a long sweep to the bank. On the level plain was a concourse of thousands, horsemen, who sat their lean-flanked Marwari or Cabul horses as though they waited to swing into a parade, the march past. The *sowars* Barlow had seen in the town were in front of him, riding four abreast, and at a command from their leader, opened up and formed a scimitar-shaped band, their horses' noses toward the river. As he came close Barlow saw Kassim in a group of officers, and Hunsa, a soldier on either side of him, was standing free and unshackled in front of the Commander. Save for the clanking of a bit, or the clang of a spear-haft against a stirrup, or the scuffle of a quick-turning horse's hoofs, a silence rested upon that vast throng. Wild barbaric faces held a look of expectancy, of wonderment, for no one knew why the order had been passed that they were to assemble at that point.

Kassim caught sight of Barlow as he drew near, and raising his hand in a salute, said: "Come close, Sahib, the slayer of Amir Khan, in accordance with my promise, is to go from our midst a free man. His punishment has been left to Allah, the one God."

Without more ado he stretched forth his right arm impressively toward the murky stream, that, where it rippled at some disturbance carried on its bosom ribbons of gold where the sun fell, saying:

"Yonder lies the way, infidel, strangler, slayer of a follower of the Prophet! Depart, for, failing that, it lacks but an hour till the sun reaches overhead, and thy time will have elapsed—thou will die by the torture. You are free, even as I attested by the Beard of the Prophet. And more, what is not in the covenant,"—Kassim drew from beneath his rich brocaded vest the dagger of Amir Khan, its blade still carrying the dried blood of the Chief—"this is thine to keep thy vile life if you can. Seest thou if the weapon is still wedded to thy hand. It is that thou goest hand-in-hand with thy crime."

He handed the knife to a soldier with a word of command, and the man thrust it in the belt of Hunsa. Even as Kassim ceased speaking two round bulbs floated upon the smooth waters of the sullen river, and above them was a green slime; then a square shovel just topped the water, and Barlow could hear, issuing from the thing of horror, a breath like a sigh. He shuddered. It was a square-nosed *mugger* (crocodile) waiting. And beyond, the water here and there swirled, as if a powerful tail swept it.

And Hunsa knew; his evil swarthy face turned as green as the slime upon the crocodile's forehead; his powerful naked shoulders seemed to shrivel and shrink as though blood had ceased to flow through his veins. He put his two hands, clasped palm to palm, to his forehead in supplication, and begged that the ordeal might pass, that he might go by the bridge, or across the desert, or any way except by that pool of horrors.

Kassim again swept his hand toward the river and his voice was horrible in its deadliness: "These children of the poor that are sacred to some of thy gods, infidel, have been fed; five goats have allotted them as sacrifice and they wait for thee. They serve Allah and not thy gods today. Go, murderer, for we wait; go unless thou art not only a murderer but a coward, for it is the only way. It was promised that no Pindari should wound or kill thee, dog, but they will help thee on thy way."

Hunsa at this drew himself up, his gorilla face seemed to fill out with resolve; he swept the vast throng of horsemen with his eyes, and realised that it was indeed true—there was nothing left but the pool and the faint, faint chance that, powerful swimmer that he was, and with the knife, he might cross. Once his evil eyes rested on Kassim and involuntarily a hand twitched toward the dagger hilt; but at that instant he was pinioned, both arms, by a Pindari on either side. Then, standing rigid, he said:

"I am Hunsa, a Bagree, a servant of Bhowanee; I am not afraid. May she bring the black plague upon all the Pindaris, who are dogs that worship a false god."

He strode toward the waters, the soldiers, still a hand on either arm, marching beside him. On the clay bank he put his hands to his forehead, calling in a loud voice: *"Kali Mia,* receive me!" Then he plunged head first into the pool.

A cry of "Allah! Allah!" went up from ten thousand throats as the Bagree shot from view, smothered in the foam of the ruffled stream. And beyond the waters were churned by huge ghoulish forms that the blood of goats had gathered there. Five yards from the bank the ugly head of Hunsa appeared; a brown arm flashed once, in the fingers clutched a knife that seemed red with fresh blood. The water was lashed to foam; the tail of a giant *mugger* shot out and struck flat upon the surface of the river like the crack of a pistol. Again the head, and then the shoulders, of the swimmer were seen; and as if something dragged the torso below, two legs shot out from the water, gyrated spasmodically, and disappeared.

Barlow waited, his soul full of horror, but there was nothing more; just a little lower down in the basin of the sluggish pool two bulbous protrusions above the water where some crocodile, either gorged or disappointed, floated lazily.

A ghastly silence reigned—no one spoke; ten thousand eyes stared out across the pool.

Then the voice of Kassim was heard, solemn and deep, saying: "The covenant has been kept and Allah has avenged the death of Amir Khan!"

# CHAPTER XXV

Commander Kassim touched Barlow on the arm: "Captain Sahib, come with me. The death of that foul murderer does not take the weight off our hearts."

"He deserved it," Barlow declared.

Though filled with a sense of shuddering horror, he was compelled involuntarily to admit that it had been a most just punishment; less brutal, even more impressive—almost taking on the aspect of a religious execution—than if the Bagree had been tortured to death; hacked to pieces by the *tulwars* of the outraged Pindaris. He had been executed with no evidence of passion in those who witnessed his death. And as to the subtlety of the Commander in obtaining the confession, that, too, according to the ethics of Hindustan, was meritorious, not a thing to be condemned. Hunsa's animal cunning had been over-matched by the clear intellect of this wise soldier.

"We will walk back to the Chamber of Audience," Kassim said, "for now there are things to relate."

He spoke to a soldier to have his horse led behind, and as they walked he explained: "With us, Sahib, as at the death of a Rana of Mewar, there is no interregnum; the dead wait upon the living, for it is dangerous that no one leads, even for an hour, men whose guard is their sword. So, as Amir Khan waits yonder where his body lies to be taken on his way to the arms of Allah in Paradise, they who have the welfare of our people at heart have selected one to lead, and one and all, the jamadars and the hazaris, have decreed that I shall, unworthily, sit upon the *ghuddi* (throne) that was Amir Khan's, though with us it is but the back of a horse. And we have taken under advisement the message thou brought. It has come in good time for the Mahrattas are like wolves that have turned upon each other. Sindhia, Rao Holkar, both beaten by your armies, now fight amongst themselves, and suck like vampires the life-blood of the Rajputs. And Holkar has become insane. But lately, retreating through Mewar, he went to the shrine of Krishna and prostrating himself before his heathen image reviled the god as the cause of his disaster. When the priests, aghast at the profanity, expostulated, he levied a fine of three hundred thousand rupees upon them, and when, fearing an outrage to the image these infidels call a god, they sent the idol to Udaipur, he way-laid the men who had taken it and slew them to a man."

"Your knowledge of affairs is great, Chief," Barlow commented, for most of this was new to him.

"Yes, Captain Sahib, we Pindaris ride north, and east, and south, and west; we are almost as free as the eagles of the air, claiming that our home is where our cooking-pots are. We do not trust to ramparts such as Fort Chitor where we may be cooped up and slain—such as the Rajputs have been three times in the three famed sacks of Chitor—but also, Sahib, this is all wrong."

The Chief halted and swept an arm in an encompassing embrace of the tent-studded plain.

"We are not a nation to muster an army because now the cannon that belch forth a shower of death mow horsemen down like ripened grain. It was the dead Chief's ambition, but it is wrong."

Barlow was struck with the wise logic of this tall wide-browed warrior, it *was* wrong. Massed together Pindaris and *Bundoolas* assailed by the trained hordes of Mahrattas, with their French and Portuguese gunners and officers, would be slaughtered like sheep. And against the war-trained Line Regiments of the British foot soldiers they would meet the same fate. "You are right, Chief Kassim," Barlow declared; "even if you cut in with the winning side, especially Sindhia, he would turn on you and devour you and your people."

"Yes, Sahib. The trade of a Pindari, if I may call it so, has been that of loot in this land that has always been a land of strife for possession. I rode with Chitu as a jamadar when we swept through the Nizam's territory and put cities under a tribute of many *lakhs*, but that was a force of five thousand only, and we swooped through the land like a great flock of hawks. But even at that Chitu, a wonderful chief, was killed by wild animals in the jungle when he was fleeing from disaster, almost alone."

They were now close to the palace, and as they entered, just within the great hall Kassim said: "There will be nothing to say on thy part, Captain Sahib; the officers will come even now to the audience and it is all agreed upon. Thou wilt be given an assurance to take back to the British, for by chance the others have great confidence in me, even more in a matter of diplomacy than they had in the dead leader, may Allah rest his soul!"

And to the audience chamber—where had sat oft two long rows of minor chiefs, at their head on a raised dais the Rajput Raja, a Seesodia, one of the "Children of the Sun," as the flaming yellow gypsum sun above the dais attested—now came in twos and threes the wild-eyed whiskered riders of the desert. They were lean, raw-boned, steel-muscled, tall, solemn-faced men, their eyes set deep in skin wrinkled from the scorch of sun on the white sands of the desert. And their eyes beneath the black brows were like falcon's, predatory like those of birds of prey. And the air of freedom, of self-reliance, of independence was in every look, in the firm swinging stride, and erect set of the shoulders. They were men to swear by or to fear; verily men. And somehow one sharp look of appraisement, and one and all would have sworn by Allah that the Sahib in the garb of an Afghan was a man.

As each one entered he strode to the centre of the room, drew himself erect facing the heavy curtain beyond which lay the dead Chief, and raising a hand to brow, said in a deep voice: "Salaam, Amir Khan, and may the Peace of Allah be upon thy spirit."

"Now, brothers," Kassim said, when the curtain entrance had ceased to be thrust to one side, "we will say what is to be said. One will stand guard just without for this is a matter for the officers alone."

He took from his waist the silver chain and unlocked the iron box, brought forth the paper that Barlow had carried, and holding it aloft, said: "This is the message of brotherhood from the English Raj. Are ye all agreed that it is acceptable to our people?"

"In the name of Allah we are," came as a sonorous chorus from one and all.

"And are ye agreed that it shall be said to the Captain Sahib, who is envoy from the Englay, that we ride in peace to his people, or ride not at all in war?"

"Allah! it is agreed," came the response.

He turned to Barlow. "Captain Sahib, thou hast heard. The word of a Pindari, taken in the name of Allah, is inviolate. That is our answer to the message from the Englay Chief. There is no writing to be given, for a Pindari deals in yea and nay. Is it to be considered. Captain Sahib; is it a message to send that is worthy of men to men?"

"It is, Commander Kassim," Barlow answered.

"Then wait thou for the seal."

He raised his *tulwar* aloft,—and as he did so the steel of every jamadar and hazari flashed upward,—saying, "We Pindaris and Bundoolas who rode for Amir Khan, and now ride for Kassim, swear in the name of Allah, and on the Beard of Mahomet, who is his Prophet, friendship to the Englay Raj."

"By Allah and the Beard of Mahomet, who is his Prophet, we make oath!" the deep voices boomed solemnly.

"It is all," Kassim said quietly. "I would make speech for a little with the Captain."

As each officer passed toward the door he held out a hand and gripped the hand of the Englishman.

When they had gone Kassim said: "Go thou back, Sahib, to the one who is to receive our answer, and let our promise be sent to the one who commands the Englay army and is even now at Tonk, in Mewar, for the purpose of putting the Mahrattas to the sword. Tell the Sahib to strike and drive the accursed dogs from Mewar, and have no fear that the Pindaris will fall upon his flank. Even also our tulwars and our spears are ready for service so be it there is a reward in lands and gold."

The Pindari Chief paced the marble floor twice, then with his eyes watching the effect of his words in the face of Barlow he said: "Captain Sahib, it is of an affair of feeling I would speak now. It relates to the woman who has done us all a service, which but shows what a perception Amir Khan had; a glance and he knew a man for what he was. Therein was his power over the Pindaris. And it seems, which is rarer, that he knew what was in the heart of a woman, for the Gulab is one to rouse in a man desire. And I, myself, years of hard riding and combat having taken me out of my colt-days, wondered why the Chief, being busy otherwise, and a man of short temper, should entail labour in the way of claiming her regard. I may say, Sahib, that a Pindari seizes upon what he wants and backs the claiming with his sword. But now it is all explained—the wise gentleness that really was in the heart of one so fierce as the Chief—Allah rest his soul! What say thou, Captain Sahib?"

"Bootea is wonderful," Barlow answered fervidly; "she is like a Rajput princess."

Kassim coughed, stroked his black beard, adjusted the hilt of his *tulwar*, then coughed again.

"Inshalla! but thou hast said something." He turned to face Barlow more squarely: "Captain Sahib, the one who suffered the wrath of Allah today last night sent a salaam that I would listen to a matter of value. Not wishing to have the hated presence of the murderer in the room near where was Amir Khan I went below to where in a rock cell was this Hunsa. This is the matter he spoke of, no doubt hoping that it would make me more merciful, therefore, of a surety I think it is a lie. It is well known, Sahib, that the Rana of Udaipur had a beautiful daughter, and Raja Jaipur and Raja Marwar both laid claim to her hand; even Sindhia wanted the princess, but being a Mahratta—who are nothing in the way of breeding such as are the Children of the Sun—dust was thrown upon his beard. But the Rajputs fly to the sword over everything and a terrible war ensued in which Udaipur was about ruined. Then one hyena, garbed as the Minister of State, persuaded the cowardly Rana to sacrifice Princess Kumari to save Udaipur.

"All this is known, Sahib, and that she, with the courage of a Rajputni, drained the cup that contained the poison brewed from poppy leaves, and died with a smile on her lips, saying, 'Do not cry, mother; to give my life for my country is nothing.' That is the known story, Sahib. But what Hunsa related was that Kumari did not die, but lives, and has the name of Bootea the Gulab."

The Chief turned his eyes quizzically upon the Englishman, who muttered a half-smothered cry of surprise.

"It can't be—how could the princess be with men such?"

"Better there than sacrifice. Hunsa learned of this thing through listening beneath the wall of a tent at night while one Ajeet Singh spoke of it to the Gulab. It was that the Rana got a yogi, a man skilled in magical things, either drugs or charms, and that Kumari was given a potion that caused her to lie dead for days; and when she was brought back to life of course she had to be removed from where Jaipur or Marwar might see her or hear of this thing, because they would fly to the sword again."

Kassim ceased speaking and his eyes carried a look of interrogation as if he were anxious for a sustaining of his half-faith in the story.

"It's all entirely possible," Barlow declared emphatically; "it's a common practice in India, this deceit as to death where a death is necessary. It could all be easily arranged, the Rana yielding to pressure to save Mewar, and dreading the sin of being guilty of the death of his daughter. Even the Gulab is like a Princess of the Sesodias—like a Rajputni of the highest caste."

"Indeed she is, Captain Sahib, the quality of breeding never lies."

"What discredits Hunsa's story," Barlow said thoughtfully, "is that the Gulab was in the protection of Ajeet Singh who was but a *thakur* at best—really a protector of decoits."

"To save Kumari's life she had been given to the yogi, and he would act not out of affection for the girl's standing as a princess, but to prevent discovery, bloodshed, and, her life. It is also known that these ascetics—infidels, children of the Devil—by charm, or drugs, or otherwise, can cause something like death for days—a trance, and the one who goes thus knows not who he was when he comes back," Kassim argued.

"Well," Barlow said, "it is a matter unsolvable, and of no importance, for the Gulab, Kumari or otherwise, is a princess, such as men fight and die for."

There was a little silence, Barlow carrying on in his mind this, the main interest, so far as he was concerned, Bootea; as a woman appealing to the senses or to the subtlest mentality she was the sweetest woman he had ever known.

There was a flicker of grim humour in Kassim's dark eyes: "Captain Sahib," he said, "that evil-faced Bagree has a curious deep cunning, I believe. I'll swear now by the hilt of my *tulwar* that he made up the whole story for the purpose of having audience with me, and in his heart was a favour desired, for, as I was leaving, he asked that I would have his turban given back to him to wear on his going; he pleaded for it. Of course, Sahib, a turban is an affair of caste, and I suppose he was feeling a disgrace in going forth without it. It appears that Gulab had taken it as an evidence that he had been killed, but when I sent a man for it she told him that the cloth was possessed of vermin and she had burned it."

"But still, Chief, though Hunsa has an animal cunning, yet he could not make up such a story—he has heard it somewhere."

Barlow felt his heart warm toward the grizzled old warrior as he, dropping the nebulous matter of Kumari, said: "And to think, Captain Sahib, that but for the Gulab we would have slain you as the murderer of Amir Khan. As a Patan, even if I had wished it, I could not have fended the *tulwars* from your body. And you were a brave man, such as a Pindari loves; rather than announce thyself as an Englay—the paper gone and thy mission failed—thou wouldst have stood up to death like a soldier."

He put his hand caressingly on Barlow's knee, adding: "By the Beard of the Prophet thou art a man! But all this, Sahib, is to this end; we hold the Gulab in reverence, as did Amir Khan, and if it is permitted, I would have her put in thy hands for her going. Those that were here in the camp with her fled at the first alarm, and my riders discovered today, too late, that they hid in an old mud-walled fort about three miles from here whilst my Pindaris scoured the country for them; then when my riders returned they escaped. So the Gulab is alone. I will send a guard of fifty horsemen and they will ride with thee till thou turnest their horses' heads homeward, and for the Gulab there will be a *tonga*, such as a Nawab might use, drawn by well-fed, and well-shod horses. That, too, she may keep to the end of her journey and afterwards, returning but the driver."

"My salaams to you, Chief, for your goodness. Tomorrow if it please you I will go with your promises to the British."

"It is a command, Sahib—tomorrow. And may the Peace of Allah be upon thee and thy house always!"

He held out a hand and his large dark eyes hovered lovingly over the face of the Englishman.

# CHAPTER XXVI

Captain Barlow walked along to the tent of Bootea to tell her of the arrangement that had been made for their leaving the camp so that she might be ready. He could see in the girl's eyes the reflection of a dual mental struggle, an ineffable sweetness varied by a changing cloud of something that was apprehension or doubt.

"The Sahib is a protector to Bootea," she said. "Sometimes I wondered if such men lived; yet I suppose a woman always has in her mind a vague conception that such an one might be. But always that, that is like a dream, is broken—one wakes."

Prosaically taking the matter in hand Barlow said, "You would wish to go back to your people at Chunda—is it not so?"

The girl's eyes flashed to his face, and her brows wrinkled as if from pain. "Those who have fled will be on their way to Chunda, and they will tell of the slaying of Amir Khan. The Dewan will be pleased, and they will be given honour and rich reward; they will be allowed to return to Karowlee."

"Yes," Barlow interposed; "that Hunsa goes not back will simply be taken as an affair of war, that he was captured and killed; there will be nobody to relate that you revealed the plot. When you arrive there you, also, will be showered with favours, and Ajeet Singh will owe his life to you; they will set him at liberty."

"And as to Nana Sahib?" Bootea asked, and there was pathetic dread in her eyes.

"What is it—you fear him?"

"Yes, Sahib, he will claim Bootea; a Mahratta never keeps faith. There will be a fresh covenant, because he is like a beast of the jungle."

Barlow paced back and forth the small confine of the tent, muttering. "It's hell!" He pictured the Gulab in the harem of Nana Sahib—in a gaudy prison chained to a serpent. To interfere on her behalf would be to sacrifice what came first, his duty as an officer of state, to what would be called, undoubtedly, an infatuation. Elizabeth would take it that way; even his superiors would call it at least inexpedient, bad form. For a British officer to be interested or mixed up with a native woman, no matter how noble the impulse, would be a shatterment of both official and personal caste.

"I won't allow that," he declared vehemently, shifting into words his mental traverse.

Bootea had followed with her eyes his struggle; then she said: "The Sahib has heard of the women of the Rajputs who, with smiles on their lips faced death, who, when the time of the last danger came were not afraid?"

"Yes, Gulab. But for you it is not that way. You have said that I am your protector—I will be."

There was a smile on the girl's lips as she raised her eyes to Barlow's. "It is not permitted, Sahib; the gods have the matter in their lap. For a little—yes, perhaps. It is the time of the pilgrimage to the shrine of Omkar at Mandhatta, and Bootea will make the pilgrimage; at the shrine is the priest that told Bootea of her reincarnations, as I related to the Sahib."

A curious superstitious chill struck with full force upon the heart of Barlow. Kassim's story of Kumari revivified itself with startling remembrance. Was this the priest that, to save Kumari's sacrifice, had wafted her by occult or drug method from one embodied form into another, from Kumari to Bootea? It was so confusing, so overpowering in its clutch that he did not speak of it.

The girl was adding: "It is on the Sahib's way to Poona; there will be many from Karowlee at Mandhatta and I can return with them."

This seemed reasonable to Barlow; she would there be in the company of people not at war. And then, erratically, rebelliously, he felt a heart hunger; but he cursed this feeling as being vicious—it was. He smothered it, shoving it back into a niche of his mind, thinking he had locked it up—had turned a key in the door of the closet to hide the skeleton.

He temporised, saying; "Well, we'll see, Gulab; perhaps at Mandhatta I could wait while you made an offering and a prayer to Omkar, and then you could journey on to Chunda." To himself he muttered in English: "By God! I'll not stand for that slimy brute,

Nana Sahib's, possession of the girl—she's too good. I know enough now to denounce him."

In council with himself, standing Captain Barlow firmly on his feet to face the realities, he realised the impossibility of being anything more to Bootea than just a Sahib who had by fate been thrown into her path temporarily. And then, feeling the sway, the compelling force of a fascinating femininity he almost trembled for himself. Weaker sahibs—gad! he knew several, one a Deputy Commissioner. A beautiful little Kashmiri girl had nursed him through cholera when even his own servants had fled. The Kashmiri, who had the dainty flower-like sweetness of a Japanese maid, and practically the same code, had lived in his protection before this. After the nursing incident he had married her, with benefit of clergy, and the result had been hell, a living suicide, ostracism. A good officer, he still remained Deputy Commissioner, the highest official of the district, but the social excellence was wiped out—he was a pariah, an outcast. And the girl, who now could not remain just a native, could not attain to the dignity of a Deputy-Commissioner Memsahib.

Barlow knew several such. Of course of drifters he knew also, the white inland beach-combers—men who had come out to India to fill subordinate positions in the telegraph, or the railroad, or mills; and, as they sloughed off European caste, and possessed of the eternal longing for woman companionship, had married natives. Barlow shuddered at mentally rehearsed visions of the degradation. Thus everything logical was on that side of the ledger—all against the Gulab. On the other side was the fierce compelling fascination that the girl held for him.

Yes, at Mandhatta they would both sacrifice to the gods. Curiously Elizabeth stood in the computation a cipher; probably he would marry her, but the escapement from disaster, from wreck, would not be because of any moral sustaining from her, any invisible thread of love binding him to the daughter of the Resident. He knew that until he parted from Bootea at Mandhatta his soul would be torn by a strife that was foolish, contemptible, that should never have originated.

# CHAPTER XXVII

And next day when Barlow, sitting his horse, still riding as the Afghan, went forth, his going was somewhat like the departure of a Nawab. Chief Kassim and a dozen officers had clanked down the marble steps from the palace with him and stood lined up at the gates raising their deep voices in full-throated salaams and blessings of Allah upon his head.

The horsemen of the guard, spears to boot-leg, fierce-looking riders of the plain, were lined up four abreast. The *nakara* in the open court of the palace was thundering a farewell like a salute of light artillery.

The *tonga* with Bootea had gone on before with a guard of two out-riders.

All that day they travelled to the south, on their left, against the eastern sky, the lofty peaks of the Vindhya mountains holding the gold of the sun till they looked like a continuous chain of gilded temples and tapering pagodas. For hours the road lay over hard basaltic rocks and white limestone; then again it was a sea of white sand they traversed with its blinding eye-stinging glare.

At night, when they camped, Barlow had a fresh insight into the fine courtesy, the rough nobility that breeds into the bone of men who live by the sword and ride where they will. The Pindaris built their camp-fires to one side, and two of them came to where the Sahib bad spread his blankets near the *tonga* and built a circle of smudge-fires from chips of camel-dung to keep away the flies. Then they went back to their fellows, and when Barlow had pulled the blanket over himself to sleep the clamour of voices where the horsemen sat was hushed.

And Bootea had been treated like a princess. At each village that they passed some would ride in and rejoin the cavalcade with fowl, and eggs, and fruit, and sugar cane, and fresh vegetables; and a mention of payment would only draw a frown, an exclamation of, *"Shookur!* these are but gifts from Allah. There has been more than payment that we have not cut off the *kotwal's* head, not even demanded a peep at the money chest. We are looked upon as men who confer favours."

It was the second day one of the horses in the *tonga* showing lameness, or perhaps even weariness, for the yoke of the *tonga* across their backs did not ride with the ease of a man, the jamadar went into a village and came forth with his men leading two well-fed horses. Again when Barlow spoke of pay for them the jamadar answered, "We will leave these two with the unbelievers, and a message, in the name of Allah, that when we return if the horses we leave are not treated like those of the Sultan there will be throats slit. *Bismillah!* but it is a fair way of treating these unbelievers; they should be grateful."

The road ran through the large towns of Bhopal and Sehore, and at each place Jamadar Jemla explained to all and sundry of the officials that the Patan, meaning Barlow, was a trusted officer with Sindhia and they were escorting a favourite for Sindhia's harem. It was a plausible story, and avoided interference, for while the Pindaris might be turned back if there was a force handy, to interfere with a lady of the King's harem might bring a horde of cut-throat Mahrattas down on them with a snipping off of official heads.

On the fourth day, and now they were on a good trunk road that ran to Indore, and branching to the left, that crossed the Nerbudda River at Mandhatta, they were constantly passing pilgrims on their way to the Temple of Omkar. In the affrighted eyes of the Hindus Barlow could read their dread of the Pindaris; they would cringe at the roadside and salaam, as fearful were they as if a wolf-pack swept down the highway.

The jamadar would laugh in his deep throat, and twist his black moustache with forefinger and thumb, and call the curse of Mahomet upon these worshippers of stone images and foul gods. He loved to ride stirrup to stirrup with the Englishman, and Barlow found delight in the man's broad conception of life; the petty things seemed to have no resting place in his mind, unless perhaps as a matter for ridicule. The sweep of a country with free rein and a sharp sword, and always the hazard of loot or death was an engrossing subject. Even the enemy who fought and bled and died, were like themselves—by Allah! men; but the merchants, the shop-keepers, and the money-lenders, who cringed and paid tribute when the Pindaris drove at them in a raid, were pigs, cowardly dogs who robbed the poor and gave only to the accursed Brahmins and their foul gods. He would dwell lovingly upon the feats of courage of the Rajputs, lamenting that such fine men should be excluded from heaven, dying as they did such glorious deaths, sword in hand, because of their mistaken infidelity; they were souls lost because of being led away from a true god, the one god, Allah, through false priests.

"Mark thou, Sahib," Jemla said once, "I do not hold that it is a merit in the sight of Allah to slay such except there is need, but when it is a *jihad*, a question of the supremacy of a true god, Allah, or the Sahib's God—which no doubt is one and the same—as against the evil gods of destruction and depravity such as Shiva and Kali, then it is a merit to slay the children of evil. Mahomet did much to put this matter right," he declared; "he made good Musselmen of thousands who would otherwise have been cast into *jehannum* (hell), at times holding the sword over their heads as argument. Therein Mahomet was a true prophet, a saver of souls rather than a destroyer of such."

By noon they were drawing toward Mandhatta, and when they came to where the road from Indore to Mandhatta joined the one they were travelling, there was an increase in the stream of pilgrims and Barlow could see a look of uneasiness in the jamadar's eyes.

There was a grove of wild mango trees on the left, running from the road down to a stream that gurgled on its way from the hills to the Nerbudda river, and Jemla said, "We might camp here, Sahib, for there is both good water and fire-wood."

They could see, as they rested and ate, a party of Hindus down by the stream where there was a shrine to Krishna that nestled under a huge banyan that was like the roof of a cave from which dropped to earth to take roots hundreds of slender shoots, like stalactites, and whose roots, creeping from the earth like giant worms, crawled on to lave in the stream. When they had finished eating, Jemla said, "That is a temple of the Preserver;" then he laughed a full-throated sneer: *"Allah hafiz!* (God protect us), give me a fine-edged *tulwar*,—and mine own is not so dull—methinks yon grinning affair of stone would not preserve a dozen of these infidels had there been cause for anger."

"What do the pilgrims there, for they go, it would seem, to Omkar?" Barlow queried.

"There has been a death—perhaps it was even a year ago, and at a shrine of Krishna, especially this one that is on a water that is like a trickle of holy tears to the sacred Narbudda, *straddhas* (prayers for the dead) are said. Come, Sahib, we will look upon this mummy, the only savour of grace about the infidel thing being that it perhaps brings to their hearts a restfulness, having the faith that they have helped the soul of the dead."

Barlow rose from where he sat and they went down to where a party of a dozen were engaged in the service of an appeal to the god for rest for the soul of a dead relative. The devotees did not resent the appearance of the two who were garbed as Moslems. The shrine was one of those, of which there are many in India, that, curiously enough, is sacred to both Hindus and followers of the Prophet. On a flat rock, laved by the stream, was an imprint of a foot, a legendary foot-print of Krishna, perhaps left there as he crossed the stream to gambol with the milkmaids in the meadow beyond. And it was venerated by the Musselman because a disciple of Mohammed had attained to great sanctity by austerities up in the mountain behind, and had been buried there.

But Barlow was watching with deep interest the ceremonial form of the *straddha*. He saw the women place balls of rice, milk, and leaves of the *tulsi* plant in earthenware platters, then sprinkle over this flowers and kusa-grass; they added threads, plucked from their garments, to typify the presenting of the white death-sheet to the dead one; a priest all the time mumbling a prayer, at the end of the simple ceremony receiving a fee of five rupees.

As the two men turned back toward their camp Jemla chuckled: "Captain Sahib, thou seest now the weapon of the Brahmin; his loot of silver pieces was acquired with little effort and no strife; as to the rice-balls the first jackal that catches their wind will have a filled stomach. It is something to be thought of in the way of regard for a long abiding in heaven that such foolish ones will not attain to it. The setting up of false gods, carved images, I was once told by a priest of thy faith, is sufficient to exclude such. It makes one's *tulwar* clatter in its scabbard to see such profanation in an approach to God."

Then Jemla spoke of the matter that had engendered the troubled look Barlow had observed: "The Captain Sahib has intimated that the One"—and he tipped his head toward the girl—"would proceed to the temple of Omkar to make offerings at the shrine?"

"Yes, she goes there."

"There will be a hundred thousand of these infidels at Mandhatta, and when they see fifty Pindaris, *tulwar* and spear and match-lock, there will be unrest; perhaps there will be altercation—they will fear that we ride in pillage."

"I was thinking of that," Barlow replied; "and it would be as well that you turned your faces homeward."

"We have received an order from our Chief that our lives are at the disposal of the Captain Sahib, and we will drive into the heart of a Mahratta force if needs be, but if it is the Sahib's command we will ride back from here," Jemla said.

"Yes; there is no need of a guard for the Gulab now—just that the *tonga* carries her as far as she wishes it," Barlow concurred.

"Indeed we are not needed; those infidels come to worship their heathen gods, not to combat men, and Mandhatta is but a matter of twelve *kos* now," Jemla affirmed.

When Captain Barlow, and Bootea in the *tonga*, drew out from the encampment to proceed on their way the Pindaris rode on in front, and then, at a command from Jemla, wheeled their horses into a continuous line facing the road, stirrup to stirrup, the horsemen sitting erect with their *tulwars* at the salute. As Barlow passed a cry of, "Salaam, aleikum! the protection of Allah be upon you," rippled down the line. Then the horsemen wheeled with their faces to the north. Jemla swept a hand to his forehead and from his deep throat welled a farewell, "Salaam, bhai! (brother)."

# CHAPTER XXVIII

The Jamadar's tribute from man to man, one encased in a dark skin and one in a white, was akin to the tribulation that would not be driven from Barlow's mind over the Gulab, that in their case made the matter of a skin colourisation the bar sinister. He rode in a brooding silence. And now the way was one of ascent toward the pass through the Vindhya mountains; a red gravelly undulating formation had given place to basaltic rocks. They passed from groups of *mhowa* trees and left behind a wide shallow stream, its bed dotted with pools fringed by great *kowa* trees, and its banks lined by a thick green cover of *jamun* and *karonda*. Thorny *babul* thrust their spiked branches out over the roadway, white with tufts of cotton torn by its thorns from bales, loose pressed, on their way to market in buffalo carts; "Babul the thief," the natives called this acacia. Higher up a torch-wood tree gleamed as if sprayed with gold, its limbs, lean and bare of foliage, holding at their extremities in wisp-like fingers bright, yellow, solitary blooms. From a *tendu* tree a pair of droll little brown monkeys chattered and grimaced at the clattering cart.

A spotted owlet, disturbed by the driver's encouraging, "Pop-pop! Dih-dih-dih! Ho-ho-ho! children of jungle swine; brothers to buffalo!" addressed to the horses lagging in the climb, fluttered away with his silly little cackle.

These incidents of travel were almost unnoticed of Barlow. All up the climb the retrospect was with him, claiming his thoughts. Just that—all that was in evidence, a pigment in the skin, *caste*; and yet reacting away back to God's mandate against the union of the white and black. And verily a sin to be visited even unto the third and fourth generation, for the bar sinister would be upon his children; they would be half-castes with all of the opprobrium the name carried. Even the son of a king, the offspring of such a union would be spoken of in mess and drawing-room as a half-caste: the indelible sign would be upon him, the blue tint to the white moons in his finger nails. Barlow shuddered. Why contemplate the matter at all—it was impossible. Nana Sahib had named the barrier when he had spoken of *varna*, meaning colour, as *caste*, a shirt-of-mail that protected from disaster.

Sometimes as he dropped back past the *tonga*, the face of Bootea would appear beneath the lifted curtain, and though on the lips would be a sweet ravishing smile, the eyes were pathetic, full of heart hunger. Sometimes he vowed that he would put off the parting—dream on; carry her on to her people at Chunda. Then he would realise that this was cowardice, a desire flooding his sense of nobility into a chasm of possible disaster; not fair to the girl; the animal mastery of male over female, the domination of sex. Beyond doubt, wrapped in his arms, not even the omnipotence of the gods would take her away from him. If there were less innate nobility in his avatar, if he were like men that were called red-blooded men, yet lacking the finer sensibility, this might be; not a villainous rush, just drifting. That was it, the superlative excellence of the Gulab; the very quality that attracted, was the shield, the immaculate robe that clothed her and preserved her like a vestal virgin from such violation. Barlow could not word all these things; subconsciously they swayed him—like the magnetic needle, always toward the pole of right.

When they had topped the pass and descended into the valley of the Narbudda, clothed in arboreal beauty, passed from a forest of evergreen *sal* to giant teak trees with huge umbrella-like leaves that formed a canopy over the straight column-like boles of eighty feet, and on amidst topes of wild mango and wild date, down, down, to the lower levels where the *dhak* jungles gave way to feathery bamboo and plantain and waving grass, the sun, like a great ball of molten gold, was splashing its yellow sheen upon the waters of a stream that hurried south to Mother Narbudda.

There was a small village of Gonds, or Korkus, like a toy thing, the houses woven from split bamboo, nestling against the billowing hills.

"Here we will rest and eat," Barlow said to the Gulab.

"As the Sahib wishes," she answered, and smiled at him like a child.

The huge medallion of gold had slid down in the west from the dome through which were shot great streamers of red and mauve, and a peacock perched high in a sal tree far up on the mountainside sent forth his strident cry of "Miaou! miaou! miaou!" his evening salute to the god of warmth.

As the harsh call, like an evening *muezzin*, died out, the sweet song of a shama, in tones as pure as those of a nightingale, broke the solemn hush of eventide.

Barlow turned his face to where the songster was perched in the top branches of a wild-fig, and Bootea, said in a low voice: "Sahib, it is said that the shama is a soul come back to earth to sing of love that men may not grow harsh."

Soon a silver moon peeped over the walls of the Vindhya hills, and from the forests above the night wind, waking at the fleeing of the sun, whispered down through feathered *sal* trees carrying the scent of balsam and from a group of *salei* trees a sweet unguent, the perfume of the gum which is burnt at the shrines of Hindu gods.

When they had eaten, Barlow said: "I wonder, Gulab, if this is like *kailas*, the heaven those who have passed through many transitions and become holy, attain to."

"It is just heaven, my Lord," she replied fervently.

"And tomorrow I will be plodding on through the sands and dust, and I'll be all alone. But you, little girl, you will be making your peace with Omkar and dreaming of the greater heaven."

"Yes, it will be that way; the Sahib will not have the tribulation of protecting Bootea, and she will be in the protection of Omkar."

There was so much of pathetic resignation in the timbre of the girl's voice, for it was half sigh, that Barlow shivered, as if the chilling mist of the valley had crept up to the foothills. Why had he not treated her as an alien, kept all interest in abeyance? His self recrimination was becoming a disease, an affliction.

He rose, muttering, "Damn! I'm like the young wasters that swarm up to London from Oxford and get splashed with the girls from the theatres—that's what I'm like."

As he strode over to where his horse was tethered, munching his ration of grain, Bootea followed him with her eyes, wondering why he had broken into English; perhaps he was chanting an evening prayer.

When Barlow came back he fell to wishing that they were at Mandhatta so that he would start on the rest of his journey in the morning; he dreaded the long evening with the girl. He could have sat there with Elizabeth, although their marriage hovered on the horizon, and talked of trivial things: of sport, of shooting; or damned the Executive sitting beneath *punkahs* in offices with windows all closed, far away in Calcutta. Or could have traversed, mentally, leagues of sea and rehabilitated past scenes in London. It would be like talking to a brother officer. But with the Gulab, and the hush and perfume of the forest-clad hills, and the gentle glamour of moonlight, his senses would smother placid intellectuality; he would be like a toper with a bottle at his elbow mocking weak resolve.

Then the girl said something: a shy halting request that set his blood galloping: "Sahib, it is not far to Mandhatta—four *kos*, or perhaps it is five; would it be unpermitted to suggest that we go there, for the moon is beautiful and the road is good."

"All right, girl!" and remembering that he had spoken in English, he added, "It will be expedient, for you will there find shelter."

"Yes, Sahib, Guru Swami will be there, and I am known of him; and there are places where one may rest."

"I'll tell the driver to hitch up," Barlow declared, rising.

But she laid a detaining hand upon his arm: "Sahib, the sweetest thing in all Bootea's life was the time she rode on the horse with him. Then, too, the moon, that is the soul of Purusha, smiled upon her. Would it be permitted to Bootea just one more happiness, for tomorrow—tomorrow—"

The girl turned away, and seemed busy adjusting her gold-embroidered jacket.

"So you shall, Gulab," Barlow declared. And he, too, thought of the sweetness of that ride where she lay like a confiding child in his arms; and also for him, too, was tomorrow—tomorrow; and for him, too, just one more foolish, useless happiness—just a sensuous burying of his face in flowers that on the morrow would have shrivelled.

"I'll send the *tonga* on ahead," he declared, "and we'll just have that jolly old farewell ride together, girl—I'd love it."

Now she turned back to him and her face was placid, soft, content, as though Mona Lisa had stepped out from the painted canvas, and, now embodied, was there listening to the sigh of the night-wind through the feathered *sal* forest.

With ejaculations of "Bap, bap, bap! *Shabaz!*" and queer gurgling clucking of the throat, and a sonorous rumble from the wide, low wheels, the driver drove the tonga on into the moonlight. Barlow had saddled his horse and thrown his blanket loosely behind the saddle. The air was chilling, but his sheepskin coat would turn its cold breath; the blanket was for Bootea.

As he had done once before, his feet in stirrups, he reached down a hand and swung the girl up in front of him. Then he enveloped her in the blanket as she nestled against his chest, arms about his waist. Her warm body was like a draught of wine and he muttered, "My God! I shouldn't have done this!" But he knew that he would have had that ride if devils had jeered at him from the jungle that lined the road.

As the horse swung along in leisured walking stride, the girl seemed to have gone to sleep; her cheek lay against Barlow's shoulder, and he could feel the pulsating throb of her heart. Once a sigh came from her lips, but it was like a breath of deep content. Barlow felt that he must talk to the girl; his senses were rampant; he was sitting like the lotus-eaters drinking in a deadly intoxication.

But it was Bootea who broke the silence as though she, too, felt herself slipping. She took from beneath her vestment a little bag of silk and taking from it a ruby she put it in Barlow's hand, saying: "Here is the 'Lamp of Akbar;' it protects and gives power."

"Where did you get this magnificent ruby, girl—it is of great value?" Barlow queried in amazement.

"Do you remember, Sahib, when Bootea asked for the turban of Hunsa, the time it was stripped from his head, and the paper of message found hidden in it?"

"Yes, you said you would take it back to the Bagrees to show them that Hunsa was dead."

He could hear the Gulab chuckle. "That was but the deceit of a woman, Sahib; the simple things that a woman says to deceive a clever man. I knew that Hunsa had the ruby sewn in a corner of the turban, and when I had taken the stone I burned the turban in the fire, for it was like Hunsa—very dirty."

"Where did Hunsa get it?"

"When the Bagrees killed the jewel merchant, that time the Sahib saved Bootea, he stole it from the other decoits, hiding it in his turban, because the Dewan wanted it."

"But I don't want the stone—I can't take it," Barlow expostulated.

"It is for a service, Sahib. Nana Sahib will assuredly cause Ajeet to be put to death if Bootea does not return to his desire, but the Sahib can buy his life with the ruby of great price."

"But if it were stolen would not Nana Sahib demand it, and then kill Ajeet?"

"No; it was not his ruby; and to obtain it he will set Ajeet free."

"I'll do that, Gulab," Barlow agreed, and the girl's hand pushed up from the folds of the blanket to caress his cheek, and her face nestled against his shoulder.

The fingers thrilled him, and, though he had made solemn vow that he would ride like an anchorite, he bent his head and kissed her with a claiming warmth that caused her to cry out as if in misery.

Presently a whimsical fancy swayed the girl, and she said, "Ayub Alli!"

Barlow laughed, and answered: "Bismillah!"

"So, Afghan, riding thus, it is not disrespect, just that we be of different faith, Hindu and Musselman."

"If it were thus, we'd not part at Mandhatta. And as to the faith, thou wouldst become a follower of the Prophet."

"Yes, Bootea would. If she could go forever thus she would sacrifice entrance to *kailas*. But this is heaven; and perhaps Omkar, when I make the sacrifice—I mean offering—will listen to Bootea's prayers, and—and—"

"And what, Gulab?" Barlow asked, for the girl turned her face against his breast, and her voice had smothered.

Their thoughts were distracted by a din in front that shattered the solemn hush of the night. There was a thunderous beat of tom-toms, the shrill rasping screech of conch-shells, and in intervals of subversion of instrumental clamour they could hear women's voices, high-pitched, singing the *scahailia* (song of joy). Loud cries of "Jae, Jae, Omkar!" rose in a chorus from a hundred swelling throats.

At a turning around a huge banyan tree they saw the flickering flames of torches, and Barlow knew that plodding in front was a large body of pilgrims.

He quickened his horse's pace, drawing Bootea closer to hide her from curious eyes, and as he passed the Hindus he knew from their scowling faces and cries of, "It is a Kaffir—a barbarian!" that they took him for a Mussulman, perhaps one of Sindhia's Arabs.

At the head of the procession, carried on a platform gaily decorated with gaudy cloths, borne on the shoulders of four men, was a figure of Ganesha. The obese, four-armed, jovial son of Shiva, bobbing in the rhythmic stride of his carriers, seemed to nod his elephant head at the horseman approvingly, wishing him luck as was the wont of Ganesha. The procession drove in upon Barlow's mind the thought that they were nearing Mandhatta; he realised it with a pang of reluctance. It seemed but a matter of just minutes since he had lifted Bootea to the saddle.

It had hurried the Gulab's mind, too, for at another turn where the road slid into the valley, bringing to their nostrils the soft perfume of *kush-kush* grass and the savour of *jamun* that grew luxuriantly on the banks of the Narbudda, the Gulab asked: "The Sahib will marry the young Memsahib who is at the city of the Peshwa?"

Barlow was startled. It was like a voice crying out in the night that shattered a blissful dream.

"Why do you ask that, Gulab?"

"Because it was said. And the Missie Baba's heart will be full of the Sahib, for he is like a god."

"Is the Gulab jealous of the Missie Baba?" Barlow asked mundanely, almost out of confusion.

"No, Sahib, because—because one is not jealous of a princess; because that is to question the ways of the gods. If I had been an Englay and he loved me, and the Missie Baba claimed him, Bootea would kill her."

This was said with the simple conviction of a child uttering a weird threat, but Barlow shivered.

"And now, Gulab," he persisted, "if you thought I loved you would you kill the Missie Baba?"

"No, Sahib, because it is Bootea's fault. It can't be. It is permitted to Bootea to love the Sahib, but at the shrine Omkar will take that sin and all the other sins away when she makes sacrifice—"

"What sacrifice, Gulab?"

"Such as we make to the gods, Sahib."

Then something curious happened. The girl broke, she clung to Barlow convulsively; sobs choked her.

He clasped her tight and laid his cheek against hers soothingly, and said, "Gulab, what is it? Don't go to the Shrine of Omkar. Come with me to your people at Chunda, and if you do not want to remain with them I will have it arranged, through the Resident, that the British will reward you with protection. You have done the British Raj a great service."

"No, Sahib." The girl drew herself erect, so that her eyes gazed into Barlow's, They were luminous with an intensity of resolve. "Let Bootea speak what is in her heart, and be not offended; it is necessary. There is, at the end of the journey the place that is called *jahannam* (hell) for Bootea. The Nana Sahib waits like a tiger crouched by a pool at night for the coming of a stag to drink."

"The Resident will protect you against the Mahratta," Barlow declared.

"Bootea could do that," and in her small hand there gleamed in the moonlight the sheen of her dagger blade. She thrust it back into her belt.

"What then do you fear, Gulab?" he queried.

"The Sahib."

"*Me*, Gulab?"

"Yes, Khudawand. To see you and not be permitted to hear your voice, nor feel your hand upon my face, would be worse than sacrifice. Bootea would rather die, slip off into death with the goodness, the sweetness of tonight upon her soul. There, where the Sahib would be, Bootea's heart would be full of evil, the evil of craving for him. No, this is the end, and Bootea will make offering of thanks—marigolds and a cocoanut to Omkar, and sprinkle attar upon his shrine in thankfulness for the joy of the Sahib's presence. It is said!" and the girl nestled down against Barlow's breast again as though she had gone to sleep in content.

But he groaned inwardly: there was something of dread in his heart, her resignation was so deep—suggesting an utter giving up, a helplessness. She had named sacrifice; the word rang ominously in his mind, beating at his fears. And yet, what she had said was philosophy—wise; a something that had been worded, perhaps differently, for a million years; the brave acceptance of Fate's decree—something that always triumphed over the weak longings of humans.

# CHAPTER XXIX

Now they could see the wide silver ribbon of Mother Narbudda lying serene and placid in the moonlight, in the centre of the river's wide flow the gloomy rock embrasures of Mandhatta Island. Where it towered upward in cliffs and coned hills the summit showed the flickering lights of many temples, and like the sing of a storm through giant trees there floated on the night wind the sound of many voices, and the beating of drums, and the imperious call of horns and conch-shells.

They came upon the *tonga* waiting by the roadside, and Barlow, thrusting back the covering from the girl's face said: "Now, Gulab, I will lift you down. We must find a place in the village beyond for you to rest tonight; I, too, will remain there and in the morning we will make our salaams."

Then he drew her face to his and kissed her.

He slipped from the saddle and lifted the girl down, carrying her in his arms to the *tonga*.

As they neared the village that was situated on the flat land that swept back from the Narbudda in a wide plain, and nestled against the river bank, they were swept into a crowd such as would be encountered on a trip to the Derby. The road was thronged with people, and the village itself, from which a bridge reached to the Island of Mandhatta, was a town in holiday attire, for to the Hindus the *mela* of Omkar was a union of festivity and devotion.

Both sides of the main street were lined with booths for the sale of everything; calicoes from Calicut, where these prints first got their name; hammered Benares ware; gold-threaded cotton puggris from Mewar; tulwars and khandas from Bhundi. In some of the little shops, bamboo structures that thrust an underlip out into the street, there was Mhowa liquor, and *julabis*, and *kabobs* of goat meat. Open spaces held tiny circuses—abnormal animals and performing goats, and a moon-bear on a ring and strap.

The street was full of gossiping men and women and children dodging here and there; it was an outing where the *ryot* (farmer) had escaped from his crotched stick of wood that was a plough, and the village tradesmen had left his shop, and the servant his service, to feel the joyousness of a holiday. Mendicants were in abundance prowling in their ugliness like spirits in a nightmare; some naked, absolute, others with but a loin-cloth, their lean shrivelled bodies smeared with ashes—sometimes the ashes of the dead—and cow-dung, carrying on their arms and foreheads the red and white horizontal bars of Shiva—who was Omkar at Mandhatta. In their hands were either iron-tongs, with loose clattering ring, or a yak's tail, or the three-ribbed horn of a black-buck.

Some of the *yogis*, perhaps Goswamies that had come from the country where Eklinga was the tutelary deity, had their hair braided and woven around their foreheads, holding in its fold lotus seeds; beneath the tiara of hair a crescent of white on their foreheads. A flowing yellow robe half hid their ash-smeared limbs. A tall Sannyasi—the most ascetic of sects—his lean yellow-robed form supported by a long staff at the end of which swung a yellow bag, strode solemnly along with eyes fixed on a book, the Bhagavad Gita, muttering, "Aum, to the light of earth, the divine light that illumines our souls. Aum!"

To Barlow it was like a grotesque pantomime with no directing head. Nautch girls tripped along laughing and chatting, bracelets jingling, and tiny bells at their ankles tinkling musically. It depressed him; it was such a terrible juxtaposition of frivolity and the gloomed shadow of idol worship that lay just the bridge's span of the sullen Narbudda: the gloomy, broken scraps of the long since deserted forts that cut with jagged lines the moonlit sky; and beyond them again the many temples with their scowling Brahmin priests, and the shrine wherein the god of destruction, Omkar, sat athirst for sacrifice. He shivered as though the white mist that veiled the river crept into his marrow.

The Gulab seemed at home amongst these gathered ones. Two or three times she had bade the driver stop his creeping pace, and looking out from beneath the curtain had questioned a man or woman. At last, as they were stopped by a wall of people watching the antics of some strolling players upon a platform, Bootea spoke to a stout woman who was pressed against the opening into the cart by the mob.

"*Lucker khan Bhaina, Bowree,*" the Gulab said in a low voice, and the woman's eyes took on a startled look for it was a decoit password, and the Bowrees were a clan of decoits akin to the Bagrees. From the woman Bootea learned where she could find a good resting place with the family of a shop-keeper. There was no doubt about it, the Bowree woman assured her, for the *tonga* would impress him, and he was one who profited from the loot of decoits.

The Gulab was given a place to sleep in the shopkeeper's house that extended back from his little shop. The driver was ordered to return in the morning to the Pindari camp. Barlow was for keeping the *tonga*, hoping that perhaps Bootea would change her mind and go on to Chunda, but the girl was firm in her determination to end it all at Mandhatta.

Before Barlow left her to seek some camping place in hut or serai, and food for himself and horse, the girl said: "If the Sahib will delay his going tomorrow for a little, Bootea will proceed early to the shrine to see the Swami—then she will return here, for she would want to see his face once more before the ending."

"I'll wait, Gulab," he acquiesced; "I'll be here at the tenth hour." He felt even then an unaccountable chill of their parting, for, many being about, he could not take her in his arms to kiss her; but their eyes spoke, and the girl's were luminous, and sweet with a look of hunger, of pathetic longing, of sublime trust.

As Barlow turned away leading his horse, he muttered over and over, "Gad! it's incomprehensible that a Sahib should feel this over a—yes, a native woman; it's damnable!"

He reviled himself, declaring that it was harder on the Gulab than on him—and he was actually suffering. It would be better if he swung to the saddle and fled from the misery that prolongation but intensified. And the girl's brave resignation in giving him up was wonderful, was so like her.

Then the sight of Mahratta *sowars*, who, it being Sindhia's territory, were a guard to watch the pilgrim throng, flashed him back to a sense of duty, his own mission. But it had not suffered because of Bootea; it had benefitted through her; but for her the written message from the British would have been lost—stolen by Hunsa, and would have landed in Nana Sahib's hands; and he would have been slain as the Patan, killer of Amir Khan.

But the Gulab was right; from that time forward should she listen to him and go on to Poona, God alone knew where it would lead to—misery. It would be utter ruin morally, officially, in a caste way; even in time passionate enthusiasm, engendered by her lovableness, dulled, would bring utter debasement, degradation of spirit, of man fibre. It was the wisdom of God that entailed upon the union of the white and dark-skinned the bar sinister.

Until he slept, wrapped in his blankets on the sand beside his tethered horse, Barlow was tortured by this mental inquisition. Even in his troubled sleep there was a nightmare that waked him, panting and exhausted, and the remembrance was vivid—Bootea lay beneath the mighty paws of a tiger and he was beating hopelessly at the snarling brute with a clubbed rifle.

# CHAPTER XXX

In the morning Captain Barlow underwent a sartorial metamorphosis; he attained to the sanctity of a Hindu pilgrim by the purchase of a tight-ankled pair of white trousers to replace the voluminous baggy ones of a Patan, and a blue shot-with-gold-thread Rajput turban. He shoved the Patan turban with its conical fez in his saddle-bags, and wound the many yards of blue material in a rakish criss-cross about his shapely head, running a fold or two beneath his chin. The Patan sheepskin coat was left with his horse.

When Bootea came at ten to where Barlow—who was now Jaswant Singh—paced up and down with the swagger of a Rajput in front of the *bunnia's* shop, she stood for a little, her eyes searching the crowd for her Sahib. When he laughed, and called softly, "Gulab," her eyes almost wept for joy, for not seeing him at once, a dread that he had gone had chilled her.

"You see how easy it is, in a good cause, to change one's caste," he said.

"With you, Sahib, yes, because you can also change your skin."

There it was again, the indestructible barrier, the pigmented badge. It drove the laugh from Barlow's lips.

"Why has the Afghan Musselman become a Hindu?" Bootea asked.

"I have no wish to anger these people who are on a holy pilgrimage by going into their temples as a Moslem."

"You are going to the shrine of Omkar?" the Gulab asked aghast.

"Are you—again?" Barlow parried.

"Yes, Sahib, soon."

"I am going with you," Barlow declared.

Bootea expostulated with almost fierce eagerness; with a fervour that increased the uneasiness in Barlow's mind. He had a premonition of evil; dread hung on his soul—perhaps born of the dream of a tiger devouring the girl.

"The Sahib still has the Akbar Lamp—the ruby?" the girl queried, presently.

"I have it safe," he answered, tapping his breast.

"If the Sahib is not going to the shrine Bootea would desire that we could go out beyond the village to a *mango tope* where there are none to observe, for she would like to make the final salaams in his arms—then nothing would matter."

"Perhaps we had better go anyway," Barlow said eagerly— "though I am going over to the shrine with you; for now, being a Hindu, I can pass as your brother—and there there would not be opportunity."

The girl turned this over in her mind, then said: "No, we will not go to the grove, for Bootea can say farewell to the Sahib in the cloister where Swami Sarasvati has a cell for vigils."

Then asking Barlow to wait she went into the house and soon returned clothed in spotless white muslin. He noticed that she had taken off all her ornaments, her jewellery. The bangle of gold that was a twisting snake with a ruby head, she pressed upon Barlow, saying: "When the Sahib is married to the Englay will he give her this from me as a safeguard against evil; and that it may cause her to worship the Sahib as a god, even as Bootea does."

The simplicity, the genuine nobleness of this tribute of renunciation, hazed Barlow's eyes with a mist—almost tears; she was a strange combine of dramatic power and gentle sweetness.

"Now, come, Sahib," she said, "if you insist. It will not bring misery to Bootea but to you."

Barlow strode along beside the girl steeped in ominous misgivings. Perhaps his presence at the temple would avert whatever it was, that, like evil genii seemed to poison the air.

There was a moving throng of pilgrims that poured along in a joyous turbulent stream toward the bridge. No shadow of the dread god, Omkar, gloomed their spirits; they chatted and laughed. Of those who would make devotions the men were stripped to the waist, their limbs draped in spotless white. And the women, on their way to have their sins forgiven, were taking final license—the *purdah* of the veil was almost forgotten, for this was permitted in the presence of the god. Even their beautifully formed bodies and limbs, the skin fresh anointed, gleaming like copper in the sunlight, showed entrancingly, voluptuously, with a new-born liberty.

Once, half way of the bridge, a man's voice rang out commandingly, calling backward, admonishing some one to hurry, crying, "It is the *kurban!*"

Barlow started; the *kurban* meant a human sacrifice. He looked at Bootea—he could have sworn her head had drooped, and that she shivered. The girl must have sensed his thoughts, for she turned her eyes up to his, but they held nothing of fear.

Beyond the bridge they passed across a lower level, jungle clad with delicate bamboos and dhak, and sweet-scented shrubs, and clusters of gorgeous oleanders. The way was thronged with white-clothed figures that seemed like wraiths, ghosts drifting back to the cavern of the Destroyer.

Then they commenced the ascent following the bed of a stream that had cut a chasm through black trap-rock, leaving jagged cliffs. And the persistent jungle, ever encroaching on space, had outposts of champac and wild mango, their giant roots, like the arms of an octopus, holding anchorage in clefts of the rock. And from the limbs above floated down the scolding voices of *lungoor*, the black-faced grey-whiskered monkeys, who rebuked the intrusion of the earth-dwellers below. Where the path lay over rocks it was worn smooth and slippery by naked feet, the feet of pilgrims for a thousand years. On the right the mouth of a deep cave had been walled up by masonry. Within, so the legend ran, the High Priest of Mandhatta, centuries before, had imprisoned the goddess Kali to stop a pestilence, making vow to offer to Bhairava, her son, a yearly human sacrifice. Higher up, approaching the plateau where were the ruins of a thousand gorgeous shrines, both sides of the pathway were lined by mendicants who sat cross-legged, in front of them a little mat for the receipt of alms—cowries, pice, silver; the mendicants muttering incessantly *"Jae, Jae, Omkar!"* (Victory to Omkar).

In front of the temple within which sat the god, was a conical black stone daubed with red, the Linga, the generative function of Siva, and before it, the symbol of reproduction, women made offering of cocoanuts, and sweets, and garlands of flowers,—generally marigolds,—and prayed for the bestowal of a son; even their postures, carried away as they were by desire, showing a complete abandon to the sex idea. A Brahmin priest sat cross-legged upon a stone platform repeating in a sing-song cadence prayers, and from somewhere beyond a deep-toned bell boomed out an admonishing call.

Holy water from the sacred Narbudda was poured into the two jugs each pilgrim carried and sealed by the Brahmins, who received, without thanks, stoically, as a matter of right, a tribute of silver.

Towering eighty feet above the temple spire was a cliff, and from a ledge near its top a white flag fluttered idly in the lazy wind. It was the death-leap, the ledge from which the one of the human sacrifice to Omkar leapt, to crash in death beside the Linga.

Almost without words Barlow and the girl had toiled up the ascent, scarcely noticed of the throng; and now Bootea said: "Sahib, remain here, I go to speak to the High Priest."

Barlow saw her speak into the open portal of one of the cloister chambers that surrounded the temple, then disappear within. After a time she came forth, and approaching him said, "The Priest would speak with thee, Sahib; for because of many things I have told him who thou art, though mentioning not the nature of the mission, for that is not permitted."

Barlow's foreboding of evil was now a certainty as he strode forward.

The priest rose at the Captain's entrance. He was a fine specimen of the true Brahmin, the intellectual cult, that through successive generations of mental sway and homage from the millions of untutored ones had become conscious of its power. Tall, spare of form, with wide high forehead and full expressive eyes, almost olive skin, Barlow felt that the Swami was quite unlike the begging yogis and mendicants; a man who was by the close alliance of his intellect to the essence of created things a Sannyasi. Larger in his conceptions than the yogis who misconstrued the Vedas and the Law of Manu as imposing an association of filth—smeared ashes, and uncombed, uncleansed hair—as a symbol of piety and abnegation of spirit, a visible assertion that the body had passed from regard—that it, with its sensualities and ungodly cravings, had become subservient to the spirit, the soul.

Swami Sarasvati was austere; Barlow felt that he dwelt on a plane where the trivialities of life were but pestilential insects, to be endured stoically in a physical way, with the mind freed from their irritation grasping grander things; life was a wheel that revolved with the certainty of celestial bodies.

It was so curious, and yet so unfailing, that Bootea, with her hyper-intuition should have found, selected this spiritual tutor from the horde of gurus, byragies, and yogis that were connecting links between the tremendous pantheon of grotesque gods and the common people. Here she had come to an intellectual, though no doubt an ascetic; one possessed of fierce fervour in his ministry. There would be no swaying of that will force developed to the keen flexible unflawed temper of a Damascus blade.

Now the priest was saying in the *asl* (pure) Hindustani of the high-bred Brahmin: "The Sahib confers honour upon Sri Swami Sarasvati by this visit, for the woman has related that he is of high caste amongst the Englay and has been trusted by the Raj with a mission. That he comes in the garb of my people is consideration for it avoids outrage to their feelings. I am glad to know that the Englay are so considerate."

"I came, Swami, because of regard for Bootea for she is like a princess."

The priest shot a quick, searching look into the eyes of the speaker, then he asked, "And what service would the Sahib ask?"

The question caught Captain Barlow unaware; he had not formulated anything—it had all been nebulous, this dread. He hesitated, fearing to voice that which perhaps did not exist in the minds of either the priest or Bootea.

The girl perceived the hesitancy and spoke rapidly in a low voice to the priest.

"Captain Sahib," the Swami began, "I see that thy heart is inclined to the woman, and it is to be admired, for she is, as thou thinkest, like a flower of the forest. But also, Captain Sahib, thy heart is the heart of a soldier, of a brave man, the light of valour is in thine eyes, in thy face, and I would ask thee to be brave, and instead of being cast in sorrow because of what I am going to tell thee, thou must realise that it is for the good of the woman whose face is in thy heart. Today she insures to her soul a place in kattas, the heaven of Siva, the abiding place of Brahm, the Creator of all that is."

Barlow felt himself reel at this sudden confirmation of his fears—the blow. The cry *"Kurban"* that he had heard on the bridge was a reality—a human sacrifice.

"God!" he cried in a voice of anguish, "it can't be. Young and beautiful and good, to die—it's wrong. I forbid such a cruel, wanton sacrifice of a sweet life."

The Swami, taking a step toward the door, swept his long thin arm with a gesture that embraced the thousands beyond.

"Captain Sahib," he said solemnly, "if thou wert to raise thy voice in anger against this holy, soul-redeeming observance thou wouldst be torn to pieces; not even I could stop them if insult were offered to Omkar. And, besides, the Englay Raj would call thee accursed for breeding hate in the hearts of the Hindus through the sacrilege of an insult to the High Priest of the Temple of Omkar. This is the territory of the Mahrattas, and the English have no authority here."

Barlow knew that he was helpless. Even if there were jurisdiction of the British, one against thousands of religious fanatics would avail nothing.

The priest saw the torture in the man's face, and continued: "The woman has told me much. Her heart is so with thee that it is already dead. Thou canst not take her to thy people, for the living hell is even worse than the hell beyond. If thou lovest the woman glory in her release from pain of spirit, from the degradation of being outcast—that she judges wisely, and there is not upon her soul the sin of taking her own life, for if she went with thee, proud and high-born as she is, it would come to that, Sahib—thou knowest it. There are things that cannot be said by me concerning the woman; vows having been taken in the sanctity of a temple."

A figment of the rumour Barlow had heard that Bootea was Princess Kumari floated through his mind, but that did not matter; Bootea as Bootea was the sweetest woman he had ever known. It must be that she had filled his heart with love.

Again Bootea spoke in a low voice to the priest, and he said: "Sahib, I go forth for a little, for there are matters to arrange. I see yonder the sixteen Brahmins who, according to our rites, assemble when one is to pass at the Shrine of Omkar to *kailas.*"

His large luminous eyes rested with tolerant placidity upon the face of this man whom he must consider, according to his tenets, as a creature antagonistic to the true gods, and said, in his soft, modulated voice: "Thou art young, Sahib, and full of the life force which is essential to the things of the earth—thou art like the blossom of the *mhowa* tree that comes forth upon bare limbs before the maturity of its foliage, it is then, as thou art, joyous in the freshness of awaking life. But life means eternity, the huge cycle that has been since Indra's birth. Life here is but a step, a transition from condition to condition, and the woman, by one act of sacrifice, attains to the blissful peace that many livings of reincarnated body would not achieve. It is written in the law of Brahm that if one sacrifices his life, this phase of it, to Omkar, who is Siva, even though he had slain a Brahmin he shall be forgiven, and sit in heaven with the *Gandharvas* (angels). But it is also written that whosoever turns back in terror, each step that he takes shall be equivalent to the guilt of killing a Brahmin."

The priest's voice had risen in sonorous cadence until it was compelling.

Bootea trembled like a wind-wavered leaf.

To Barlow it was horrible, the mad infatuation of a man prostrate before false gods, idols, a rabid materialism. That one, to fall crushed and bleeding from the dizzy height of the ledge of sacrifice upon a red-daubed stone representation of the repulsive emblem, could thus wipe out the deadly sin of murder, was, even spiritually, impossible.

The priest, his soul submerged by the sophistry of his faith, passed from the gloomed cloister to the open sunlight.

And Barlow, conscious of his helplessness unless Bootea would now yield to his entreaties and forswear the horrible sacrifice, turned to the girl, his face drawn and haggard, and his voice, when he spoke, vibrating tremulously from the pressure of his despair. He held out his arms, and Bootea threw herself against his breast and sobbed.

"Come back to Chunda with me, Gulab," Barlow pleaded.

"No, Sahib," she panted, "it cannot be."

"But I love you, Bootea," he whispered.

"And Bootea loves the Sahib," and her eyes, as she lifted her face, were wonderful. "There," she continued, "the Sahib could not make the *nika* (marriage) with Bootea, both our souls would be lost. But it is not forbidden,—even if it were and was a sin, all sins will be forgiven Bootea before the sun sets,—and if the Sahib permits it Bootea will wed herself now to the one she loves. Hold me in your arms—tight, lest I die before it is time."

And as Barlow pressed the girl to him, fiercely, crushing her almost, she raised her lips to his, and they both drank the long deep draught of love.

Then the Gulab drew from his arms and her face was radiant, a soft exultation illumined her eyes.

"That is all, Sahib," she said. "Bootea passes now, goes out to *kailas* in a happy dream. Go, Sahib, and do not remain below for this is so beautiful. You must ride forth in content."

She took him by the arm and gently led him to the door.

And from without he could hear a chorus of a thousand voices, its burden being, "The *Kurban!*"

Barlow turned, one foot in the sunshine and one in the cloister's gloom, and kissed Bootea; and she could feel his hot tears upon her cheek.

Once more he pleaded, "Renounce this dreadful sacrifice."

But the girl smiled up into his face, saying, "I die happily, husband. Perhaps Indra will permit Bootea to come back in spirit to the Sahib."

The High Priest strode to the entrance of the cloister, his eyes holding the abstraction of one moving in another world; he seemed oblivious of the Englishman's presence as he said:

"Come forth, ye who seek *kailas* through Omkar."

As Barlow staggered, almost blind, over the stony path from the cloister, he saw the group of sixteen Brahmins, their foreheads and arms carrying the white bars of Siva.

Then Bootea was led by the priest down to the cold merciless stone Linga, where she, at a word from the priest, knelt in obeisance, a barbaric outburst of music from horn and drum clamouring a salute.

When Bootea arose to her feet the priest tendered her some *mhowa* spirit in a cocoanut shell, but the girl, disdaining its stimulation, poured it in a libation upon the Linga.

From the amphitheatre of the enclosing hills thirty thousand voices rose in one thundering chorus of "Jae, jae, Omkar!" and, "To Omkar the *Kurban!*"

Many pressed forward, mad fanaticism in their eyes, and held out at arm's length toward the girl bracelets and ornaments to be touched by her fingers as a beneficence.

But Swami Sarasvati waved them back, and turning to Bootea tendered her, with bowed head, the *pan supari* (betel nut in a leaf) as an admonition that the ceremony had ceased, and there was nothing left but the sacrifice.

As the girl with firm step turned to the path that led up through shrub and jungle growth to the ledge where fluttered the white flag, a tumult of approbation went up from the multitude at her brave devotion. Then a solemn hush enwrapped the bowl of the hills, and the eyes of the thousands were fixed upon the jutting shelf of rock.

A dirge-like cadence, a mighty gasp of, "Ah, Kuda!" sounded as a slim figure, white robed, like a wraith, appeared on the ledge, and from her hand whirled down to the rocks below a cocoanut, cast in sacrifice; next a hand-mirror, its glass shimmering flickers of gold from the sunlight.

For five seconds the white-clothed figure disappeared in the shrouding bushes; men held their breath, and women gasped and clutched at their throats as if they choked.

Then they saw her again, arms high held as though she reached for God. And as the white-draped, slender form came hurtling through the air women swooned and men closed their eyes and shuddered.

An Englishman, clothed as a Hindu, lay prone on his face on the hillside sobbing, the dry leaves drinking in his tears, cursing himself for a sin that was not his.

THE END

CPSIA information can be obtained
at www.ICGtesting.com
Printed in the USA
LVHW012009100820
662833LV00004B/600

9 781437 523744